NOT MY MOTHER

BOOKS BY MIRANDA SMITH

Some Days Are Dark
What I Know
The One Before

NOT MY MOTHER

MIRANDA SMITH

bookouture

Published by Bookouture in 2021

An imprint of Storyfire Ltd.
Carmelite House
50 Victoria Embankment
London EC4Y 0DZ

www.bookouture.com

ISBN: 978-1-80019-310-9
eBook ISBN: 978-1-80019-309-3

For Lucy

PROLOGUE

Then

Amelia

Amelia's senses returned. First, the feeling of grainy cement beneath her fingers. A warm breeze blew over her, carrying with it the scent of chlorine and iron and decay. Her vision came into focus, unlocking a hauntingly vivid image. The fruit from the charcuterie board had wilted in the heat, buzzy flies drinking up the juices. The sun was almost gone now. She stood, shakily, trying to find balance. That's when she saw the blood. Slippery stripes stained the concrete surrounding their backyard pool. Her hands were sticky with it. At her feet, lay her husband. His face was still. His eyes were closed. A stream of blood oozed from his left ear.

Even that terrifying image wasn't the scariest part. What truly terrified her was the silence. No footsteps, no whispers. Worst of all, no crying. She ran inside the house, up the stairs. Horrified, she tore through the nursery, each detail searing itself into her brain. The open window. The empty crib. She ran outside a second time and was greeted again by that stony silence.

She knew it then, could feel it in her bones. Her baby was missing.

Baby Caroline was gone.

CHAPTER 1

Now

Marion

I wish Ava had taken a longer nap. I wish I'd started the party at two, instead of noon. I should have ordered cupcakes instead of a specialty-made, two-tiered sugar monstrosity that I'll be responsible for dissecting into a dozen pieces.

My first year of motherhood has taught me this: I'm always second-guessing myself.

And it's not like I have a partner to tell me otherwise, contradict my own insecurities. I have no husband. No boyfriend. It's just Ava and me. I'm responsible for every doctor's visit, every sleepless night, every celebration. Of course, I chose this path. But sometimes, in moments like this, when every shortcoming seems on full display, I really feel it. That heavy responsibility.

Then Ava smiles, a reminder parenthood is worth it. Even the hard parts, the lonely parts. Her happiness sends out a silent signal that I'm enough.

If I'm being honest, I'm not as alone as I may feel. I look around the room, cataloging each person who has come to celebrate Ava's first birthday. Some people I felt I had to invite for the sake of the business, like Holly Dale, the hotel manager across the street. The words she uttered when she first learned I was pregnant stay with me: *A baby is a lot to take on by yourself.* She irks me, but I have to remain friendly with her because she always provides tourists with coupons for The Shack. There are a few mothers from Mommy and Me I know on a first name basis; I invited them so Ava isn't the only baby at her party.

And then there are the people who've really helped Ava and me during this first year. Carmen, my best friend, her long black hair falling over one shoulder. Over by the pinball machines, I spot her two kids: Preston and Penny. Preston is manically punching the ball grip on the machine, despite nothing happening. Penny has taken a roll of streamers and is wrapping them around her brother's ankles.

"Cut it out, you animals," Carmen shouts when she spots them.

"It's a party," says Michael, her husband, standing by her side. "Let them have fun."

My business partner, Des, walks into the dining hall carrying a pan of handmade cheese pizza. The older kids take their seats at the decorated table.

"Time to eat," Des says, in her husky voice. "If you want toppings, I have another one coming."

None of the kids care. I know from years of working here most kids only want cheese and balk at anything else.

Des is also my honorary aunt, of sorts—I've known her as long as I've known anyone, it seems. She's owned The Shack for years, inviting Mom to step in as co-owner some years back. After graduating college, I joined them, taking over the management of the place. This little eatery has proven to be a stable support system for all involved, favored by both locals and the tourist crowd visiting the nearby beaches.

North Bay is a small beach town by the Atlantic, and it's the only place I've ever called home. I love everything about it. The bronze sands, the blue skies. I love that the place only feels touristy during the months of July and August; the rest of the time, it's like this beautiful landscape is a secret, only to be enjoyed by our few thousand residents. We moved here when I was a toddler. I certainly don't remember living anywhere else, and once I was old enough to swim in the ocean, I knew I'd never want to leave.

Des catches sight of me holding Ava and shuffles over.

"There's the birthday princess," she says, her voice climbing a few octaves. The only time that happens is when she's around my child. Normally, Des despises children, but Ava works some kind of magic on her. "Let me hold her."

"She looks adorable," Carmen says, walking over to join us. Michael is only a few steps behind. "This dress is perfect on her."

"It was very generous of you," I say.

"It's a shame she'll mess it up once she tears into that cake," Des says, giving Ava a hearty cuddle.

"A true fashionista wouldn't be caught dead in the same outfit twice," Carmen says, nudging Des.

Looking at them, you wouldn't think Carmen and Des had anything in common. Carmen is tall and slim, while Des is short and squat. Carmen appears polished in her high-waisted pants and blouse, where Des looks thrown together in flour-dusted joggers. It only takes a short conversation with the two women to see how like-minded they are. They both give as good as they get.

"The place looks great," Michael says, giving the room another once-over. I've turned The Shack's dining room into a pink and gold wonderland, an almost exact replica of the Pinterest board I started creating three months ago.

"Thank you." And I am thankful. I need this reassurance.

I reach my hand out to Ava, letting her tiny fingers clench around mine. Her light blue eyes flit about, taking in the colors, the presents, the people. She appears happy. That's all that matters.

My phone vibrates in my pocket. I scan the screen to see who is calling.

It's Evan.

Of course he'd be calling today. *He probably doesn't remember it's Ava's birthday,* I tell myself. Or maybe he does and that is why he's calling. Either way, I won't answer. I switch the phone on silent, tucking it into the back pocket of my jeans.

"Who's that?" Carmen asks, having caught the look on my face.

"No one," I say, looking around the room. "Anyone seen Mom?"

"She's upstairs wrapping her gift," Des answers.

"I'll go get her. I'm sure the other parents are getting antsy. It's probably time to cut the cake," I say, giving Ava another smile before walking away.

When we moved to North Bay, Mom rented the upstairs apartment above The Shack, which is how she met Des. They sparked a friendship, and the rest is history. We continued to live there, even though Mom eventually made enough money to move elsewhere. She's still never left. It's her home, I suppose.

I climb the narrow stairwell connected to the kitchen, gently pushing open the apartment door. Mom is sitting on the living room floor in front of a massive gift-wrapped box.

"I'm coming, I'm coming," she mumbles, a strip of tape between her teeth.

"You spent too much time decorating for the party." I lean against the doorframe, my arms crossed.

"I know. I just wanted the place to look perfect. And it does, doesn't it? You picked the most adorable decorations. I love the cake. And that little sign for her high chair."

Mom tacks the tape to the box and sits back, pleased. She leans on the present for stability and stands.

"Do I even want to know what you've bought her this time?"

"I've got one granddaughter. Let me spoil her." She walks over and squeezes my hand. "Speaking of gifts, I got you a little something."

I poke my head into the hallway to hear what's going on downstairs. "We have people waiting."

"It'll only take a second." She pushes the hair off her face, and I notice the sparse gray strands starting to peek through. She takes a small pink box out of her pocket. "Today is about Ava, yes. But it's a special day for you, too. People always forget the mother's role."

Here I am, thinking my efforts go unseen, thinking I'm not enough. Mom always has a way of reminding me that I am. She's the partner I need when the weight becomes too heavy. And she's right: throughout the day, my mind has revisited where we were a year ago, the intimate details of Ava's birth story. Somehow, the event seems like yesterday, and yet here we are a year later, celebrating it. The joy and the pain. It takes both to make a life. It takes both to live one.

I open the gift. It's a ring with three pearls. Each is a different color: black, white and pink.

"Mom, you didn't have to—"

"I wanted to get you something. You've sacrificed a lot over this past year, and, honestly, I couldn't be prouder. I thought I was lucky having you for a daughter. You're an even better mother."

We've not always had this friendship, Mom and me. Most mothers argue with their teenage daughters, and we were no exception. But since I entered adulthood, we've become much closer. Best friends, really. And since I've had Ava—my goodness, I don't know what I'd do without her.

"It's beautiful," I say, sliding the ring down my finger.

"The different colors reminded me of the three of us. You, Ava and me."

I hug her, resting my cheek against her shoulder. "Thank you, Mom. For everything."

I help her carry Ava's gift downstairs. We place it by the present table, where the cake sits at the center. There's a unicorn cake topper on the top layer. Carmen's idea. It's fitting, I suppose. Like Ava herself is a mythical creature, rare and beautiful. Ava was never a guarantee, that's for sure. She's a gift. My little miracle. Now she's here, smiling at everyone that passes, equal parts overwhelmed and mesmerized.

Carmen is holding her, probably so Des can fetch the next pizza. Carmen is deep in conversation with Holly Dale. I only catch the tail end as I approach.

"I'm just saying, I think it would get to me," Holly says, one hand on her hip, the tattoo on her bicep on full display. "How can you defend people who willingly break the law?"

I puff out my cheeks, bracing for Carmen's response. Holly is a wannabe activist, the causes ever-changing. Of course, she can't understand Carmen's career as a defense attorney.

"It's about due process. I'm doing my part for justice, even if others don't see it that way," Carmen says, shifting her weight to better hold Ava. "People tend to view crime as black or white. Did they do it, or didn't they? I focus on the less obvious question: why? That *why* provides more than motive, it provides context. It can take a straitlaced juror and make them question their own ideals. Would they react in the same way? Was the action justified, or at least understandable?"

"Maybe we should get some pizza," Michael tries to interject. Neither Carmen nor Holly acknowledge him, and he slowly backs away.

"Wrong is wrong," Holly says, crossing an arm over her torso. "There is no justifying it. Just admit it. You're in it for the money, even if that means letting criminals roam the streets."

"I believe in second chances. I believe we all make mistakes, and in the depths of failure, we aren't in the right headspace to find our way out of it. That's where I come in."

"Hey, guys," I say, loud enough to gain control of the conversation. "We're about to cut the cake if you want to head over there."

"Please," Carmen says. She's not one to turn down a good debate, even if we are at a one-year-old's birthday party. As she's about to hand Ava to me, I spy a cluster of people hovering by the front door.

"Put her in the high chair for me? I'll be right back."

I step outside, propping the door open with my foot. The afternoon heat hits me all at once.

"We're hosting a private party," I explain. "If you want to come back in an hour—"

"Is there a Sarah Paxton here?" a man asks.

Only then do I register their dark clothing. Their badges. These are police officers. I look behind him, spying a trio of squad cars, their lights blinking.

"I don't know anyone with that name," I say, wondering why there seems to be so many officers on the scene.

The man looks to the person next to him. They're both wearing sunglasses, so it is hard to read their expressions. Something tells me they were expecting that response.

"And your name?" asks the second officer, his uniform tight across his shoulders and chest. The Shack is big with the local police department. I think I've seen him before, but it's hard to tell.

"I'm Marion Sams. I own this restaurant. I don't know a woman named Sarah Paxton."

"How about Eileen Sams?" asks the first officer. I'm sure he picked up on the last name.

My stomach clenches tight. Mom? What could they possibly want with her? All these men wouldn't show up for a simple traffic violation. And their overall tone, combined with their sheer quantity, makes me think this is serious.

"Can you tell me what is going on?" I ask, my voice calm, practical. "I'm hosting my daughter's birthday party."

"I need to know if Eileen Sams is on the premises. We have a warrant—"

"I'm Eileen Sams," Mom says, standing behind me. She looks between me and the officers, her face as surprised as mine.

"Step outside, ma'am," says the officer.

Mom looks down, obeying his order. From inside, I can hear Des.

"Marion, are we doing the cake or what?"

I don't answer her. I'm following Mom outside. With the front door closed, they ask her to turn around. They're placing her hands behind her back and reaching for handcuffs.

"Sarah Paxton, you have the right to remain silent—"

"What are you doing?" I push the arresting officer's arm away. "I just told you I don't know a Sarah Paxton. This is my mother."

The second officer, the one with the tight uniform, steps forward, pulling me back. "Miss, we're going to need you to step away—"

"Not until you tell me what is going on. You've got the wrong person."

"Marion?" Mom's voice is broken, as though she has been underwater too long, and struggling to gulp air. I sense she wants to say more, but she doesn't. Or can't.

"Mom, tell them who you are."

Mom starts breathing fast and heavy. Her gasping continues as they walk her toward a police cruiser, opening up the back door. She's having an anxiety attack. I've seen her have them in the past, but it has been years since the last one. Not since I graduated high school. I'm back in that moment, watching my mother turn fragile, feeling unequipped to do anything.

The second officer still has a hand on my arm, trying to keep me from approaching the car. "Miss, if you'll go back inside—"

"Stop with the miss and ma'am routine," I shout. I can feel my blood running hot beneath my skin, feel my heart thud faster and faster. I don't know what's happening, but I know Mom is in trouble, and there's nothing I can do about it. "Tell me what's going on. Why are you arresting her?"

The officer takes a step back and holds up both hands. "Fine." He walks to another officer, this one wearing a navy suit, and takes a folded stack of papers. He hands them to me. "This is the warrant. Everything you need to know should be in there."

I hold the bundle in my hands, staring ahead. I watch, helplessly, as the squad car carrying Mom drives away.

CHAPTER 2

Now

Marion

Out here, beneath the burning sun, I'm frozen. My mind is thawing, slowly familiarizing to this new world, the one where my mother has been placed in handcuffs and driven away in a police car.

A breeze whooshes past, carrying with it the scent of the sea, and crinkles the papers clenched between my fingers. I look down. The warrant. I'm too rattled to begin reading. Around me, more officers descend upon the parking lot. I see them clearly, but can't grasp their reality, like they are a mirage, a side effect of the desperation and fatigue washing over my body.

"Marion. Are you okay?" It's Carmen. Her heels smack against the pavement, the volume increasing as she approaches like a crescendo. The sound pulls me out of my own thoughts, back to the present.

Des is only a few steps behind her. "Where's Eileen?"

"They took her." My words drift without purpose, like I'm in a dream, a nightmare. I'm disconnected from this life that feels nothing like the one I was living ten short minutes ago.

"Who took her?" Carmen asks, her hand raised to block the sun's glare, her head bowed, trying to get a better look at my face.

"The police."

Only then does she seem to connect the dots. She looks at the police cars pulling into the restaurant lot, at the officers approaching the front door.

"They arrested her? What for?" Des looks from me to Carmen. Already, we are expecting answers from her. She's the lawyer. This is her world, not ours.

I hand Carmen the papers. I'd read them myself, but I'm not in my right mind. It's like I'm inhabiting an entirely different body, and my brain's synapses are not fully firing. All I can think about is Mom being stuffed into the back seat of a squad car, her broken cries before the door slammed shut.

"They weren't using her name," I mumble, remembering. "They called her Sarah."

Des, boiling with anger, looks around the parking lot, her gaze stopping on an officer in uniform. She marches toward him, but I don't follow. I watch Carmen's face as she reads over the arrest warrant, hoping she will have an explanation.

"What does it say?"

Carmen bites her bottom lip, holding the warrant in her hands, as though the ink and paper bear hieroglyphics, some indecipherable code. I've watched her practice opening and closing arguments a dozen times, usually from the comfort of her living room over glasses of wine. Typically, each word leaves her lips with confidence and intention. But not now. When she does speak, her tone is as shaky as my comprehension.

"There's a list of charges. Custodial interference. Kidnapping. Murder."

I'm not even sure what the first phrase means, but it doesn't matter. All I can hear is that last word over and over again. *Murder.* The police think my mother murdered someone?

"Carmen, this can't be right. There must be a mistake." My stomach sinks further. "The name—"

We're both distracted by the sound of Des' yelling. She's standing in front of The Shack entrance, her wide frame blocking the officers from walking inside.

"What are you doing?" I ask the officer, jogging toward him. He looks to be a decade my junior, his face free from any lines or creases.

"I tried telling her," he says, nodding to Des. "We have a warrant to search the premises."

"But why?" I ask. "I don't understand what you're looking for."

"The suspect is listed as an owner of this establishment."

"Well, I own the building," Des shouts, defiantly. "And I say you can't come in."

"It says here this is also her residence," he says, pointing at another piece of paper. "Does she live here?"

"Upstairs," I say. The word falls out.

"Desiree, please," Carmen says, giving her a sympathetic stare. She turns to the officer. "I'm Carmen Banks, and I'll be acting as Ms. Sams' defense attorney. We're in the middle of a private party. At least let us ask the guests to leave."

The officer looks to his partner a few steps back, then nods at Carmen. "Five minutes. And I'll be standing inside until everyone exits the building."

"Thank you," Carmen says, placing her hand on Des' shoulder. "Let's explain to the guests that something has come up."

I'm still in a state of shock, trying to process what is happening. I'm thankful for Carmen and that logical, beautiful head on her shoulders. She's taking back control of this predicament, something I should be doing, but shock has restricted my abilities. She identified herself as Mom's attorney. Hearing that title startled me. This is real. Whatever *this* is, it's happening.

The party. Suddenly, I remember Ava. It's as if for the past ten minutes she hasn't existed. I've been so lost in this foreign predicament I'd forgotten about her, and the birthday celebration that has been ruined.

When I re-enter the restaurant, Michael is holding her, bouncing her rhythmically on one knee. She reaches for me, as she always does, oblivious to the tense air in the room. I hold her close, and, for several seconds, do nothing but breathe, allowing Carmen and Des to wrangle the remaining guests.

"Looks like quite the commotion out there," Holly says, craning her neck to get a better look outside. I ignore her.

"Is everything okay?" Michael asks. He's standing now, his eyes wide and full of confusion.

"I... I don't know." I squeeze Ava tighter, nuzzling my jaw against her soft curls.

People gather their belongings and leave. They must be curious, even shocked. The people here know me. They know Eileen Sams. Who is Sarah Paxton? I push the thought out of my mind, focusing instead on Ava. Her powdery smell, the confetti clinging to her dress.

I feel a hand on my back. I turn and see Carmen, but she is not looking at me. Her face is fixed on the front door, where the young officer is standing.

"I'm going to the police station." Her eyes fall on Ava, but her smile is strained, pretending for both our sakes the situation isn't as bad as it appears.

"I'm coming with you."

"I can't figure out what's happening if you're right beside me," she says. "Take Ava home. By the time you arrive at the station, hopefully I'll have more information."

I know Carmen is right, and she's already thinking with her lawyer brain, not as my best friend, but I feel an unexplainable desire to be near my mother. I can't erase the image of her sitting in the back seat of that police cruiser.

"I want to speak with her. I have to know she's okay. You didn't see her face when they arrested her. She was—"

"Just trust me to figure out what's going on." She gives Ava's arm a gentle squeeze, then pats my back.

"I'll drive you home," Des says, jingling her key ring. "I can watch Ava when you leave for the station."

"What about the restaurant?" I ask, disregarding the trail of police officers and technicians making their way inside.

"We've got bigger problems that need attending," Des says, her eyes bouncing between Carmen and me. "That was my best friend in handcuffs."

Des and Ava are safe at the condo. Carmen has had more than an hour's head start at the station. I'm hoping she can make sense of this. Why Mom is being charged with kidnapping... and murder. Why the police are calling her a different name.

The guy behind the counter looks fresh out of the academy, even younger than the cop back at The Shack. He sees me standing, but purposely ignores me for a few seconds. When he finishes writing, he looks up. "Help you?"

"I need to see my mother. She was brought in earlier today."

"Name?"

"Eileen Sams." Or should I say Sarah Paxton? I don't even know what name I should use.

"Your name?"

"Marion Sams." I look past the cop. There are a few more uniformed officers standing around, chatting. No one seems to mirror my state of rush.

A door to my right opens, and Carmen walks out. I turn, no longer seeking assistance from the deputy at the desk.

"Where's Mom?" I ask her.

"She's still being processed. It'll be a while before she can have visitors," she says.

"I want to see her now."

"Marion, you're going to have to wait."

"Have you at least figured out what's going on?" My voice is louder than normal, almost a shriek. "Can you tell me anything?"

Carmen yanks my arm, leading me outside. A cement bench rests to the left of the door. She forces me to sit.

"I understand you're upset right now, but from this moment forward you need to keep your emotions in check. Everything you say and do should be to help your mother's case. You're a big part of this, which means you'll have to listen to me."

"I'm a part of this—" I can't even form a question. There are too many antagonistic thoughts at the forefront of my mind, fighting for priority. "Please, just tell me what's going on. Who do they think she kidnapped? Who do they think she killed?"

Carmen takes a deep breath, looking over her shoulder before she continues.

"Back in the eighties, there was an infant abduction. A rich couple out of New Hutton. A woman broke into their home, attacked the mother and killed the father. Their three-month-old daughter was kidnapped. The press has aired several stories about it over the years. It's known as the Baby Caroline case. Any of this sound familiar?"

Some of what she says connects, in the same way any high-profile mystery would. I'm not sure of the details. I don't follow much media coverage, and anything on the crime channels gives me the creeps, especially after having Ava.

"I don't know. What does any of this have to do with Mom?"

"A woman named Sarah Paxton is considered the prime suspect. The police are alleging your mother was responsible for that kidnapping." She swallows hard, failing miserably at disguising her dread. "They think you're Baby Caroline."

CHAPTER 3

Then

Eileen

Dear Marion,

I'm writing this letter in the hope you'll never have to read it. I know that's selfish, as many of my decisions must seem to you in this moment, but I hope that by reading this you'll understand some of the selfless choices, too.

Today you are ten years old, and you've come to me just now, asking a question. You wanted to know about our family. I assured you the term only applied to the two of us. In a selfish chamber of my heart, it's true. But you're becoming so bright and curious. You're exactly as I always imagined you'd be, and that ushered in the realization you might one day be confronted with the truth. That's why I want you to hear it from me, in my own words, and I'm writing everything down, in case I'm no longer around to tell you myself.

Before we get started, you must understand why the idea of family is so important to me. I've avoided telling you about my upbringing because one child shouldn't have to live through it, let alone two. But now you need to know. To understand.

My father was a violent man. There wasn't a deputy in our county who couldn't recall some run-in with him. A bar fight they busted up. A high-speed chase down the narrow dirt roads that snaked around our house. But most often, they knew him from when they'd get a call from the neighbors. He was either beating on Mama or me, sometimes both.

Living like that, it wasn't a family. Not a good one, anyway. From the time I was a little girl, I promised myself I'd have better. I wouldn't cower in the corner, like Mama, or take out my anger on those smaller than me, like Daddy.

Of course, I stumbled a few times along the way. Being a screw-up is genetic, I think. It is as hereditary as any other trait. I come from a long line of screw-ups, and although I was able to persevere, I had my missteps. Like Mama, I fell into the trap of believing that maybe a man could solve my problems. I started dating Albert Crawford when I was sixteen. He convinced me to drop out of school and move into his apartment in New Hutton. I did it, mainly because I finally had a roof over my head that wasn't owned by my father. But I also did it because it felt, in a sad, convoluted way, like I was one step closer to getting that family I'd always dreamed about.

As you'd expect, things with Albert didn't last. He gave me more trouble than anything. He was the one who convinced me to rob that convenience store. *Beer and smokes*, he said. *No one cares about beer and smokes.* But once we got in there, he was reaching for the cash register. I didn't know until the police showed up—turns out the lady behind the counter had one of those buttons that silently made them aware—that Albert was carrying a gun.

Screw-up.

Like I said, it was in my genes. I took that moment to evaluate where my life was headed if I didn't start changing. I didn't have any role models to look up to, so I had to put in the work myself. It was like rewiring the chambers of my brain, teaching my cells to operate in different ways. Screwing up felt so natural. I'd actually ask myself, *What would Mama and Daddy do?* Then I'd try the opposite.

My lucky break was that I was still seventeen at the time of the convenience store incident. And I think, deep down, the police believed me when I told them I didn't know about the gun. I spent a couple of months at a juvenile facility—that's where I began changing, started rewiring my brain—and I was released. I was sentenced to probation for the next five years, but all that meant was intermittent stints of community service and counseling. I was told if I did everything the way I was supposed to—if I didn't screw up—my future employers wouldn't be able to see my criminal record.

During those early years, I drifted. I lived in cheap apartments you could lease for six months or less and worked wherever I thought I could make my next buck. *Honestly.* I want to stress that part. I never asked for anything I didn't deserve, and I certainly didn't take.

I'd worked at five, maybe six, different places over the years when I got a job at Buster's. It was a small eatery tucked between a few other nameless businesses in the downtown area. It was far from the Ritz, but it was in a nice enough part of town. There weren't addicts and prostitutes camped outside the front door, like at a few places I worked before. The food was good enough that we had some wealthier customers drive to our side of town for our famous toasted Italian. A hidden gem, locals called the place.

I didn't see Buster's like that at first. It was just another room, another place for me to work and make rent. I'd served in restaurants before, but I'd never done the cooking. At Buster's, I did a little bit of everything. Took orders at the register and shoved subs into the oven. Mopped floors and scrubbed the urinals after closing. It was more than I was used to doing, but it also paid better. A whole $1.25 more per hour than my last job, plus tips, and I didn't have to fight for more hours like I did at other places.

That's not what I liked the most about Buster's, though. It was the first place where I felt I was rubbing shoulders with people like me. In most settings, I was the poorest girl there, or the youngest. At Buster's, I looked around and I saw myself. People in their early twenties, a little rough around the edges, but willing to work, trying to smile. Just like me.

Jamie was the one who hired me. She was petite, looked like a cheerleader you would see somersaulting through the air, except she dressed like she was in a punk rock band and constantly smelled of cigarettes. There was a hardness to her that let me know she understood the world around us. When I handed over my application, she ignored my credentials, reading me instead.

"Drug problem?" she asked.

"No."

"Guy problem?"

"No." I didn't have time for guys, not since I left Albert.

"Got a car?"

"I only live three blocks away. I can walk."

She held my gaze a few more seconds, then nodded. It was as good as a handshake. Just like that, I was hired to work six days a week, open to close.

Jamie was the manager of sorts, which struck me as odd because she was only a few years older than me. Her uncle owned the place, although I never met him in all the years I worked there. Jamie had all sorts of family, as it turned out. They'd come in the restaurant sometimes, but they rarely spoke, and they all looked the same with their dark hair and black coats.

Most restaurants were like revolving doors. People worked a few shifts, then quit. Buster's had a reliable crew. Tucker was our security. Sometimes he'd help us clean, but he mainly stood by the door and made sure no one got jumped for tips at the end of the night. There was a tall girl—I can't remember her name all these years later—who worked only weekends. And there was Cliff. At twenty-five, he was a few years older than me, but his face still had that boyish charm. His spirit, too.

He was the cut-up of the place, the one pulling pranks and making others, even customers, laugh. During the day, we had all sorts of people visit. Students from the university across town. Lots of young moms with their babies. When Cliff wasn't making the moms laugh, I'd make funny faces at the children. I loved watching them giggle.

As the mothers would strap their babies into strollers, I'd think to myself, *that's going to be me. I won't be a screw-up anymore. One day, everything I've ever wanted will happen for me.*

You have to know, from the start, that's all I've ever wanted. Better for me, and the best for you.

CHAPTER 4

Now

Marion

Who is Baby Caroline?

That's the only question in my mind. I'm back in that trance I found myself in at the time of Mom's arrest. As though I'm uprooted, falling in the world around me, struggling to find stability. The blue patches of sky, lush greenery lining the sidewalk and the unmistakable scent of the ocean surround me, a kaleidoscope I find dizzying.

"Marion?"

It's Carmen's voice I hear. My tongue, a dry lump in my mouth refusing to work.

Who is Baby Caroline?

"Marion?"

I see her now. She's kneeling in front of me. The dirty sidewalk will probably leave stains on her expensive pants, I think. She touches my arm.

"Do you understand what I'm saying?"

"No. I don't," I say, shaking my head slightly. "The police have it wrong."

"They've been searching for Sarah Paxton for years and they believe Eileen might be her." Carmen looks over her shoulder, back at the building. "I'll need more time to figure out—"

"Fix this." I'm angry now. "Mom isn't capable of something so horrific. It would mean she kidnapped me as a child. That she murdered a man. That she's not even my real mother. They can't possibly think that?"

"Yes." She looks down. "That's exactly what they think."

"They've got the wrong person."

Carmen squeezes my hand. "I have to go back inside. Should I call Des?"

"No. Don't." I raise my head to look at her; my beautiful friend looks abnormally pale. My own appearance must be frightening. "Just go."

She remains on her knees another moment, debating whether she should leave me. "I'll call you as soon as I know more, okay?"

I nod. She stands and brushes off her thighs before walking inside the police station. I'm alone again, trying to iron out the information I've just been given. The woman who has raised me, shown me nothing but a gentle hand, couldn't be responsible for such crimes. It would mean my entire existence was no more than a fabrication. It would mean my mother... was something else. A deranged woman who stole me away, leaving a dead body and decades of mystery in her wake.

Who is Baby Caroline?

They've got the wrong person. They've made a mistake. Police fumble investigations all the time, don't they? Every documentary leads you to think so. There's no way my mother, the only parent I've ever known, could have done something so heinous. My mother is caring. Thoughtful. She puts everyone before herself, me more than anyone. She's not the type of person who could have done something like this.

A car door slams beside me. Two officers exit a vehicle and walk toward the station, their badges glinting as they pass. I take several deep breaths and stand. I'm not sure where I should go, but I know I have to leave. I need to think, list every reason why this outlandish accusation is false. They have the wrong person. That's the best explanation—the only explanation.

I drive past The Shack. The police cars have multiplied. Inside, they are no doubt tearing apart the business and Mom's upstairs apartment. The place where I spent the bulk of my childhood. My home. The business quadrant of my brain has a fleeting thought about what a PR nightmare this could be. Holly Dale has probably posted on Facebook by now. I imagine the confused faces of our local customers when they realize their favorite restaurant isn't an option for dinner tonight. I imagine their horror when they learn what I've just been told: that their neighbor and friend stole a child and raised her as her own.

Who is Baby Caroline?

I park my car in a vacant lot by the pier. I can't deal with Ava's needs or Des' questions right now. I just can't. I have to grapple with my own understanding of these allegations first. Besides, the beach has always been my personal place of refuge. I remain in the car, watching as the sun sinks into the water in the distance. It has always been so beautiful here in North Bay. There's rarely a scandal; now my mother is immersed in one.

The crime itself is so unnerving. I can't quite grasp the horror of it, of walking into the nursery and finding an empty crib. My own heart leaps into my throat when I think of Ava being part of such an ordeal—it would be every parent's worst nightmare. To one minute have your child safe at home, the next having that security ripped away from you. Being helpless to prevent it.

I lean back the seat and pull out my phone. *Baby Caroline.* Already, there are articles being published—forty-five minutes ago, thirty-eight minutes ago—about the arrest, although Mom's name hasn't been released. Looking back further, I see several stories have been written about the case. There are numerous thirty-year anniversary features from a few years back. I begin reading, taking it all in.

Baby Caroline, born Caroline Parker in 1987. An infant abduction. A woman named Sarah Paxton broke into the home of Amelia and Bruce Parker. Amelia was attacked, Bruce was murdered, and Baby Caroline was taken. Paxton's whereabouts remain unknown. It was one of those cases that had a dozen different theories, breadcrumbs leading nowhere. Were the parents responsible? Unlikely, considering one of them was murdered and Amelia Parker was able to name a suspect. Was it human trafficking? An attempted ransom gone wrong? Endless possibilities, all fruitless and forgotten, until a slow news day brought the story back into the spotlight. Never any solid leads. Never any answers.

At the end of the article, there is a picture of Sarah Paxton; it's the only known picture of her. It was taken when she was seventeen, after she was arrested for a previous crime. I pinch the screen, zooming in on the girl's face. The girl in the photo has a different hair color and a bitter scowl. Could it be Mom? Even I'm not sure. There is limited information about Sarah Paxton. In the few articles I've read, most of the information focuses on Baby Caroline's parents.

Amelia and Bruce Parker. I can't imagine their heartache, and yet, I feel compelled to attach faces to their names. They are real people after all. Real victims of an unspeakable tragedy. Most of the pictures are of Amelia post-attack. She is wearing structured dresses, sitting in front of interviewers or standing behind a podium. In some photos, she is crying, yet somehow she appears stoic and calm. A determined woman on the hunt for answers, guided by hope.

Finally, I find a photo of Bruce and Amelia together. It seems to have been taken on their wedding day. She's not wearing the frivolous layers of the time, but her hair has just enough height to let you know it's the eighties. Her décolleté is exposed, the hem folding beneath her shoulders, and the dress is fitted at the waist and ankles, giving her hips a classic pear shape.

The couple look happy. Ready. Rich. It's painful knowing what tragedy awaited them. You'd never know by looking at this picture.

They didn't know, and there's a lump in my throat just thinking about it. I zoom in, squinting to take in every feature on Amelia's face. Do we look alike? Is it possible? We both have narrow noses and green eyes. Her hair is a mousy brown, the same color mine used to be. Is that coincidence, or connection? Do I look more like her, or Mom? Do I look like that young girl in the mugshot?

Two Moms, I think with a shudder.

I keep scrolling through online archives. We have so few pictures of my childhood before we moved here, but there are multitudes of Amelia's family, the Boones, and Bruce's, the Parkers. They were both wealthy families who, when not committed to charity, devoted their lives to leisure. There are tons of pictures from both sides of the family: picnics under trees, water skiing on lakes and horseback riding on beaches. That nugget of envy returns, the one I felt growing up, watching my friends go about life with their normal, traditional families.

They think you're Baby Caroline.

I toss my phone onto the passenger seat, as though the secrets it contains are a contagion. I place my fingers against my temples, staring at the sinking sun in the sky. A mistake must have been made. An explanation must be imminent. And yet, there is a sinking feeling in my gut that I'm missing part of this story.

I need to talk to Mom.

CHAPTER 5

Now

Marion

Hours seem to pass. I'm still staring at that same stretch of sky, noticing how it changes. Streaks of orange splash against the blue as evening begins, a view that, on any other night, would leave me feeling peaceful, appreciative. Like the world is exactly as it should be.

The phone rings. It's Carmen.

"Where are you?"

"At the beach. I needed some time alone to try and make sense of all this."

"You can't see your mom tonight." She drops the news, unceremoniously. The last thing she must want is to extend the uncertainty. "You should probably go home."

Your mom. Is she my mom? The police don't think she is. Could she be anyone else?

"I have to speak with her, Carmen. I've been looking into Baby Caroline and—"

"It's not a choice, Marion. Visiting hours are over. It's been a long day, for her especially. She could probably use a night's rest."

"Did you get to speak with her?"

"A little."

"And? What did she say?"

There's a pause, which makes me nervous. "I think she's still in shock. She's not really answering any of my questions. Like I said, rest would do her good."

I close my eyes, wondering what Mom must be going through. She should have jumped at the opportunity to speak with Carmen, given her any information necessary to prove her innocence.

"I might be able to set up something tomorrow," Carmen says. "Right now, the best thing you can do is go home. Take care of Ava. Take care of yourself. The foreseeable future will be exhausting."

She pauses again. It's like we're thinking along the same track. Police. Press. If this case is what it's looking like, the repercussions will be huge. Insurmountable.

"Thank you for this, Carmen. Thank you for helping her."

The research I've been doing into the Baby Caroline case has left me with more questions than answers. I know little about the Parkers and their daughter and the mysterious Sarah Paxton. The only person I do know in all this is Mom, and what they're saying about her can't be true. With Carmen on our side, I'm hoping we'll be able to prove it.

I must have sat in that parking lot for hours. During that time, the police completed their search of The Shack. Des insisted on looking over the place, checking what, if any, damage had been done. She took Ava with her, so I go there to meet them.

I'm not sure what I was expecting the place to look like. It's not been this bad since the renovation. I can see where they've pulled up the tiles in certain areas of the floor, not taking the time to put them back. They've moved the furniture around, sifted through every drawer and left the contents strewn on the counters. They've taken the computer we use to track orders and process payments. I'm sure they did more damage upstairs, where Mom lives, but I don't think I have the energy to walk up the steps. I used what little I had left to tell Des everything I knew about the case, watching her bewildered reaction.

"The police have got it wrong. I've never heard the name Sarah Paxton in my life," Des says, passionately. "I think I would know if my best friend used a different name."

She pours a cup of coffee and slides it in front of me. To my right, Ava sways in her baby swing. It remained untouched by the police. As usual, she's in her happy, infant daze, nearing the edge of sleep. I hope she won't put up a fight tonight.

"Thanks," I say, my fingertip stroking the warm ceramic before I take a sip.

"I'm putting in a pizza for us, too."

At least the appliances work. It will take several days of labor before we're able to open the dining room back to the public, not to mention the cost of repurchasing our computer equipment. Even then, I'm not sure how many customers we'll have left. These accusations are severe. I wouldn't blame people for wanting to stay clear of the restaurant right now.

"I'm not hungry."

"You have to eat something. I bet you've not put anything in your stomach since the party."

She's right. Food has been the last thing on my mind, but I know there's no sense in arguing with Des. I watch as she prepares the pizza from scratch. Pounding the dough, curving her hands to make the crust. Staying busy is her coping mechanism, whether she's making food or offering childcare.

"I still can't believe any of this," I say, watching Ava across the room.

"Eileen has no business being thrown in a cage with a bunch of criminals. Don't you worry. Carmen will get her out."

It sounds like Des is trying to calm herself as much as she is me. Thing is, Mom's charges are as severe as you can get. Kidnap and murder. North Bay doesn't have a lot of crime. It's mostly civil violations. I'll read about a domestic abuse arrest in the paper from time to time, but there aren't random shootings and stabbings. There's more activity in the summer months, but that's usually tourists getting a little too bold.

"What do you think about all this?" I ask, needing some honest input from someone who knows Mom as well as I do.

"Which part?"

"Do you think the things people are saying about her could be true? Do you think she kidnapped me? Murdered my biological father?"

Des turns, reaching into the ingredients' galley for toppings. Did she turn intentionally? I wonder. She literally doesn't want to face me.

"I have no reason to think any of it's true. The Eileen I know isn't capable of such violence."

"You've been friends with Mom for a long time. Since we moved here. Did she ever talk to you about where we lived before? Did she tell you anything?"

"Nothing about kidnapping and murder."

Again, her subdued reaction tells me she's deflecting. She knows something but won't say what. "Des, I need someone to be honest with me. I need answers."

She turns around, keeping her eyes low. "When I met Eileen, all I saw was a young mother and her bright-eyed little girl. It was obvious she didn't come from much, but she needed a place to stay, which is why I rented her the apartment. I assumed she'd been through something, but she never told me what. And I didn't ask."

"But what about after that? You've been friends for over thirty years. She never opened up about her life before North Bay?"

"Friends tell each other everything. Better friends know when to stay quiet."

Des is a confrontational person, but she's not nosy. Damn it. I believe her when she says she didn't pry into Mom's past. Still… surely… there must be something.

"Did she tell you about my father?"

"She said he wasn't in the picture. Said it was just the two of you."

That's the same thing she told me. That my father took off when she told him about the pregnancy. They were both young, and I was better off not having him around. When I asked for a name, she refused to tell me. Half my life I've suspected there was more to the story, but as with any other lingering questions about my childhood, I let it go. Out of respect for Mom and all she'd done for me. Now the police are saying Mom murdered my real father. They're saying she had to kill him in order to take me.

And that woman. Baby Caroline's mother. I can't imagine her pain. Losing a husband. Losing a child. Never knowing what happened until your daughter was already grown, an adult and mother herself. An entire lifetime stolen. Whoever did that to her is a monster, but I can't believe Mom is that person.

"Do you think the police have arrested the wrong woman?"

Des has the raw pizza centered on a wooden spatula. She slides the pizza into the industrial oven and the door creaks closed. After setting the timer, she walks toward the table. She's about to sit, when a loud noise startles us.

Clack.

We jump, turning toward the front window where the sound originated. Something has been thrown against the building. I can't tell what it is. Some kind of fruit, possibly. It's a mushy mound slowly sliding down the glass.

"Son. Of a. Bitch."

Des investigates, opening the front door and using a nearby broom to slide the mass to the ground. I can hear another commotion outside. It sounds like voices and footsteps. Des closes the door and pushes the lock.

"What was it?" I ask.

"A bunch of hooligans," she says, still looking out the window. "There's some press out there, too. They know we're in here now."

Press. They've found the restaurant. How much longer until they show up at the condo? The Baby Caroline story is gaining traction. I fear what people will have to say about Mom. And me.

"Close the blinds," I say.

Des pulls the tassel beside each window, until the blinds are flat from floor to ceiling.

"They're the ones I don't get," she says. "They're not impacted by any of this. Don't they realize real people are hurting?"

"They don't care, Des."

She sits next to me, her arms outstretched across the table. "Whatever they say about Eileen doesn't matter. Your mom is the best friend I've ever had. She doesn't have it in her to do the things they're saying."

Des is loyal to a fault. I feel the same way. *Unless…*

"Do you think she did it?" I ask, dryly. I can't ignore the fact that the police wouldn't have made a move after so long unless they had solid evidence. "Do you think she was so desperate for a baby she kidnapped me? Attacked my mother? Killed my father?"

"The only mother you've ever known is Eileen."

"I know that. But do you think she did it?"

"I don't know." It hurts her to say this. Again, she's honest. "If she did, I'm sure she had her reasons. Either way, it won't change how I feel about her."

The timer behind the counter dings. Des seems thankful for an escape. She might wear her emotions on her sleeve, but she's not one to talk about them. Beside me, Ava is now asleep. I'm happy the fruit thrown against the glass hasn't disturbed her the way it did us. None of this bothers her the way it does us. Oh, to be so naive.

When Des returns, she has two plates. She places one in front of me.

"Mushroom and pepperoni. Your favorite. Now eat."

I stare at the greasy toppings, the molten cheese frayed at the edges. The smell is tempting, but Des got it wrong. This isn't my favorite pizza. It's Mom's. And I still don't think I can eat.

CHAPTER 6

Then

Eileen

I was used to people looking at me and wanting something. My father demanded respect. Albert Crawford recognized my naivety. When Cliff, the scrawny line cook at Buster's, looked at me, there wasn't anything self-serving about his gaze.

It was the way he spoke to me, too. Inquisitive. Interested. He wanted to know more about me, and I felt I could tell him all the little thoughts in my mind. Even the dark ones. I could tell him without fear he would use the information against me, manipulate my trust to fulfill his own needs.

So, I'd tell him about the awful events I saw growing up. With only a little shame, I told him about my first relationship which ended after my arrest. I was overwhelmed by his acceptance, unafraid he might judge me. Cliff didn't judge. He cared. He listened. He understood.

And he told me about himself, too. Our breaks at Buster's were supposed to be ten minutes every three hours, but we had memorized the lunch schedule. We knew when it was safe to stretch ten minutes into twenty, and we'd fill the extra minutes with conversation. Like me, he came from a long line of screw-ups. Raised by parents who had no business parenting, in a neighborhood whose inhabitants did anything but act neighborly. He'd found his way out, as I had, but the consequences of those experiences followed him, like a mangy mutt tracking a scent.

There was a darkness inside him I liked because it reflected a part of myself. The screw-up. He'd tell me about his life, about the particular things he felt shaped him. Unfortunately, his schoolmates were as oppressive as his family members. Cliff and his younger brother had been selected to attend a nearby private school, a scholarship program reserved for the poorest of the poor. By his own admission, Cliff fit the bill. What was meant to introduce him to a better life only provided a glimpse into more cruelty. The students there were mean to him, never wasted an opportunity to remind him how low he was.

The khaki pant pricks. That's what he called them. They weren't just his tormentors at school, but afterwards, too. They'd follow him along his walk home, daring to enter the secluded alleyways from which their privilege protected them. Even though they were the same age as Cliff, in the same grade, wearing the same clothes, their worlds were entirely different.

"I used to hate them," Cliff said, sitting on that dirty stoop behind Buster's.

"What would they do when they'd follow you home?"

"Whistle and holler. Call me names. I'd ignore them half the time. Getting in a fight with one of them would have ended my free ride at Peppermill, even if they were the pricks who started it. Their parents' generosity is what paved my way, you know."

He shook his head, sliding the rolled cigarette from behind his ear. He didn't light it right away. He twiddled it between his fingers. Cliff rarely smoked, really.

"So you just ignored them?"

"For the most part. Against my better judgment." Cliff made this face. It was hard to tell whether he was proud of his tolerance, or ashamed of his inaction. "There was only one time I fought back."

"Yeah?"

"They knew they weren't getting to me, right? On one hand they liked it, I guess. They wouldn't know how to handle themselves if

I actually turned around and popped them a good one. They were just bored. They'd waste a good twenty minutes after school following me around, and they'd never get a rise out of me. One day, they were at it again. We made it three or four blocks away from school. I turn down the alley leading to my neighborhood, and they're snickering and whispering the whole way. I keep walking, like I always did, like I wasn't fazed by their little games.

"There was this bum crawled up asleep by the dumpster. They usually didn't sleep that late in the day, but fall was creeping into winter, which meant the nights were becoming less and less tolerable. He probably curled up to take in the sunlight and fell asleep. Anyway, the khaki pant pricks are only a few steps behind me. They see this guy, sleeping on the pavement. They stop. I keep going, like I always do. But then, their laughing gets louder. I'd about forgotten about the bum next to the dumpster."

"What happened?"

Cliff's face was somber, his tone level. Like he was stuck in this moment, this memory from long ago. The intensity in his expression startled me.

"I had to backtrack a couple of steps to see. One of the guys, Ben I think was his name, pulled his pecker out and was pissing all over the guy."

I raised a hand to my mouth. "He didn't."

"To this day, I can't tell you what happened. It's like I blacked out or something. Next thing I know, I'm standing over 'ole Ben. He's got blood streaming out both his nostrils, and in my hand, I was holding some plank I'd picked up from a broken crate." He stopped, looked up at me. I recognized his shame. It's the same I felt every time I told the story of my arrest. He was afraid he'd lost me. Afraid my judgment had taken over. "Growing up where I did, fighting wasn't anything new. I know it was wrong, though."

"No. What you did was right. They were messing with that guy for no reason. You stood up for him."

"Yeah. Yeah, I guess I did."

"What about his friends? What did they do?"

"They stood there and watched the whole thing. They were afraid to intervene. Hell, when I backed away, it's like they were afraid to touch him."

"Is that why you ended up leaving Peppermill?"

I knew from previous conversations he'd never graduated. He dropped out and earned his GED.

"That's the craziest part about it. All that night and the next morning, I kept waiting for my slap on the wrist. It never came. My teachers didn't mention it. The students didn't. Ben didn't come back until the following week, after the swelling in his nose went down. Even he didn't say anything to me about it. Or his friends. It's like they knew they'd crossed a line. Me beating up Ben may not have been the best move, but they weren't wanting to admit what they'd done either."

"You must be an all right guy if that's the worst thing you've ever done." I smiled, tucking my chin to my chest. "All you were doing was standing up for a guy who wasn't in a position to defend himself."

"I guess you're right." He looked up at the sky, perhaps searching for forgiveness, still rolling the cigarette between his fingers. "Thing is, I think about that day all the time. I think about those guys. It's like I still see them everywhere. Whenever some guy in a snazzy car drives through my neighborhood or some douchebag with shiny shoes slums it at Buster's for his afternoon lunch. I want to just start beating his face in. I know they're different guys, maybe even good guys… but that's not what I see."

His honesty was refreshing, yet startling. "You wouldn't do that, right? Unless they deserved it?"

"Right." He laughed, nervously. "You only give someone a beating that bad if they deserve it."

I realized that day, sitting in that dirty alleyway behind Buster's, this was the first time anyone had looked at me in a long time and seen me. Not seen the screw-up or the criminal or the extra mouth to feed. Otherwise, he wouldn't have told me that story. And although I didn't tell him the truth about what was going on in my life then—that I was struggling to get by, hoping I'd still have the same job and apartment come Christmas—I felt like it was the happiest I had been in a while.

"Break's over," Jamie said, swinging the door wide so that it smacked the brick.

Cliff took his cigarette, still not smoked, and tucked it behind his ear. He scrambled back inside, leaving me alone with Jamie.

She leaned against the building. She pulled out her own cigarette and lit it immediately. "You feeling it yet?"

"Feeling what?"

"Butterflies. You two have been flirting back and forth for weeks."

"You think?" I had little experience with guys. I wasn't sure if they liked me, if I liked them, or if we were just passing the time.

"He's into you, that's for sure."

I couldn't hide the smile on my face. It seemed to ignite a chain reaction through the rest of my body, my bony frame filling with warmth.

"When I hired you, you said you didn't have a boy problem." She smiled. Like she was looking for the same acceptance from me I found in Cliff.

"I still don't."

She raised her chin. "The three of us should get a drink after work. It'd be good to get out, maybe act my age for a change. Who knows? Maybe you two will hit it off."

"I'd like that," I said, practically floating back into the building. I was on track to make friends, maybe even more. I couldn't help but think Buster's, and the people inside it, had come into my life for a reason.

Maybe it was fate. I thought that then. I still think that sometimes.

CHAPTER 7

Now

Marion

In the morning, I have a brief moment of ignorance. All I hear is the ocean crashing into the shore on the other side of my patio. I hear Ava through the baby monitor, wrestling with the covers in her crib, starting to wake. I smile.

Then I remember yesterday. Everything that happened. Everything I was told. All the things I still don't know. And I remember Mom is gone. She's being detained at the jail, and I've still not had the chance to speak with her.

I stumble into the kitchen and turn on the coffee machine. I'm alone, and yet the usual quiet of the morning seems disturbed. There's an unusual background noise seeping in from outside. I walk to the window and push back the curtain. A cluster of news vans are parked on my street.

Shit. The press. Like Carmen said, Baby Caroline was once a big news story. A cold case people aren't likely to forget. I pull the curtains tight, making sure no one can see inside. I retrieve my phone to call Carmen, but there's already a text from her.

It reads: *Stay calm. I'm on my way.*

Just then, Ava lets out a cry. Not an upset wail, more a curious caw that asks, *Did you forget about me?* I've been so enveloped in my own problems I'm neglecting her.

I walk into her room. She is standing in her crib, bouncing in anticipation of being picked up. I immediately go to the windows in her room, making sure they are locked and covered. Her bedroom doesn't face the street, but I feel an unusually strong urge to protect her now that I know there is a horde of tragedy vultures outside our complex.

The minutes spent waiting for Carmen to arrive pass slowly. The entire time I've been with Ava—holding her, rocking her, cleaning her—I've felt guilty. Aside from me, Mom is undoubtedly the most important person in my daughter's life. She's nowhere to be found now, and I'm not sure when I'll see her again. I realize Ava is too young to understand what is going on, and yet, I believe she can sense Mom's absence. I know I can.

When Carmen arrives, she walks into the living room wearing red slacks and a silk, sleeveless blouse. I would guess she has been in court again, but Carmen often dresses like a raven-haired Grace Kelly in a classic film. Confident and sleek, yet feminine. Her chic aura scatters when she collapses on the couch, overcome with exhaustion. The past twenty-four hours have clearly taken an emotional toll.

Before I close the door, Rick, Carmen's assistant, walks in carrying a briefcase. That's his title, at least. Over six feet tall and two hundred pounds, Rick looks more like he stepped off the football field than out of the courtroom. He's basically a private investigator Carmen enlists when she needs information on people. I can only imagine the amount of digging he'll be tasked with when it comes to Mom. More than thirty years' worth.

"Marion." Rick nods, then sits beside Carmen on the sofa, placing his case on the floor.

"Get any sleep?" she asks.

"Not enough. Still trying to wrap my mind around everything."

"I can't imagine what you're going through, but police officers will be arriving soon. They'll start asking questions. I'll tell you everything I know, but it's important we go over what you might say to them, too."

"Where do we start?"

"Have you ever heard the name Sarah Paxton?" she asks, sitting upright on the couch.

"No," I answer, honestly. "Not until yesterday."

"Good. That's good. Was your mother ever called anything else when you were growing up, that you can remember?"

"No. Eileen Sams. I've never known her under any other name."

"Okay. Has she ever told you anything about your life before moving to North Bay? Do you remember living anywhere else?"

In the wee hours of the morning, I sat in bed trying to remember the exact same thing. We moved here when I was a toddler. I don't have any memories before that time. It's more like glimpses, a sensory connection to a certain song or smell. I don't remember where we lived. When I was older, I asked Mom. She said we moved around a lot, usually based on her ability to find work. When something didn't pan out, we'd pack up and move again. Then we found North Bay, our perfect place, she said, and stayed.

I tell Carmen all of this. She nods as she listens, taking notes. "What about New Hutton? Did she ever mention having lived there?"

"Never. She always said we lived in small towns. I think one might have been Ringold. Maybe East Ridge."

"I'm guessing you don't remember any people from these places?"

"My first memory of someone aside from Mom is meeting Des at The Shack."

Our first week in North Bay was spent in a motel. I have vague memories of it; the vending machines right next to our room made it hard to sleep. I think the main reason I remember our first week here is because it was my first time seeing the ocean. I'd never seen anything so big, so beautiful. It's like the landscape washed away any fragmented memories I had before.

After the week at the motel, we moved into the upstairs apartment at The Shack. Des hired Mom to work at the restaurant, which at the time was called something else. It would be another two years before Mom and Des decided to revamp the place together, making Mom a partial owner.

"Can you write down all the places your mom said you lived before North Bay?" Carmen pushes over a notepad and pen. I'd forgotten I was in the thick of an interrogation, preparing for an even bigger one.

"Yeah. Sure."

"Everything you say needs to be clear. It's okay if you don't remember all the details. You were young. But you don't need to change anything you say. Got that?"

Carmen has been in full lawyer mode since the party, but there is a part of me that longs for her friendship. That longs for someone to tell me everything will be okay, even if it won't be.

"You've told me a little bit about your father before," she says, her tone softer. "But I need you to tell me everything you know. Specifically, everything your mom told you about him."

"You know she's not said much," I say, looking down at Ava. "She said they weren't married. They were young. He left before I was born."

"Has she ever given you a name? Told you anything about his family?"

No and no. Not for lack of trying. When I was younger, the idea of not having a father didn't bother me. I'd never known a family unit outside the one I had with Mom. As I got more involved with school, I realized something was off. Most of my friends had a dad. Even the ones with absent fathers knew something about them. Their mothers at least referenced them from time to time, calling them scumbag or deadbeat.

Mom actively avoided talking about my father, or any other family members, for that matter. Grandparents: dead. Father:

gone. No siblings. No aunts and uncles. No cousins. It's like Mom and I were the last two standing. Like we'd been plucked out of nothingness and placed in North Bay. But saying that definitely wouldn't help Mom's case.

As a teenager, I was more vocal with my questions. Every time Mom and I had a fight about curfew or her ironclad rules, I'd bring him up. It's like I could use this person I'd never met against her. I knew this was hurtful, which during an argument was my aim, but I also hoped she might tell me something about my father in a fit of passion and rage, this man I knew nothing about.

It never worked, and as I grew older, I made peace with the situation. Maybe there were things about my father she didn't want me to know. Maybe it was easier for her to pretend he never existed. After a while, it didn't bother me anymore. The not knowing. I was used to the dynamic of Mom and me against the world. I preferred it, really. But again, I can't tell the police that.

"Marion?"

My mind is wandering, and Carmen's waiting for an answer.

"She never told me anything about him. Even when I asked. I don't know anything. Sorry."

"You don't need to apologize," Carmen says, her tone kinder.

I clear my throat, handing Ava a block just out of her reach. "It's overwhelming having to sift through my entire life in a matter of minutes."

"I know. That's why we're talking now. It's better to get the emotional stuff out of the way. When the police arrive this afternoon, it needs to be all facts." Carmen shifts in her seat, placing her hand over mine. "Really, you've done nothing wrong here. Even if what they're saying about Eileen is true—"

"Do you think it's true?" I stare at her, hoping she'll be honest. Although, honesty is hard in this complicated situation. She's my mother, and even I don't know if I believe what they're saying about her. I know I don't want to believe it.

"It's never my responsibility to decide whether a person did the crime they're accused of committing. My job is to argue reasonable doubt. I find the holes in the prosecution's case and go from there."

"Do you think there is reasonable doubt? Are there holes in the case?"

"You already know the police are alleging your mother's birth name is Sarah Paxton. There has not been any sign of that woman since the late eighties. Her last known whereabouts were in the New Hutton area. That's where Caroline Parker was kidnapped. She was only three months old. It was a media circus at the time. Bruce Parker was found dead at the scene. Trauma to the head."

"That's all they have? That Mom might have gone by the name Sarah Paxton and lived in the same area?"

"They're comparing her DNA and fingerprints to what was found on the scene back then. Results could take a few more days. Other than that, they're trying to find out as much as they can about Eileen's past and compare it to Sarah's."

Good luck with that, I think. Even I'm unsure about Mom's history. It never seemed important until now.

"And they think I'm Baby Caroline?"

"Yes."

Silence fills the room.

"Why now? It's been so long."

"Any case that big is always a priority. Also, the parents were wealthy. The mother—" Carmen's eyes dart to the left. I know what she's thinking. *Your mother*. Maybe. "Mrs. Parker named Sarah Paxton as a suspect from the beginning. The two women met at a counseling center where Mrs. Parker worked. She believes Sarah developed an unhealthy obsession with her. Sarah broke into their home, attacked them and left with Caroline."

"All these years this woman has known who stole her baby? And she's been trying to find her?"

"She never stopped searching for answers. No telling how much money she has poured into dead ends over the years. An anonymous tip let them know Sarah Paxton was living in North Bay, which is what led them here. All they need is to prove you were... are Baby Caroline."

"I'll do it right now," I say, my body bucking with adrenaline, answers feeling within reach. "Let's submit a DNA test."

"It would help Eileen's case if you didn't volunteer anything. A test is inevitable, but let the police come to you. No need to speed up the process. Your priority should be helping your mom."

I recall the look on Mom's face as they cuffed her wrists behind her back. She was broken, afraid. I want to help her, but there is a knot of anger tangling in my gut. Maybe she's not who they say she is, maybe I'm not who they say I am, but something isn't adding up. After all these years, the police wouldn't make a move unless they were confident they had found the right person. The fact Carmen insists I don't take a test suggests she's worried about what the results might be.

"When will I get to speak with her?"

"I'm hoping this afternoon. After your talk with the investigators." Carmen looks down, pretends she's fiddling with something, although her hands are empty. "Meanwhile, I'll have Rick look into everything he can find about Sarah Paxton."

He's been sitting with us the whole time in silence. Occasionally, he'll scribble something on his notepad. He sits up, lifting his briefcase from off the floor and unlocking it.

"I wanted to give you this," he says, handing over a business card. "It's got my cell phone number. If you run into any problems or feel like you're not safe, call me. Day or night."

"Not safe?" I look to Carmen. "Why wouldn't I be safe?"

"Again, when a case is this big, it brings the crazies out," she says. "I'm already trying to make the press back off."

"I'm leaving you with this, too," Rick says. He pulls out a black baton. It looks like the type of weapon a policeman might carry on his utility belt.

I release a quick laugh. "You've got to be kidding me. You don't think I'll really need that thing, do you?"

The look on Carmen's face is serious. "It wouldn't hurt to carry it around. Leave it within arm's reach whenever you're inside the house. It's better to be safe than sorry."

I exhale, taking the baton from Rick's hand. Owning one of these is out of character, let alone having to use it. Then I remember the fruit being chucked at The Shack's front window last night. I think of what other actions people might take to get my attention, or worse, punish us for what they think Mom has done. My life has become so bizarre in such a short amount of time.

"I have a bad feeling," I say. "This seems like a losing battle. How will we prove to the police they have the wrong person?"

"Right now, it's like we're getting pummeled with all the evidence the prosecution has already gathered. They've had a head start, after all." Carmen leans back, crossing her legs and placing her hands on her stomach. "As hopeless as things might appear, there's plenty of holes. The crime happened thirty years ago. That's a lot of time for evidence to decay and stories to change. It won't be a slam-dunk until—"

"Until they do a DNA test." It would take one flimsy cotton swab to determine whether or not Mom is my biological mother.

"The test will come. Wait for it. If the results aren't in our favor, we can think of other strategies."

Strategies. Carmen can predict how one outcome will bleed into the next. She knows what those results will do to me. The devastation I'll feel. I wonder if Carmen is trying to gather as much information as she can from me now, before I'm a blubbering mess. It's a manipulative tactic, but that's what makes her good at her job.

"Let's start over," she says, propping her elbows on her knees. "We'll review the main questions again and again. Until you're ready to share them with investigators."

I nod. "Okay."

CHAPTER 8

Now

Marion

Carmen's visit did help prepare me for my conversation with investigators. By the time they arrived, I was able to retell what limited information I had in a calm, methodical manner. In fact, the detectives, both of them male and in their fifties, didn't push too hard. They didn't provide much information about Mom's case, either. There seemed to be an unspoken understanding that, whatever my mother had done, I was a victim. This was painful for me, and they weren't wanting to add to that agony. They left with a warning there would be future conversations as the case developed.

Now I'm riding in the passenger seat of Carmen's Range Rover. Ava is buckled into her car seat behind me. The seat is rear facing, but I can hear the occasional sound of her babbling and cooing. I long for her obliviousness. Ava's life was also upended yesterday, but she doesn't know it.

"Are you sure Michael can handle the kids?" I ask. We're taking Ava to Carmen's house, so that we can go to the county jail and talk with Mom.

"Probably not. But Esme is there, so they'll be fine. Besides, he'll have to get used to more time with the kids now that he's not working."

In all that's happened in the past two days, I've forgotten the Banks family is also going through a transition. Carmen's job is demanding. She works long, unpredictable hours. Michael's job was equally taxing, until he abruptly quit last month. He was some kind of financial advisor, which meant he spent a good portion of the month traveling outside North Bay. He grew tired of constantly being away from his family, so he quit and has been studying for his real estate license ever since.

They still have extra help from Esme, a part-time nanny Carmen hired last year. It would be nice, having a second set of hands. Of course, Carmen and Michael had two large salaries to fund this expense; I make a decent living from The Shack, but as a single parent, I'm basically still getting by.

"How is Michael doing?" I ask. "Does he miss his job yet?"

"Sometimes." Carmen, for the first time since the party, drops the lawyer role. "He won't admit it, though. Everyone talks about wanting to take time off, but when you work the hours we do, you kind of get used to it. It becomes addictive. We're hoping we can make it to the end of summer, go on a nice vacation before he starts working in the fall."

"That's great."

Carmen has a lot of help. She has Esme and me and even Des, if she needed to ask. But it's nice to know Michael also supports her. It's important to have that person, the one who is always in your corner. I thought I had it with Mom, but now I'm not so sure.

As though timed, my phone buzzes. It's Evan again. He called yesterday during the party, but then chaos ensued. I never got back to him, and I'm still not sure I'm ready. I silence the phone, staring out the window as we pull into Carmen's neighborhood.

Carmen's house also faces the water, but the single residence is almost the size of my entire complex. I carry Ava into the living room. Esme has just prepared dinner, some kind of pasta with a red sauce. As usual, Esme's face lights up when she sees Ava. Babies are magical in that sense. They're able to temporarily make people forget the negative aspects of the world, just with their bright eyes and pudgy rolls.

Michael comes over. He kisses Carmen on the cheek, then pulls me in for a half hug.

"I'm so sorry, Marion," he whispers, quiet enough so the children can't hear.

"Thank you."

The last time I saw him was at the party. He was one of the many guests who watched the scandal unfold. The whole thing was so humiliating. Holly Dale and my friends from Mommy and Me were likely horrified. Yesterday seems like a lifetime ago.

"Eileen is in good hands with Carmen," he says. "Don't worry about a thing."

Carmen and Michael lock eyes. I can tell she appreciates his comment but doesn't want to blush too much in my presence. I always thought they were a compatible couple. They prioritize business, allow each other the independence needed to succeed in their given fields, but they also strive to make time for family. I hope to build a connection like that with someone one day.

I can't follow Michael's instructions not to worry, though. Carmen is good at her job, but she is usually tasked with making a bad situation better. As hopeful as I try to be, I know Carmen won't be able to restore the normalcy that was stolen yesterday. No one is that good.

"Call us if you need anything," Carmen says, her eyes flitting between Michael and Esme.

Once we're in the car, the magnitude of what is about to happen sets in. I'm about to ask my mother the truth about these charges. I'm about to ask her if she did the horrible things the police say she did. Did she steal me as an infant? Raise me in secret all these years? Did I—do I—belong to another family entirely? In my head, the answers to these questions is a resounding no, but I need to hear Mom say it.

Carmen's told me I can't ask direct questions, of course. Any admission Mom gives could be used against her at trial. But I'm not about to sit across from her without asking. If anyone deserves the truth, it's me.

There isn't any music playing in the car. I only hear the whistling wind as we zoom along quiet streets. The sun is setting, an orange orb dipping into the gray waters on the horizon. As much as I've thought about Mom in the past twenty-four hours, she's not the only person on my mind.

"Tell me about them. About the Parkers."

Carmen, cool as ever, doesn't flinch. She keeps her eyes on the road.

"I don't know much. It appears Amelia Parker worked as a counselor. Bruce Parker worked for her father, at Boone Enterprises. She comes from big money." She clears her throat. "Mr. Parker was killed on the same day Caroline was kidnapped. Mrs. Parker was attacked, too, but survived. She's spent a small fortune trying to track down leads over the years."

I know Carmen is trying to sound objective, but I can hear a hint of sympathy in her voice. She feels sorry for them. For this poor woman who found her husband dead and daughter missing. For this woman who has lived without answers for over thirty years. I'm buckling from stress after only a day of this. I can't imagine if suddenly Ava was taken from me.

I stop. I can't go down this road again. It's a horror I can't fathom, and I don't envy anyone who has lived it.

"Did Amelia Parker have any other children?"

Carmen shakes her head. "She never remarried. No kids, either." Carmen's hands tighten around the steering wheel. "Maybe talking to Eileen right now isn't the best—"

"I have to see her, Carmen. I'm going crazy reading theory after bizarre theory. She's the only person who can make sense of this."

Carmen's jaw clenches, but she doesn't say anything. She knows nothing can talk me out of having this conversation.

CHAPTER 9

Now

Marion

It's not until I enter the waiting room that I really think about what the last twenty-four hours must have been like for my mother. Over the years, Carmen has whispered details about the criminal justice system. What really happens when you are arrested, on trial, convicted. I imagine my mother's fingertips dipped in ink, her squinting under the bright flash from the camera for a mugshot that will forever document this accusation. She has been stripped and searched, dressed in stiff clothes and uncomfortable shoes. Last night, she slept alongside a dozen strangers, or more likely, didn't sleep. She probably stayed awake, contemplating how many more nights like this were to come. Contemplating so much.

All of this runs through my mind as I wait for Carmen to invite me into the meeting room. She has pulled some strings, allowing me to visit Mom privately, instead of in the rowdy visiting room.

A deputy taps on the glass door in front of me, nodding for me to follow.

"Ms. Banks wants you to wait here," he says, as I stand in the vestibule on the other side of the door. It's colder here, it seems. Or maybe it's just my nerves. I pull on the sleeves of my shirt, finding it difficult to look anywhere other than the floor.

A door opens. I enter the room and see Mom sitting behind a table, Carmen standing at her back. Whatever anger and fear I have felt leading to this moment dissipates. As Mom stands, I rush to her.

"Are you okay?"

It's like my nerves have transferred to her. Suddenly, she's shaking, like it's taking all the strength she has left just to stand. She doesn't answer. She only nods, before whispering in that broken tone: "I'm sorry."

I hold her a second longer, wanting her to see I'm strong. I'm with her. But as I sit in the chair across from her, I can already feel my buried curiosity returning. There is so much I need to ask her. There is so much she needs to tell me.

"Are you okay?" I repeat.

Now composed, Mom takes a deep breath, wiping her cheeks with her hand. "You shouldn't have come here."

My mouth opens, but I don't know what to say. Rather, I don't know how to say it effectively. We've both been through trauma in the past two days, and all she can say is I shouldn't have come?

"Mom, you need to tell me what's going on. I've read up on the Baby Caroline case, but I need to know why the police think you're involved."

Suddenly, she's shaking again. First her arms, then her head. Like she's trying to wipe this moment away. "I can't do this. Not here. Not like this."

"We aren't left with many options," I say, leaning across the table to be closer to her. "What they're saying isn't true, is it?"

"We can't discuss specifics of the case," Carmen says, a simple but stern reminder.

I ignore her, focusing instead on Mom.

"The police are saying your real name is Sarah Paxton," I begin, but I'm distracted by Mom's manic behavior.

Her head still shaking, she covers her ears. "I can't. I can't."

"Mom, please." I lurch closer, the table between us. "You have no idea what I've been going through. You have to tell me something. The police have you mixed up with someone else, right? Your name isn't Sarah Paxton, is it?"

"Yes." The word, a whisper. She puts a hand to her mouth, like she can somehow take it back. And she begins to cry.

I'm stunned. The hope I had that the police had the wrong person is gone. There must be some truth to these accusations, but she's refusing to tell me.

"What about everything else they've been saying? That you kidnapped me? That I'm not your daughter?"

"I can't." Mom stands so quickly the chair clatters against the tile floor. She backs toward the door against the far wall.

"Mom, calm down," I say, and now I'm standing too. "I'll support you either way. Nothing will ever change what you mean to me. But I need to know the truth."

"I can't do this," Mom wails.

"Maybe we should try this another time," Carmen says, her voice a little more soothing.

But I can't be soothed. I'm enraged. You would think Mom might show a little concern for me. For Ava. For what we must have been going through. Not only is she refusing to answer my questions, she is trying to ignore me altogether, wishing me away.

"You can't do this," I tell her, my voice cracking, but my anger providing strength. "You've avoided questions my entire life. You hid things from me, like about my father, without ever thinking how it might impact me. You can't do that anymore. You have to start being honest."

Now Mom is sitting on the floor next to the door. She is hunched over, like a child grappling with a nightmare. Her eyes remain closed, her hands cover her ears. "No, I can't. I won't."

A guard rushes in, brushing past me to get to Mom. He swoops her up in one swift movement, escorting her through the door.

"Mom, wait. Please!"

But she is gone. The door is shut, the vertical window only giving me a small glimpse into the dark hallway. This was it. My opportunity to find out the truth. Now it's over.

"I told you not to bring up specifics of the case," Carmen says, marching toward me. "I told you she was fragile."

"She won't even talk to me, Carmen."

I've never seen my mother break down like this. Being a single mother, it's not like she didn't have trials and tribulations. She rose above each and every one. She exemplified control. Now she's crumbling before me, and I'm no closer to learning the truth.

The woman I just saw. The behavior she just showed.

I don't recognize that woman.

CHAPTER 10

Then

Eileen

Thanks to the convenience store incident, I had to attend two counseling sessions a month. This was supposed to last until I turned twenty-five or got in trouble again, whichever came first. Of course, I'd already promised myself the latter would never happen. And really, the sessions weren't as bad as you'd think. It wasn't like on TV, where some pretentious therapist with gray hair and wire glasses asks about your childhood.

Did your dad beat you? Yes.

Did your mother stop him? No.

Is that why you're a screw-up? Maybe.

No, it was none of that. We rarely talked about the past. Our sessions were focused on the present. Where was I living? Working? Who were my friends?

My encounters with the counselor were brief—Ms. Lang, if I remember correctly. She spent more time placating the people in the waiting room than she did working in her office. That's where the real show was, let me tell you. Not every person sentenced to counseling was as adjusted to the idea as I was. Some people downright refused. The younger the person, the louder they were, I noticed. Always spitting their upset at the secretary and Ms. Lang.

I don't need this shit, they'd shout. As if it was Ms. Lang's choice they were here. It's like they ignored the fact their mistakes brought them to this place, and their refusal to participate would keep them here longer.

No, I wasn't like that. I sat in my chair, legs crossed, biting my fingernails, waiting for the tired secretary to call my name. I rarely talked to the people in the waiting room. It was a private building, with only a small staff of counselors. I feel I need to stress that word. Counselors. There weren't PhDs in this place. Sessions weren't meant to provide treatment; they just wanted to know if you had plans to off yourself or someone else, so they could pass along the paperwork.

There I was, as usual. Sitting alone and minding my own business.

"Yucky day today," said a woman. Another counselor.

We'd never spoken before, but I had noticed her during previous visits. She was hard to miss. This woman was tall and thin, her brown hair pulled away from her face and fastened with a clip. She had pearl studs and a matching necklace. Simple and classy. She wore the prettiest outfit in the place—probably the prettiest outfit on the block. Always vibrant colors, the material perfectly ironed. On that day, she wore green.

Yes, I had watched her several times, but she had never spoken to me before.

"Yeah, it is," I said, staring at the same gray skies.

"Sarah, right?"

"Yeah."

I straightened my posture, as though possibly being selected for a grand prize. It surprised me this woman knew my name. Dozens of young girls came to the center; I often felt invisible. I expected this woman to see through me like everyone else, like even Ms. Lang tended to do.

"We've talked before, haven't we?"

"I don't think so."

I hated to correct her, but I had to be truthful. More than once, I had wished to speak with this woman over Ms. Lang. I wouldn't be unruly and rude, like the other girls in the lobby. They didn't know how lucky they were. Who wouldn't want to spend a few extra minutes of their day with someone who appeared so… perfect?

"That's right. You're waiting for Ms. Lang?"

"Yes."

For a moment, I had this fantasy she would whisk me away to her own office instead. *No sense in you waiting out here*, she'd say. But she didn't say any of that.

"I'm Mrs. Parker." She held out a hand. French tips on her nails. When this woman smiled at you, you wanted to return the kindness. "I work with some of the younger visitors. How do you like Ms. Lang?"

"She's great."

It was an overstatement, but I felt compelled to be positive in this woman's presence. In Mrs. Parker's presence. She seemed perfect. The exact type of woman I wanted to one day be. It's like her talking to me made me special, if only for a few seconds.

"Good. You know, my family helps fund this place. It's important to hear people are getting the help they need, even if some are more reluctant than others."

Both our eyes fell upon a girl sitting across from us. She had her feet kicked up onto an empty chair, headphones over her ears. She couldn't hear anything we were saying, but she fit Mrs. Parker's description to a tee. In fact, she was one of the girls I'd seen yelling during my last visit.

"Amelia?" The receptionist called her by her first name, and just like that, Mrs. Parker was gone, disappearing into one of the counseling rooms on the other side of the wall.

Not long after, I had my meeting with Ms. Lang. I barely remember what our sessions were about. Probably we talked about my job at Buster's and my relationship with Cliff and everything else going on in my life. Our conversations are a blur, and yet, all these years later, I can remember my exchange with Amelia Parker verbatim. That's the kind of impact she had on me.

I thought about her for the rest of that day, as I worked my closing shift at Buster's. I had been working there for almost two years at that point, my most serious job by far. The pay was good and the neighborhood was safe, but I know it was the people—mainly Jamie and Cliff—that kept me coming back. Not long after we went out for drinks, Cliff and I started dating, and Jamie became our best friend.

Most of my life I'd been a loner, but now I saw the benefit in talking to others. Really talking. Counseling wasn't like that; that was just reciting facts, offering updates. With Jamie and Cliff, it was different. When I spoke to them, I felt heard. I told them about my abusive upbringing, which became easier to accept because they had their struggles, too.

Like Cliff, Jamie was more than her outward appearance. She had people in her past she was trying to forget. She told me about an aggressive teacher at her private school. *A known predator*, she said. *We used to call him Fuzzy Sweater Gray Gums.* As usual, she did her best to make light of the ordeal. He'd gotten away with it with students in the past. This teacher and his behavior had become a running joke at the school, half rumor, half ghost story.

Until he targeted Jamie.

"There was a line for the girl's bathroom," she said, exhaling a puff of smoke. It was one of those nights I'd offered to stay and help her close, but as usual, we wasted time talking. "This teacher tells me I can use the restroom in the employee lounge if I didn't want to be late to class. So I thought, what the hell? Anything beats a call to my parents about too many tardies, right?

"I swear I locked the door behind me, but somehow he got inside. He walked up behind me while I was washing my hands. Tried to pull my skirt up."

"My goodness, Jamie. At school? What did you do?"

"At first I froze. Wasn't sure how to react. The guy was a teacher, after all. Then my fight kicked in. I pushed him off me. Tried to knee his crotch. We went back and forth for a while. In the end, I rammed him into the paper towel dispenser on the wall. It made a nasty cut on his forearm. That's when he finally stopped."

"Did you report him?"

Jamie scoffed. "No. Like I said, he'd been accused of doing things in the past. Nothing ever seemed to happen. I just left campus. Ended up grounded for two weeks for skipping school."

"Why didn't you tell your family?" I asked her, trying not to sound judgmental.

The biggest difference between Jamie and the rest of us was she actually had family. A big one. The talk around Buster's was there were mafia connections, a rumor that seemed far-fetched at first, but became increasingly believable the longer I knew Jamie. I didn't understand why she didn't go to her family, tell them about what almost happened. She at least had people to turn to, which is more than I ever did.

"My family does things," she told me. "I've had an uncle or two end up in prison. It's nothing new, but if any of the men in my family found out what that asshole did to me, they'd be sent away for life. I don't want to be the reason one of them gets locked up for good. I dodged the creep, even left him a nice little scar. That's all that matters."

And yet her explanation had holes. On nights I stayed at her place, she'd wake up with night terrors. Every now and then, during a smoke break, I'd catch her staring in the distance, as though the brick wall in front of her had something written on it.

An image.

A face.

A small, more mature voice inside me wanted to suggest she talk to someone about what happened, but I never did. Jamie was handling what happened in the best way she could. And counseling had done little for me.

Sometimes, she talked about the ordeal around Cliff, too. He listened, then would offer another yarn about the khaki pant pricks. We figured most of those guys grew up to do the type of thing that teacher did to Jamie. A different type of cycle, rooted in privilege and entitlement. *Someone needs to give these people what they deserve*, we'd say, trying to laugh about it.

These discussions were morbid, I knew that. But it seemed a natural way for us to explore our shared grief. We were all three tired of people never getting their comeuppance. The creepy teacher. The cruel bullies. My father and his abuse. Why did no one ever step in and do something about the bad that was happening? Why let it persist?

Befriending Jamie and Cliff was a form of kismet, I still believe that. They came into my life at precisely the right time, helping me process all the parts of myself I needed to accept, the parts of myself I needed to expunge. It was interesting how our past struggles played into our present desires. Jamie was determined to fend for herself. Run Buster's. Live alone. She was kind to me, but she was also hardened. Soft material sealed beneath a man-made shell.

Cliff was trying to prove he could do better than his family and his bullies, the people who had tormented him during his youth. He was on the right track, I'd tell him. But I think he was also fearful of that rage inside of him, the one that was brought to light that day in the alley.

And me. I was searching for family. For people who would love me unconditionally, and who I could protect in return. At night, I'd close my eyes and try to picture it, this future I might one day have.

Maybe I'd be like that Amelia lady at the center, I thought. All clean clothes and modest jewelry. I might not have it all right now, but I'd get it in time. If I was lucky.

CHAPTER 11

Now

Marion

I'm sitting alone in Carmen's car while she tries to talk with investigators. She wants to make sure that Mom receives medical assistance before returning to her cell for the night. The breakdown I witnessed was much worse than anything I've ever seen from Mom before.

I'm feeling my own anxiety take over, a wave crashing into my mind, carrying with it memories of the woman I thought I knew. My breathing picks up and my vision blurs. I have to close my eyes, fight to keep my emotions from taking over my ability to think.

Mom's admission is startling. Until now, I'd hoped the police had made a mistake, that they'd arrested the wrong person. Now that she's admitted to being Sarah Paxton, I dread what other parts of her past she is covering up.

I've often joked about having two Moms.

Most people assume I'm talking about Des. In many ways, she's like a second parent. She's been Mom's best friend and business partner almost my entire life, which means she's been there when I've needed her. Des never married or had children of her own, so I think she enjoys stepping into that role, offering me guidance when Mom is not enough.

But I'm not referring to Des when I mention my second mother. I'm talking about the woman Mom is now, compared to the nervous, possessive woman I remember from my childhood. The two are completely different, almost separate entities.

I don't think the label *worrier* would cut it. All parents worry. I know that now more than ever because I am one. But Mom's nervousness was more intense, almost proprietorial. I wasn't allowed to go anywhere without her, even reasonably safe places, like the local playground with Des. I didn't have my first sleepover until I was in high school, and even then, it was only after I begged a teammate's mother to convince her. I was sixteen. I had a driver's license. Still, it was like she didn't want to let me out of her sight for even one night.

Field trips were another point of contention. She'd sign permission slips for me to visit the local attractions. This was a whole new adventure to my younger self. Spending a few hours on a weekday exploring an aquarium or museum felt liberating, even if our teachers were only the next row over. In seventh grade, after watching a Christmas film at the local cinema before holiday break, I spotted Mom's car in the parking lot. She was sitting inside it, watching me as I got on the bus for our return to school. I never mentioned seeing her, and thank goodness none of my friends noticed, but knowing she was there ripped away my notions of independence. Even when I thought she wasn't watching me, I was wrong. I felt violated. Smothered. Like she somehow found me less capable than my peers.

If the trip meant venturing outside of North Bay, she wouldn't allow it. No overnight trips. No visits to D.C. with the Honor's Society. The weeklong trip to New York City my senior year of high school was out of the question.

And I hated her for it. That vitriol feels fresh even all these years later.

"Everyone is going," I shouted at her. "Why can't I?"

It was right after I told Mom I'd saved enough money to pay my own way. Des let me start working the cash register at The Shack once I entered high school. For almost an entire year, I saved every paycheck, making sure I'd have enough to pay the trip fee plus spending money.

"Those trips are overpriced," Mom said, washing the dishes, an attempt to ignore me. "They hike up the prices for school groups to take advantage of you."

"It's not about the money. I already told you, I have it right here." I dropped an envelope with cash on the counter. She barely looked at it.

"You're not going."

"But why? It's a safe trip. There will be an adult chaperone with each group. They take a trip like this every year, and nothing has ever happened before."

"New York isn't going anywhere. Maybe we'll plan a visit sometime—"

"Oh, come on! You never go anywhere. I've been asking you to take me places my whole life!"

"And you have your whole life ahead of you. You can go to New York and anywhere else you want."

"But I want to go now. With my friends. It's safe. I have the money. Please let me do this."

"You're not going." She averted her eyes. Didn't look at me for several days after that conversation, as I recall. "You're a minor, and I won't allow it. I'm sorry."

That anger festered within me, only growing worse with time. Not all moms were this overprotective. Why did mine have to be? Was it because I was all she had?

For weeks, all my friends talked about was the trip. They bought special outfits and then came back with bucketloads of souvenirs and stories. All experiences I'd never have. I spent that week moping, working my regular shifts at The Shack. Des would never disagree with Mom in front of me, but I think even she questioned Mom's stubbornness. Within a few months, I'd be off at college, if Mom would allow it. Why not give me this one week of freedom?

I first noticed the shift in Mom's behavior right after I turned eighteen. Out of all my birthdays, that one remains the clearest in my mind, and not just because it signified my entry to adulthood. Since my birthday was close to the end of senior year, it turned into a pre-graduation celebration of sorts. Mom and Des didn't spare any expense decorating The Shack. Des even set up a miniature bar in the back of the restaurant.

It was an all-around good night. I don't think I've ever felt so loved or celebrated. And I don't think I'd ever seen Mom look so proud. She seemed to float around the room, mingling with my friends and their parents. At previous parties, she always seemed to hang back. She avoided any small talk that could blossom into full-blown conversation.

But not at that party. She rejected her nervous ways, undressed her introverted layers. She laughed and danced. Danced! Even made herself a drink. It was the first time I'd seen Mom partake in the fun, not simply observe from a safe distance. From that point on, Mom became less possessive, more demonstrative. The panic attacks ceased. She became a different person.

A second Mom.

I believe reaching adulthood means you're able to view your parents as people, as the flawed, capable humans they are, not as mere authority figures. I accepted there were parts of Mom I'd never be able to change, parts of her past I'd never fully understand, but I didn't need any of that to accept her for who she was. A woman. My mother. That's when our friendship truly developed. Whatever the cause, she no longer felt compelled to protect me from the world, and together we could start living in it.

Now that eighteenth birthday party holds significance for a different reason. Could it be, if what the police are alleging about Mom is true, that that was the end of her sentence? At eighteen, no one could send me to a foster home or ship me back to my biological family. That was the deadline after which I could no longer be taken away from her.

I go over what I know about the Baby Caroline abduction in my mind. The type of person who could commit such an act would be the polar opposite of my mother. Manipulative. Ruthless. Violent. There would be a string of clues leading to their capture, a capture that should have happened a long time ago. Little mysteries surrounding that person. A warm, tingling feeling pulsates through my body.

It whispers, *Unless…*

But no, no. It can't be true. If Mom—Eileen—Sarah—stole me, it would mean I'm someone else's daughter. That can't be possible. I'm in my thirties. I would know by now if my upbringing was rooted in such deception, wouldn't I?

Unless…

The gall to commit such a crime is one thing, but to avoid detection for so many years would take another set of skills. The culprit would have to be careful about being seen, establishing residence in a normal but forgettable town. Like North Bay. We moved here when I was a toddler, and Mom never left. She never visited me when I went to college, always offering some excuse why she couldn't pull herself away from The Shack.

In fact, Mom never strays from routine. She's never even been on vacation. She'd argue, *Who needs a vacation when you live at the beach?* Even Des went on the occasional cruise over the years, but Mom never joined her. As a child, I assumed Mom didn't make enough money to fund a proper getaway, and as I got older, I labeled her a homebody. A creature of habit. An introvert.

Unless…

A woman capable of living the majority of her life under an alias would have to be strategic about where she put down roots. Like never buying property, which might explain why she's continued to live above The Shack, even when she earned enough money to buy a bigger place. She'd need to concoct a backstory. Either her past would be non-existent or precisely detailed. When it comes to Mom, it's the former. I don't know anything about my grandparents or extended family. Details—exact places and dates and names—remain murky. She has always given me more excuses about her life than actual answers. She never uttered the name Sarah Paxton.

These quirks and traits make Mom who she is, I thought. I learned to accept them, and it was that eventual acceptance that brought us closer as adults. No one would assume it meant their parent was on the run, avoiding punishment for a heinous crime.

The brutality of the crime, the bloodshed involved, gives me pause. I've never seen Mom be violent or malicious. It's hard to imagine her capable of bludgeoning Bruce Parker to death. But everything else getting away with this crime would entail—the lies, the secrecy, the compulsion—it feels like a betrayal to admit this, but it fits.

My hands start to shake. Am I actually starting to think this? That it's possible? I need to talk to someone. I need a phone call telling me this has been a mistake, that her admission is distorting my memories, forcing me to see the worst in my mother. If Mom did this horrible thing, took me from my biological parents so she could raise me as her own, it's an unforgiveable act. She's never—

Unless...

That word returns, carrying with it a thought too grisly to say aloud. We all have little mysteries surrounding our childhoods. Memories that are misremembered, stories that don't seem to add up. Now, all those misunderstandings are shifting. The pieces of my life are coming together, making everything clear.

She was hiding me.

CHAPTER 12

Now

Marion

In the time I've been waiting in this car, it feels like years have passed, and I suppose they have, as I analyze every piece of my life. If Mom were innocent, why won't she try to prove it? Why won't she talk to me?

Carmen insists she's under stress, still in shock from the arrest. But what about me? Her daughter. Didn't she think I would be just as overwhelmed, just as desperate for answers?

"You were too hard on her in there," Carmen says as she drives us back to her house. Like me, she must be rehashing what happened.

"All she had to do was talk to me. Answer my questions."

"It's hard for her to do that right now. There's a lot at stake. Her freedom, for one."

I turn to face Carmen. Passing streetlights cast shadows across her face.

"What's hard is hearing your entire childhood was a lie. I'm struggling to accept that the woman who raised me may not be my mother at all."

"Don't start thinking like that—"

"What am I supposed to think? She admitted her real name is Sarah Paxton. She's the woman police have been searching for all these years." I look out the window, at the pellets of rain sliding down the glass. "I know you're her lawyer, but you don't have to pretend for my sake. They wouldn't have made an arrest if they didn't have sufficient evidence."

Carmen knows I'm right. We sit in silence a while longer before she responds.

"As your friend, I understand your anger. Eileen's been protective of you, at times overprotective, and now you're having to accept she might have been lying. But as your mother's lawyer, I'm asking you to stay open-minded. There could be more to the story we don't understand."

"And how are we supposed to get the full story if Mom refuses to speak with us?"

"She's probably afraid to talk to you. Afraid of disappointing you."

Carmen's good at dissecting the opposite side of an argument. She's made a career out of it. Prosecutors seek the truth, defense attorneys defend. This time she'll have to do both.

The kids wore Ava out. She is asleep before we pull onto the highway. The gentle purring of rain on the car helps. I calculate how long it has been since I've had a good night's rest. I didn't get much sleep before the party. I was frenetic, filled with nervous energy, bogged down with anxieties that no longer seem to matter. I'd wanted the party to be perfect for Ava. How terrible the whole thing turned out to be.

My neighborhood is quiet. Carmen lodged a complaint to keep the media away from my complex. Now any news crews hoping for a picture have to park across the street from the community entrance, and it appears most have given up. They are still trying to contact me though; Des said the landline at The Shack hasn't stopped ringing all day.

As I pull up to the curb in front of my duplex, I see a man sitting on the front porch. He stands as I approach, the overhead light shining down to reveal his identity.

It's Evan.

I kill the ignition and release a deep breath. I've been trying to avoid him, but that's impossible now that he is in front of me. I step out of the car, leaning against it as he descends the steps. I purposely leave Ava in the back seat; I have no intention of introducing them tonight.

"I tried calling you," he says.

He looks older, a few more lines around the eyes. It has been a long time since I've seen him in person. Now he is here, returning during one of the worst weeks of my life. All the things I'd imagined saying to him dissipate, like the moisture in the air.

"How is your mom?" he asks.

"I'm guessing you've talked to Des?"

"First I saw it on the news. Then I called Des." He stuffs his hands inside his jacket. "How is she?"

"I don't know. She refuses to speak with me."

"I can't believe they arrested her at Ava's party like that."

It's strange, hearing him say her name. Evan, who used to be the most important person in my life, has never met the little girl who seized that role. My beautiful, bouncing Ava.

"What are you doing here?" I ask. A genuine question. He'd tried reaching out to me earlier, but the fact he has arrived on my doorstep the same week they took Mom away in handcuffs seems more than coincidental.

"I thought Cassie would have told you by now."

Cassie is his younger sister. She lives across town with her husband and two kids. We used to be close back when Evan and I were a couple. We keep in contact, but we don't see each other much. The family resemblance is too strong. Seeing her used to make me miss him. I'd just started to get over that, and now he's here.

"We've not talked a lot lately. I've been so busy with Ava."

"That's understandable." His eyes fall on the back seat window. He's looking inside, at where Ava is, but it's so dark he can probably only see his own reflection. "I'm guessing that's why you've missed my calls, too."

I've been avoiding his calls. Yesterday, because of the party. Today, because I was preparing to see Mom. Earlier, because... I don't know. It's difficult hearing his voice. Our breakup was ages ago but being around him now still feels raw. Evan is the most important romantic relationship I've ever had, and I'm his.

"You've talked to Des. You know I have a lot on my plate right now."

"And I don't want to add to it—"

"Then why are you here?" I stare at him, my gaze unforgiving.

He looks down, touching his forehead with his fingers. "Now isn't the best time to tell you this considering everything going on with Eileen, but I thought you'd want to know I'm moving back to North Bay."

"Moving back?" I suspected a few reasons he might want to talk, but his moving back wasn't one of them. "When? Why?"

"This is my home."

That's not what he said when he left me. That same argument that died ages ago has been resurrected. "I thought you weren't happy here?"

"Sometimes things change."

They sure do. The life I have now seems forever away from the one I was living two days ago, or the one from before when Evan was still my partner. My mind scrambles as I try to envision what this means, how the life I've worked hard to create will crumble knowing Evan is just down the street. I'd accepted him being gone. Now suddenly, he's back. It takes a few seconds to register how rude my reaction probably sounds.

"My mind is all over the place right now. Maybe I'll talk to you later. After I find out what is going on with Mom."

"Yeah, I'll go. Des told me to stop by. I wasn't sure about it, but you know how Des is."

He laughs. We both know how Des can be. No isn't in her vocabulary. The sound of his laugh makes me hurt in a place I didn't know was still there.

"Give me a call if you need anything," he says, walking past me to get to his vehicle. "I'll be around."

I remain leaning against the car, watching as he drives away. It's a strange feeling, knowing how much our paths have divided in such a short amount of time. Now, it seems they're intersecting again. I unbuckle Ava from her car seat. She's still asleep, so I scamper down the hallway into her room, placing her little body in the crib as gently as I can.

I watch her sleep. Her chest rises and falls. Her arms are outstretched, her fingers coiling and relaxing rhythmically. Sometimes in these moments of calm and quiet, it hits me. Just how much this tiny person is now the center of my world. How I'd do anything to protect her.

CHAPTER 13

Now

Marion

My phone rings. The sun burns orange across my eyelids, announcing a new day, but I don't feel rested at all. My body aches for more sleep.

The phone continues vibrating. I slap the covers, trying to find it. It's Carmen.

"Marion, you need to get to the hospital. There was an incident at the jail."

My body jolts forward. Just like that, back to that adrenal state it's occupied for the past two days. "With Mom? Is she okay?"

"Eileen was stabbed by another inmate. She's going into surgery right now."

The phone slides down my hand, landing on the tangled sheets. I'm motionless, thoughtless, trying to catch my breath. I've gone from losing Mom as the woman I thought she was to, possibly, losing her entirely.

Ava is cranky when I wake her. I rush to put her in a clean onesie, throw the diaper bag over my shoulder and get in the car. Before leaving the complex, I text Des and tell her to meet us at the hospital. Hopefully, she can take Ava if I need to stay. Waiting for her to get here feels impossible. My need to get to Mom is urgent.

Just last night, I was bruised by her deception. I'm still angry. But buried beneath that fury is the love I still have for her, regardless of what lies she might have told and horrible deeds she might have committed. She might be a kidnapper. A murderer. A liar. But she's still the woman who raised me, and that's the woman I'm racing to see.

The process of parking and finding the right floor takes forever, but now I'm standing at the hospital check-in desk, trying to find information. The lobby is too big, too bright with the morning sun shooting in through the windowed walls. There aren't many people here to help fill the space this early in the morning. The receptionist seems annoyed, if not by the muddled details I provide, then by Ava's wailing.

"Her name is Eileen Sams," I say, failing to calm Ava by bouncing her on my hip. "Or Sarah Paxton."

"Which is it?"

"I… I don't know. I'm not sure what name they admitted her under."

The woman continues typing, the computer screen reflecting off her round spectacles. Her eyebrows arch. "I see who you're trying to find. What's your relation?"

"I'm her daughter."

That much is true. No matter what information is yet to be uncovered, our relationship to one another can't be erased overnight, and in this moment, I'm the person who cares most about her recovery.

The receptionist's eyes wash over Ava, whose face is red and splotchy. My methodical bobbing does little to soothe her.

"You can't take a child back there."

"I have someone coming."

Her eyes fall across my hands, bare of any rings. "Is it the father?"

I get this all the time. Nosy people with their assuming minds. They like to write my story without knowing it. I'm a careless girl who found herself in trouble. Some miserable woman who couldn't keep a husband, let alone a father for her child.

"Does it matter?" My eyes narrow at this judgmental stranger. "Tell me what happened to my mother."

"I can't release any information. You'll have to speak with a doctor. Someone will come out shortly."

I sit by the far wall, the sun at my back casting shadows on the floor. I rock Ava, trying desperately to calm her. She must sense my own agitation and it's upsetting her, that and the fact I woke her so abruptly. After a few minutes, she's no longer crying. Her head rests on my shoulder, and I can feel her breathing begin to mellow.

"Everything is okay," I tell her, half telling myself. Even in the aftermath of a public tantrum, I'm grateful for her. Soothing her stops me from driving myself crazy with worry for Mom.

Across the room, the automatic doors slide open, and Carmen walks in. She clearly ran out of the house as fast as I did, without bothering to get herself ready. It makes me love my friend a little more knowing she is willing to drop everything to be here for me. Eileen is more than a client to her.

"What happened?" I ask.

"There was an altercation at the jail last night. I've already asked for security video to try and figure it out myself. I don't know all the details, but Eileen was stabbed."

"Stabbed?" I'm being hit with one unbelievable situation after the next. The arrest, the charges, now this. My mother, who rarely raises her voice, not even during my rebellious teenage years, stands accused of murder and has now been the victim of violence. "I don't understand. She was at the county jail. Surely she was being watched. How could this happen?"

"All the inmates are thrown together until they're transferred elsewhere before trial. It's impossible to watch them at all times." *Inmates.* She catches her use of the word, too, and blushes. "I don't know what provoked the fight, but I can guarantee you I'll find out."

"Do you think she might have been targeted? The media is already running this story everywhere."

"It's hard to say. This isn't the first time around for most of the women in the jail. They might have decided to start messing with her. But I also don't know where Eileen is mentally right now."

That rising panic returns, as I imagine what might have heralded this attack. "She was upset after we spoke to her last night. Do you think she might have gone in there and started something?"

"I'm not saying that—"

"Do you think this happened because I pushed her too hard?"

Carmen rests her hand on my knee.

"Don't do this. What happened isn't your fault. None of this is your fault." She pauses to let me know she's not only talking about the attack. "Everything I've told you came from the police station. I don't know anything about her medical condition because I'm not family. But she's here, so that has to be a good sign, right?"

It's impossible not to blame myself. Carmen tried to tell me Mom's state of mind was shaky, weary. Instead of accepting that, I pushed her further.

Des rushes in. She stomps around, her head twitching from left to right like some Amazonian bird. Finally, she spots us. I remain seated, allowing Carmen to fill her in on the details.

"You have got to be kidding me," Des says, her mouth open and long. "You've got to be freaking kidding me!"

"Lower your voice," Carmen says.

I'm not particularly bothered by Des' reaction. She's simply expressing the unrest and shock I feel inside.

"She's been there two nights. *Two nights*. After you sort this out with Eileen, we're going to sue the hell out of that honky-tonk police department."

"One thing at a time," Carmen says. "There's not a ton of violence in the county jail, but unfortunately these things do happen."

"Marion Sams?" There is a nurse dressed in blue scrubs standing behind me. Behind her, a uniformed officer. "I can take you back now."

I pass Ava to Des and follow the woman, snaking through the corridors of the massive hospital. We stop outside a room where another police officer is stationed, drinking from a Styrofoam cup. Beside him is a doctor reading a clipboard. He looks up and offers a weak smile.

"Marion Sams?" I nod, holding my breath as I wait for him to speak. "Your mother received three wounds. Two to her stomach, a third to her neck. It's the last blow that's done the most damage. She lost a lot of blood, but paramedics reached her in time. All things considered, she's lucky. We're about to take her into surgery to assess the damage."

I try my hardest to hang on to the doctor's every word, and yet the sentences float away like untethered balloons. In what world is a stabbing victim lucky?

"Surgery?"

"The blade they used was man-made, so it wasn't a clean cut. We have to make sure those arteries are intact, otherwise we run into more risks."

"What does that mean?" Maybe on any other day I could follow along, but right now I need him to spell it out for me.

"She has a chance of pulling through, but there's no guarantee. We'll have to monitor her recovery in phases."

I look at the closed door, afraid to see the mangled woman on the other side.

"She might not make it?"

"We're doing everything we can. We're aiming for more surgery tomorrow morning. You can go in for a visit, but she's heavily sedated. She won't be able to respond."

I nod, shaking the doctor's hand before he scurries away. The police officer standing by the door barely acknowledges me as I push the handle and walk inside.

The blinds aren't completely shut, cloaking half the room in dark grays and blues. The whirring of machines fills my ears. They are monitoring her breathing, her heart rate, her brain function. Mom is lying on a gurney, her head tilted back with a tube down her throat. There is a thick bandage wrapped around her neck.

Her arms, riddled with IVs, are resting beside her. There aren't any handcuffs linking her to the bed. That's the type of thing you see in the movies. This is real life, yet it feels so bizarre. Mom's not going anywhere. Not again. She might never leave this hospital, an idea that makes me want to double over with dread.

I reach for her hand, then think better of it. She already appears so fragile. I'm not sure if she can handle anything else, even my touch. Yesterday, she seemed so scared. She refused to speak with me, and now I might never get to talk to her again.

And yet, beneath my confusion and sorrow, there's a thick layer of resentment. I have questions that need to be answered, and the police and the media and Carmen can't provide them. Only Mom can. I'm afraid of being robbed of any opportunity to understand why she did what she did.

Alone with her, I cry. I realize I haven't cried at all since the arrest. I've been too preoccupied, trying to rationalize her actions without jumping to conclusions. Trying to remain strong for Ava. Mom taught me that strength. She molded me into the woman I am today, and I've yet to fully accept that same woman is a fraud. She may have done monstrous things, but I'm not ready to let her go.

As the last sobs trickle out, I look at her. I try to picture her happy face at the birthday party, not this one clinging to life.

"I don't know who you are," I say, knowing she won't be able to hear me. "But I need you here. I need you to pull through for me. For Ava. Please don't leave us."

For several minutes, I sit alone, taking in the mechanical drone. Taking in the stillness.

CHAPTER 14

Then

Eileen

And just like that, everything changed. Jamie was moving to the east coast. She had applied to a university there and was accepted. Part of me wondered if Jamie wanted to leave New Hutton and its memories in the past. Leave behind the bitter girl she was here and start over somewhere, refreshed. She had the resources for that.

I think her only regret was leaving us behind. She knew she'd miss out on everything happening in our lives, but it was time for her to take control of hers. One of her black coat cousins would be taking over at Buster's. She promised he'd take care of us, give us the best hours and higher pay.

On the day she was due to leave, Cliff and I offered to help her pack up her place, hoping to make a few more memories together.

"I've got to drop off some keys down the street," Jamie said. I can still remember she was wearing denim overalls and high-top sneakers, her hair curly and pulled to the side with a scrunchie. "Want to meet back here in twenty to finish up?"

"No, just go," I said. "We can box up the rest of this."

"Are you sure?"

"It will be waiting on the sidewalk by the time you get back," Cliff said.

"You guys are too good to me."

I let the compliment linger, even though Jamie was the one who deserved thanks. Before I landed the job at Buster's, I hadn't known what it felt like to be grounded. To have people I cared about. I'd never missed someone before, the way I would soon miss her. And yet, I'd also never carried that amount of love for someone. Part of me wanted Jamie to stay, but I also wanted her to leave and find the happiness that she couldn't seem to capture here.

Cliff and I resumed filling the last of the boxes. All that was left was dishware; everything else was wrapped, sealed and sitting by the front door for Cliff to carry outside.

"I can't believe she's actually leaving," he said, staring at his own warped reflection in the dish. "It's going to be weird not having her around."

"I know."

There was a painful knot in my throat, and I was afraid talking to Cliff about how I felt would untangle it. I was fragile back then, more devastated by Jamie's departure than I was willing to admit.

"Maybe we could save enough money to visit her," Cliff said. He put down the plate and walked closer to me.

"I've never even left the state."

"Yeah, well, I haven't either. All the more reason to plan a trip."

"We need to save as much money as we can. Now that Jamie's gone, there's no guarantee we'll keep our jobs at Buster's. The new manager might—"

"Stop worrying," he assured me, pulling me closer to him. "Buster's is still owned by Jamie's family. She'll look after us. Like she always has."

As I stood there, worrying, grieving, I knew he was right. I'd been so used to life going wrong. To having to struggle to make it to the end of the month. I'd focused on survival, not splendor. Cliff had grown up the same way, and yet, recent months had changed him.

"A trip would be nice. I've always wanted to visit the city. Go to all the landmarks. Maybe watch a play."

"We'll do all of it," he said, that glimmer back in his eyes. "Maybe we'll love it so much we'll stay there. Find jobs and a place of our own."

"That's ambitious."

"Yeah, but we could work for it. No harm in dreaming." He carried three boxes to the front door and set them on the floor. When he stood upright, he gave the room a double take, before looking at me. "What do you think of this place?"

"I've always loved it," I said.

Jamie's apartment was spacious (she was the only person I ever knew who had a two-bedroom loft) and had a security code at the front gate. We'd spent countless nights in this very room. Watching MTV and sports finals. Celebrating New Year's Eve and Halloween.

"I wonder if they've found a new tenant," he said. He lifted his head, and his eyes looked hopeful. "Maybe it could be us."

"Do you have any idea how much a place like this costs?"

"It can't be more than your rent and mine combined. If we're both living here, we could swing it. I'll pick up another part-time job if I have to."

"You think we're ready for that?"

"We have to be. We're throwing money away on two apartments, especially when we spend every night together. Besides, in time we'll be thankful for the extra space."

In time. One day. All these phrases served as confirmation Cliff wanted a future with me. He wanted to build a better one together. I'd never had that type of reassurance before. I'd never had someone place so much faith in me.

For a brief moment, I felt like a bride on her wedding day, like a giddy girl in the old movies being carried over the threshold into forever. Each day, I was getting closer to being that perfect person I wanted to be. And I enjoyed imagining it. Going new places. Making new memories. Raising a family—a real family—with a man like Cliff by my side.

He must have been fantasizing too, because when I opened my eyes again, he smiled.

"You make me so happy, Sarah Paxton."

I wanted to say the same, but the moment passed. I looked down at the floor. Cliff walked to the last stack of boxes and pushed them into the hallway.

"I can carry one—"

"Don't even think about it," he cut me off, blocking me with his shoulder. He lifted all three boxes with one squat.

"Be careful going down the stairs," I warned him.

Outside, Jamie pulled up to the sidewalk just as we were exiting the building.

"Last load?" she shouted, blocking the sun with her hand. We nodded.

"I'm going to ask her about it," Cliff said, still holding the boxes.

"About what?"

"Who's renting her old place. Maybe it could really be ours."

I smiled, knowing that even if it wasn't possible to rent a nicer apartment now, Cliff wanted that, and at some point, we would get it. My eyes darted left, then right, following Cliff as he walked across the street. For a brief second, I looked behind me. At Jamie's old home. Possibly my new one, and my heart felt like it might burst with sadness and joy all at once.

"Cliff!" Jamie shouted. "Wait!"

A dark SUV barreled down the one-way road. It came out of nowhere, this dark mass of metal and shine. Cliff, his face blocked by the boxes, couldn't see. The car slammed into him. His body somersaulting into the air, the belongings he'd been carrying spilling into the street. Everything happened in slow motion, an excruciating scene that would not end. And I couldn't stop watching.

After the hit, we were all still. *Had it really happened?*

I ran to him. As I got closer, I heard the squealing tires as the SUV continued its mad dash down the street. In that moment, I didn't care. I only wanted to be near Cliff. Make sure he was okay.

But he wasn't. You could tell just by looking at him. You could tell by the blood oozing out of his nose, trickling down his left ear. And his limbs—well, no one's body should be bent in that way. Especially not my boyfriend's, who, only moments ago, had been speaking about our future.

A future that would never happen.

CHAPTER 15

Now

Marion

It's the middle of the night when I wake up. I had a dream. It wasn't traumatic enough to be considered a nightmare, but it wasn't good, either. One of those annoying tricks of the mind that transports you to the past, and for a few moments upon waking, you think you're in a different time.

In the dream, Evan and I were at our old apartment, the one we shared before I bought this condo. The dining room table was covered with his books and papers; my clothes had a light dusting of flour from the restaurant. I sat on his lap, laced my fingers behind his neck and kissed his lips.

That's all I remember.

I once read dreams, even the winding, epic ones, last only a few seconds. I don't see how that can be true when, even as I'm awake, I'm still trapped in the vision.

It's no wonder Evan is oozing his way into my subconscious. With everything that has happened in the past few days, it's understandable why I'd want to revert back to a time when life was simpler. Happier. Before I had to start making decisions that could adversely affect those around me. It must be my mind's way of preventing me from worrying about Mom. It's a form of protection.

I think back to the events that led us to this point. Evan and I began dating when I moved back home after I graduated college.

I'd known him most of my life, the way all North Bay natives know each other. His father owned one of the leisure boating companies, taking tourists out along the coast. He was working for his dad while I had plans to reinvent The Shack. We were both part of a younger generation, trying to pay our respects to the one before us.

Des was determined to make The Shack more commercial. She aspired to make it a must-stop destination for tourists visiting North Bay, and she thought bringing me in would help make that happen. Des is a mean cook, but she's the first to admit she's not a people person. She enjoys making one-on-one connections with locals, but she lacks the kind of personality needed for wider networking.

Mom had owned The Shack for years alongside Des but couldn't really help her on this front. She wasn't a people person either. Of course, now I'm wondering if she dodged those connections because she wanted to remain unrecognizable, in an attempt to hide me and what she'd done.

For years, The Shack had kept its head above water, but now I needed it to turn a profit, to make it a thriving restaurant, not just one that existed. Mom and Des pulled funds to pay for a massive renovation of the dining room. Gone were the yellowed tiles and flimsy faux steel counters. We purchased new tables and chairs, updated the appliances. The hardest part was convincing Des to tweak the menu.

Once we'd improved the restaurant's ambience, I started reaching out to other local businesses. That's how I got into the hotel crowd, even if it meant kissing ass to people like Holly Dale. It was worth it. Within a few years The Shack earned back the investment from the renovation. Then we started making real money, enough for me to start saving.

Those early years in North Bay were some of my greatest. I'd gotten a taste of the real world while I was in college. I was able to experience all the things I felt I couldn't when I was trapped under Mom's thumb, but it had also made me realize that North Bay was where I was destined to live. I loved the scenery and the people. A big part of that peace came from Evan. Our life together felt easy.

Things became complicated after Evan's father died. The two men had had a problematic relationship. Evan admitted to always feeling like he'd simply followed the path laid out for him instead of forging his own way. After his father passed, he was juggling grief with his newfound lack of purpose.

I was there for him, of course. We'd been together over five years at that point, although neither of us had dealt with anything as traumatic as losing a parent. The Shack had just started turning a profit, and I'd been dabbling with the idea of purchasing a home. Evan assumed ownership of the boat touring business, a career that never fulfilled him.

After a few weeks, we went to dinner at one of our favorite restaurants overlooking the bay. I hadn't yet opened my menu when Evan dove into the topic on his mind.

"What would you say if I told you I wanted to go back to school?"

"School?" It wasn't a bad idea, per se. Just random. We were both just shy of thirty and had been managing our respective careers for some time. "To do what?"

"I'm thinking about applying to law schools." He looked down, his mouth twitching in the right corner, a sure sign he was nervous. He forced a laugh. "Does that sound crazy?"

It actually made perfect sense. Evan was an intellectual. If anything, running a rental company for obnoxious tourists seemed out of character. I'd seen the way his face lit up over the years hearing Carmen talk about her work. There were more than a few double dates where Carmen and Evan would get lost in their own conversation.

"I think it's a great idea," I said, truthfully.

"You think? I mean, most people starting law school are almost a decade my junior. I want you to tell me if I'm being too bold."

"It's never too late to start a career. Besides, you're sharp. Smart outweighs youth, especially in a court room."

"It's a big commitment. It'll be almost a year before I can start. Another few years of schooling after that." He cleared his throat. "Would you be willing to wait that long?"

"I don't know what else I'd be doing," I said, with a smile.

I meant it when I gave Evan my support. I knew he needed to build a life for himself that wasn't rooted in his father's shadow, and now was his time to do it. As the months passed, he studied and studied. He aced his exams. Before long, he was applying to regional law schools.

In the meantime, I'd been hunting for houses. Condos, rather, and I'd finally narrowed it down to three different options. Each had their own amenities, plus they all came with the quintessential North Bay view. One day after work, I came home to present the potential options to Evan. As I spread out the printouts and pictures, I couldn't ignore the queasy look on his face.

"Home ownership is scarier than it seems," I told him, trying to alleviate his stress. "When you consider the amount of money we throw away each year on rent, it really makes sense to buy."

"The condos are great," he said, picking up a picture, then letting it drift back down to the table. "That's not what bothers me."

"Then what is it?"

"I've been trying to find the right time to tell you this." Evan never kept anything from me, and I could see the stress corrupting his features. "I've been accepted to law school."

"That's great," I said, hugging him. His acceptance didn't come as a surprise. Thankfully, there were at least three options within a few hours' drive. "What's the lucky school?"

"Sanderson."

"Sanderson?" I asked, like I hadn't heard him right. A pocket of air seemed stuck in my throat. "But that's out west."

"I know."

"What about the schools around here? The ones where you could drive to campus during the week and be back here for the weekend."

"I'm still waiting to hear back from those." He stared at me, like he was waiting for the rest to sink in. Now I knew why he looked sick.

"But you want Sanderson?"

"Honestly, it's always been my first choice. The schools around here would be nice, but I guess there'd be a part of me that would feel like I'm settling."

We'd discussed long distance relationships in the past. We both agreed they didn't work; we wouldn't even want to try. But those conversations had been ages ago. I never knew his moving so far away was still an option. I thought we were more committed than that.

"Settling for the school? Or settling for me?"

"I definitely am not settling for you," he said, holding my hands. "I want you to move with me."

"Move with you? To another state?"

"It could be our fun little adventure."

"But what about the restaurant? My family?"

My mind immediately pictured my mother. The earlier version, the woman who barely trusted me to go to the local cinema without her supervision. I was an adult now, of course. But still, moving that far away would crush her.

Evan looked down. He knew what my answer would be before he even suggested it, but he continued to try. "It's not like we won't visit. Your mom and Des can handle the restaurant on their own. They did it before."

But whenever people make these types of decisions, those promises tend to fall apart. Plans change. Things happen. I couldn't move away from a business I'd worked so hard to revamp. Besides, I didn't want to live anywhere else. North Bay had always been my home. I loved everything about it. Had never wanted any place else. And I thought Evan had wanted those same things, until he said the word Sanderson.

"Are you saying you want to go to Sanderson, or you want to leave North Bay?"

"Both."

But they had different meanings. "Do you see yourself living here? Eventually?"

He opened his mouth, then closed it. He exhaled, shakily. "I don't know. For the longest time, it's like North Bay was my only option. It's all I've ever known. But with Dad gone and the business out of the way... it feels like this is my one shot to live life on my own terms. Decide what I want for myself without being influenced."

On one level, I understood his conflict. Evan had the right to *live life on his own terms*, find a place and career that completely fulfilled him. The difference was, I'd already made those decisions for myself. And I'd believed he was a part of that. That very day, I'd been showing him options for our future home. He was taking that all away with this decision, unbothered by how his choices might impact my life.

"I'm not leaving The Shack just because you got into school. You can't expect me to uproot my entire life. That's never been part of the plan."

"I know."

"Then what are you saying?"

"I'm saying Sanderson is on the table. It's an option."

And yet, it must have been important to him otherwise he would never have mentioned it. He would have gladly taken one of the other offers from the nearby schools, as we'd discussed, instead of trying to convince me to move halfway across the country. He wanted this, even if it meant losing me.

"Be honest with me. Is this because of the house stuff? Does it freak you out?"

"No, of course not. Why would you even think that?"

"Because guys get nervous when you start talking about the future. I've not been trying to pressure you with any of it. I'm doing this all for me."

"I know. I understand completely. I even admire it. But I feel the same way about Sanderson."

It hurt to hear our life together wasn't enough for him. Six years of happiness had led us to this fork in the road. We had our opposite directions, and neither of us was going to get what we wanted without sacrifices. I felt it immediately, everything I'd be losing.

The conversation overshadowed everything we did in the months that followed. My decision to buy the condo. His acceptance to Sanderson, and eventual move. Just like that, my relationship ended in the most anticlimactic and heartbreaking of ways.

It was one of those breakups that seemed to impact everyone in our social circle. Des was devastated. Carmen was pissed. Mom didn't say much; she'd always believed Evan and I would end up together, and she never liked admitting when she was wrong. I was upset over the breakup. He'd chosen Sanderson as clearly as I'd chosen North Bay. As the months passed, that heartbreak morphed into anger. Evan cheated me, allowing me to believe we could build a future together, only for him to take off when I was at the precipice of having everything I'd ever wanted.

I remind myself, if our relationship had worked out, I would never have had Ava.

Does it make me less of a mother to sometimes dream of that alternate life? One where Evan exists, and Ava doesn't? Except, even in my daydreams, she does exist in some capacity. Evan and I have a child together, and it's her. I know that's not possible. That's not the outcome life gave us. Sometimes I wish it had been. Evan and Ava are the two greatest loves of my life, separated by the choices I made in between them.

The doorbell rings, and suddenly I'm back in the present. As I walk to the door, I worry it might be a reporter, but Carmen has already ordered the press not to enter the complex property. It would have to be a brazen reporter to ring my doorbell this early in the morning, and if they did, they'd be slapped with a huge fine.

Pulling back the curtain, I see a woman standing outside. Alone. She's wearing white capris, a floral blouse and gold sandals. Her hair is cut short, and large sunglasses cover half of her face. Still, I can tell she looks nervous. There's that anxious fidgeting of her hands, the impatient tapping of her foot.

"Who is it?" I ask, waiting for her to answer.

My eyes scan the living room, landing on the baton Rick gave me. It's sitting next to the bureau by the breakfast table. I've not thought about it since he gave it to me. Was he right about being cautious of people following the case? I peer out the window again.

The woman looks down, then back to the door. "Does a Marion Sams live here?"

"I can't speak to the press if that's what you're after—"

"I'm not from the press," the woman says, a catch in her voice. "My name is Amelia Parker."

I wait a beat, knowing the name sounds familiar. Then it hits me, and I swing open the door.

Amelia pushes her sunglasses into her hair and stares at me, her mouth agape. Behind the smile lines and makeup, I can see the resemblance. She's the same woman featured in those pictures from long ago. The woman who lost her husband. The woman who lost her daughter. A daughter the rest of the world refers to as Baby Caroline.

CHAPTER 16

Now

Marion

There's an awkward air between us. I'm afraid to inhale. Amelia, standing in front of me, also appears to be holding her breath, like she's not sure this moment is real. Finding her daughter. Seeing her again in the flesh. This must have been only a fantasy, but now she's here. I'm here, right in front of her.

"I don't quite know what to say." She starts to say more but stops. Her eyes dance around my face. "I should have called."

Although I only learned about this woman a few days ago, she has wondered about me for years. She's worried for me since the day I was taken away. There must have been a large part of her that feared she would never know what happened to her daughter. Her life has been defined by tragedy; it's not in my nature to shut the door on her.

"Would you like to come inside?"

She nods, looking over her shoulder before entering. She looks around my living room as though it's a playhouse or a movie set. Taking in each item, committing it to memory. She sits at the breakfast table, her handbag still hanging from the crook in her arm.

"Do you have any idea who I am?"

"I do."

Ever since Mom admitted her real name is Sarah Paxton, I've been struggling to accept the truth about my childhood. Part of that means admitting this woman in front of me, Amelia, might be my biological mother.

"You have to understand, it's been over thirty years. After so many false leads and dead ends, to hear that they'd actually found you… that they'd actually made an arrest…" She stops, struggling to put her feelings into words. "I just had to see you. It's like I couldn't stop myself."

Found you. Baby Caroline. Her daughter that was taken. My shame at being at the center of this lifts momentarily, and part of me hopes it's true. If, for no other reason, to spare this woman more pain. Seeing the grief on Amelia's face makes the horror of what Mom did all those years ago much more real.

"I didn't know about any of this until a few days ago," I say, looking away. "I'm still in shock, really."

"That's understandable. You must have so many questions."

I do have questions, and with Mom in the hospital, I'm not sure if they will ever be answered. And yet, Amelia sits in front of me. She's a stranger, but she would know at least a little about my past. About the life I could have lived, if I hadn't been taken.

"I'm getting most of my information through Eileen's attorney." This seems like the best way to address my mother. I've never known her as Sarah, but calling her Mom in front of Amelia seems cruel. "If what the police are saying is true, I'm your daughter."

Amelia nods. Her eyes fill with tears, but she doesn't look sad. There's a smile spreading across her face.

"I know how bizarre this must seem. There's a lot I don't know, too. But at least I know you're all right. You're safe. That's what's most important in all of this."

We lock eyes, as though we're each trying to decipher the details of the other's face. Just then, Ava's crying breaks through the silence. It's so jarring, I don't need the monitor to hear it, and neither does Amelia. She jumps, like she's reliving a moment from long ago, turning her head in the direction of Ava's bedroom.

"Excuse me just a minute." I grab a bottle from the refrigerator and rush to Ava's room, shutting the door behind me. Some days she wakes up harder than others. Normally, I'd pick her up and soothe her, but Amelia is sitting in the other room. I want to continue our conversation, and yet, there's a part of me that wants her nowhere near my child. Not until I know more.

It only takes a few sips from the bottle for Ava to close her eyes and relax. I tiptoe back to the kitchen. Amelia is standing, looking at a series of picture frames on a nearby shelf.

"Sorry about that," I say.

"Not a problem." Amelia smiles, interlocking her fingers in front of her body. "You have a child?"

"Yes, I have a daughter. Ava just turned one."

"That's wonderful."

And yet, there's a sadness in her expression. She may have found her daughter—me—but that doesn't return all the years that have been taken from her. She's missed out on my entire childhood, my adulthood. My heart breaks a little for her. Carmen said she never had other children. How tragic it must be to have your time as a mother stolen from you, an entire chapter—arguably the most important chapter—of your life swiped away, and never be given a second chance.

Amelia lifts a silver picture frame off the shelf. It's a photograph of Mom and me on the beach. We're both wearing long skirts and tank tops, our skin tanned and our hair wispy. She holds the photo, using her other hand to cover her mouth.

"Sarah looks so different," she says, gently putting the photograph back in its place. She turns to me and offers a weak smile. It's another confirmation. The woman in the picture might look different, but she's familiar.

I want to continue talking to Amelia. I want to hear what she has to say. We've missed out on an entire lifetime together, and even though she could have given up hope a long time ago, she's here. Right in front of me. She wants to know me, and I'm curious to know about her, too.

"I'd like to talk with you more," I say. "I just need to get Ava settled first. Could we meet in an hour?"

"Sure, sure. I have all the time in the world."

She offers a cool smile. She must pick up on the fact I'm cautious having her around Ava. Then again, if anyone understands my reluctance of having strangers around my daughter, it's Amelia. Her life has been forever shaped by it.

CHAPTER 17

Now

Marion

Twenty minutes later, I'm pushing open the front door to The Shack. The restaurant is still closed, but Des spends every spare moment preparing for the reopening.

"Well, you stopped by just in time." Des plops a stack of pans on the counter. Her scowl drops long enough for her to make googly eyes at Ava.

"What does that mean?" I say, lifting Ava out of her car seat and placing her in the portable playpen we leave up behind the counter. Another item untouched by investigators.

"I just had a lengthy talk with your little friend across the street."

"Holly?" I collapse into a chair, bracing for the story. "What's she saying?"

"It's what she's asking. *Did you know Eileen's real name was Sarah Paxton? Do you think this scandal could impact North Bay's tourism?*" Des mocks Holly's voice. "Someone should tell her she's not in charge just because she runs the town's biggest hotel."

"Holly Dale loves any opportunity to put people in their place."

I'm pretending to blow off Holly's suggestion, but unfortunately, it has merit. This town functions on tourists in the summer months. It has crossed my mind more than once that Mom's arrest could hurt The Shack just as our busiest season begins. Either that, or the people that do show up will be true crime sickos seeking information about the case.

"Did she say anything else?"

"She wants to know about the hotel's ad campaign. I got the feeling she wants to drop The Shack from her list of recommendations."

"She can't do that," I say, slamming my hand on the tabletop. "If people start disassociating from us publicly, that will tank the restaurant."

"That's my fear, too. These people have known Eileen as long as I have. I can't believe they're so quick to turn their back on her."

Unfortunately, I think Des is on her own. It's natural for people to be shocked and outraged by what Mom did. I know I am. Des chooses to see the best in Mom, ignore the evidence against her, but not everyone will make that choice. Still, whether people's reasons are warranted or not, if The Shack goes down, Des and I will also plummet.

"I'll handle Holly Dale," I say. "This isn't the first time she's tried to pull a power card."

"Not that you don't have enough on your plate." Des places both hands on the counter. "What made you decide to stop by?"

"I actually need a favor," I say, looking around the place. She's done a lot of work since the police search, and I feel guilty for not pitching in. My mind has been elsewhere. Right now, it's across town with Amelia Parker.

Behind me, I hear the whooshing of the front door as it opens. Michael walks inside carrying a big box. Penny and Preston run out from behind him, chasing each other to the pinball machine.

"Michael and the little rascals are here to help me set some stuff up," Des says, walking around the counter. "I'm aiming to open up in a couple of days."

Michael walks over and leans in for a hug. I'm not used to seeing him in the middle of the day like this. Now that he's in between jobs, I'm sure he's looking for any excuse to get out of the house.

"Where's Carmen?" I ask him.

"She's in court." He starts sifting through the box he carried in.

Has there been another development in the case? Events have unfolded in such quick succession, like a flapping deck of cards, it's hard to keep up with everything.

"Is something happening with Mom?"

"No, it's one of her other cases."

Another twinge of guilt. Mom's case has uprooted my own life so much, I'm ignoring that people have responsibilities outside of it.

"I forgot she has other clients," I say, scratching the back of my neck. "She spends most her time worrying about Mom."

"She wouldn't have it any other way. Eileen's case is her top priority. How's your mom doing, by the way?"

"Surgery went well," I say, although he probably already knows that much from Carmen. "Doctors are keeping me updated, but she's still not awake."

"She'll pull through." He says it like it's a fact, not a wish.

"So, what did you need?" Des asks, draping a dishrag over her shoulder.

"I was wanting you to watch Ava for an hour or so, but since your hands are full—"

"Nothing's full here. I can do it. What's going on?"

I open my mouth and close it. I don't want to tell anyone I'm meeting Amelia. Des would think it's a betrayal. She wouldn't understand this is my way of trying to understand what happened back then. It's best I keep Amelia a secret for now.

"Just looking into a few things," I say. "For the case."

"Do you need my help with anything?" Michael asks.

"No, I'm fine. I just need a little bit of space."

"Take all the time you need," Des says.

Preston and Penny gather around Ava, helping her stack primary-colored blocks on the floor. I kiss her forehead before I leave.

CHAPTER 18

Now

Marion

Pier 15 is too far south for tourists, which is why it's a local favorite. That and because Crabby's Coffee is nearby. As usual, I take off my sandals, leaving them by the entry ramp so I can feel the sand beneath my feet. The sensation brings peace. So much of my life has been lived on this shore. Celebratory meals and firework shows and first dates. It never occurred to me it would also be the perfect place to hide away from the rest of the world.

Crabby's Coffee is about the size of a food truck. It's painted bright blue with a few local artists' murals coloring the sides. The large takeout window makes it easy for patrons to order drinks and snacks on the beach, and there are circular tables spread around for outdoor dining.

That's where I spot Amelia. She already has a drink in hand. She remains seated, watching me. Once I've ordered my coffee, I approach her, and she stands.

"Would you like to sit?"

"I thought a walk might be nice," I say. I bring a hand to my forehead, blocking out the sun so I can see further down the beach. As expected, there aren't many people.

We begin walking. For several minutes we're both silent, unsure where to start. How do you begin a conversation with someone who was meant to play a critical role in your life, who instead turned out to be a stranger? How do you get to know the child that for decades you feared you might never meet again?

"Has the press been following you?" she asks. "I know you mentioned them when I first showed up at your place."

"You too?"

"Not so much here, but the press has been a double-edged sword for me over the years. That's how I found out there was a development in the case. Certain detectives are pretty good about staying in touch, but not this time. It was Carla Phelps from Channel 10 News."

"My gosh," I say, raising a hand to my chest. "I'm sorry you had to find out that way."

"I've made the mistake of getting my hopes up over the years. There have been leads before which led to nothing. I'm happy this time was different."

I take a deep breath, slowly so she can't see. I know Amelia is just being honest with me, but it's still awkward trying to grasp what she's been through. I'm the answer to the prayers she's been whispering for all these years, and I feel unworthy.

"Anyway," she says, as though she senses my unease, "I thought maybe the press had been bothering you, too. Which is why you suggested meeting here."

"That's part of the reason," I say, squinting as the clouds part and the sun hovers ahead. "I also really love it here. I've always gone to the water when I'm feeling overwhelmed."

"I do love the ocean. I never travel as much as I used to, it seems."

We must be thinking the same thing. That this landscape is so different from the urban streets of New Hutton. Amelia's life there likely differs from most. She probably lives in a fancy suburb. I wonder what it would be like to grow up in that environment. No ocean. No sand. No two-bedroom apartment above The Shack. Every aspect of my life is different, all because of what Mom did.

"Tell me about yourself," I say.

There's no rule book for how to reconnect with a woman you never knew was your mother, or a daughter you thought you might never see again. It's an unusual predicament, but we persevere, trying to find common ground.

"I've been around New Hutton my whole life, really. I attended the local university. That's where I met your—" She stops and blinks, as though the sun has become unbearably bright. "That's where I met Bruce."

I could finish her sentence. She was about to say *your father* but thought better of it.

"After graduation, I worked as a counselor for troubled youth," she continues. "Daddy owned a big business. Boone Enterprises. After I left the counseling center, I worked there for a few years helping with marketing."

"Are your parents still—"

"No, no. They died about ten years back."

Amelia has withstood so much loss. Her husband. Her child. Her parents. And yet, you wouldn't know by looking at her. Beyond the tailored clothes and highlighted hair, she looks kind. Understanding. Perhaps she's just patient.

"Do you have any siblings?"

"I was an only child, but Bruce was the youngest of five. I keep in touch with his family. I'm close with my nephews. Seven in total. They all remember Bruce as their wacky, fun-loving uncle, and I guess I try to keep up that role."

When she speaks of Bruce, it's all I can do not to tear up. Together, they started a family that never came to fruition. A family that was finished before it really found its footing. A family destroyed by my mother.

"What do you do now?" I ask, trying to direct the conversation into less emotional territory.

"I left the family business ages ago. I do a lot of charity work and plan fundraisers for the community. For the past ten years or so, I've been involved with parents of missing children."

I find it comforting Amelia works with other parents unfortunate enough to be in the same situation as her. She shares more about the different charitable organizations she's worked with over the years. She tells me about a trip she once took to Ghana to help access clean water and a mentor program Boone Enterprises started there. I love listening to her talk, imagining a life that seems more exciting than my own.

I stand still, looking at the water. The waves are rougher, rising and falling in choppy breaks. I think I could stare at this view forever, in all its forms. It calms me, reminds me there's a world out there much bigger than myself.

"Care to sit?" I ask Amelia.

"Sure."

We hunker down into the sand. In the distance, I see a few joggers. It's a local's haven, a quiet place, perfect for thinking hard with limited interruptions.

"Can you tell me what happened that day?" I ask, hoping it's not too soon. I'm trying to be sensitive around Amelia, but I can't help asking. Ever since Mom's arrest, I've been dying to know the truth about that day. The truth about my life before.

Amelia tilts her head back. "I wasn't sure what you'd want to know—if you'd want to know."

"I want to know everything," I say, blankly, relieved Amelia is as desperate to approach the topic as I am.

She exhales shakily. She must have retold her story dozens of times, but that doesn't make sharing it with me any easier.

"I met Sarah through the counseling center. I'd been working with her while she was on probation. She was a nice enough girl, in the beginning. The more time we spent together, she seemed to become obsessed with me and my life. She was always trying to concoct reasons for us to meet outside our sessions. I kept our relationship professional, but she wasn't happy when I told her I was leaving the center to go on maternity leave."

As she tells the story, her voice is calm. It doesn't even crack. She's had years of practice. This is the first time I'm hearing any of it, and I feel like I might be sick. It's strange to picture my mother as a neurotic young girl. I've never known her to be reckless, but I also never knew her as Sarah Paxton.

"I had a difficult pregnancy and had to spend most of the time on bed rest," she continues. "Bruce and I had already been trying to get pregnant for over two years. It rarely took. Sometimes it did, but nothing ever came of it."

"I'm sorry."

"I had about accepted the reality we wouldn't get pregnant before you came along." She looks down, clawing the sand with her hands, letting it fall. "Of course, I was nervous the first several months. By the time we entered the third trimester, it really hit me. It's happening. I'm going to be a mother."

I remember having the same feelings about Ava. In fact, most of Amelia's story resembles mine. I can remember the gnawing uncertainty of whether or not motherhood would ever happen for me. It almost felt like trickery, knowing something I wanted so intensely was finally on its way.

"Every mother says this, I know," Amelia continues, "but you were the best baby. All the books try to prepare you for a newborn, and people almost scare you out of it with their horror stories, but once you were here, you were just… perfect. You rarely cried. All you needed was a few cuddles to make you happy again. I couldn't believe how lucky we were. You were worth the wait in every aspect.

"You were three months old when it happened. It was one of those perfect summer days. I can still remember how clear the sky was, how the breeze seemed to slice through the heat. I remember being so happy." She pauses, her smile fading. "Sarah showed up at the house. I hadn't seen her in months, not since I left the center. I had no idea she knew where I lived. She told me she had a gift for you. For the baby. I told her she needed to leave, that her arriving unannounced made me feel uncomfortable. When she refused, I threatened to call the police. Sarah forced her way into the house and followed me to the backyard. I'm not sure what happened. She must have hit me, and I blacked out. My next memory was waking up and finding Bruce. Then I went searching the house, but you—Caroline—my baby was gone."

I bite the inside of my cheek, trying not to react to her story. I imagine the sudden shift from an idyllic day to a tragedy. Amelia's confusion, then fear as she struggled to find her child. Of course, as she tells the story, I'm picturing Ava, how my world would be entirely lost if someone took her from me.

"I'm sorry."

They are the only words I can muster. Beneath the sadness, is rising anger toward Mom. How could she do it? There's not an excuse in the world that could justify putting another person through such pain. And Amelia, of all people. A woman who struggled so hard to have a child in the first place. Nothing about this is right or fair or tolerable.

"You have nothing to be sorry for," she says, placing a hand on my knee.

It's warm and soft, and I feel a bit better knowing she's here to comfort me, even though she's the one who has lost so much.

CHAPTER 19

Now

Marion

We wander away from the beach, back to the lot where both our cars are parked. An awkward silence falls between us. Where do we go from here? I'm not sure what either of us wants.

"Thank you for meeting with me today," Amelia says. She leans in for a hug, which I slowly accept.

"Thank you for telling me what happened." I realize that's what I've wanted most since Mom's arrest. To understand the truth about what occurred that day.

We exchange phone numbers, but don't make plans to meet again. Our relationship to each other still feels fresh. I think we're both aware of the boundary between us; we don't want to push the other away.

Amelia seems stoic about the whole thing, but I know that's a front she's putting on for me. How couldn't she be devastated by what she has been through? Her daughter stolen. Her husband murdered. It's unbelievable she's had to live through such things, and it's equally incredible to ponder how different my own life could have been.

Instead of the two-bedroom and shared bath I grew up in above The Shack, I could have lived in a house. I could have gone on vacations and visited other parts of the country, other parts of the planet. Amelia wouldn't have been scared to let me explore what was out there; she wasn't hiding from the world, unlike Mom. I could have had cousins. Cousins! Maybe even a brother or sister, had Amelia's life taken a happier turn. I remember all the other extras I asked for over the years: violin lessons and summer camps. Mom denied me all these things, blaming finances, when in reality, it was probably just another way to keep me unseen, keep me hidden.

I got over the limitations of my childhood years ago. I accepted my mother and the life we lived, tried to focus on the positive things she gave me instead of everything I lacked. But now I realize, maybe, I shouldn't have accepted it. I should have pushed for more. Pushed for answers. It wasn't that Mom couldn't provide them. Mom took those opportunities away from me, stole them from me, just as she stole me from Amelia.

By now, it's late afternoon. Des told me Carmen picked up Ava once she got out of court, giving her more time to work at the restaurant. As usual, my body leaps at the idea of seeing Ava, but I still can't shake my conversation with Amelia. I'm disgusted, still in disbelief over what my mother has done.

I exhale, puffing out my cheeks. I can't seem agitated when I walk inside. I don't want Carmen to know I've spoken to Amelia. She might predict my biological mother will want to get in touch, but her brain is busy strategizing for Mom's defense. I go in through the front door, winding past the stone columns in the entryway. Carmen is sitting at the breakfast bar eating a sandwich, her phone in her hand. When she sees me, she puts it down and stands.

"Everything okay?"

"I'm fine," I say, dryly. "Why?"

"I was worried when Michael told me you dropped off Ava. I thought maybe something was wrong."

"I just needed to get away."

I look around. I'm not exactly lying, but if Carmen looks closely enough, she'll see there is more I'm not telling her. The far wall in the living room is a series of windows overlooking the backyard and the beach beyond that. Preston and Penny are playing in the fenced-in grassy area. Esme watches over them from a lounge chair in the shade.

"Where's Ava?"

"Just finished her nap," Michael says, walking in holding Ava. He hands her to me.

She folds into my arms, resting her head on my shoulder. Despite all the chaos around us, I feel so complete with her. Close to me. A part of me never wants to let her go.

"Thank you for watching her," I say. "You know, this whole *Daddy Day Care* bit might suit you, if real estate doesn't work out."

"I'm exhausted. That's for sure."

"Did you get anything done at the restaurant?"

"I worked until Des told me to quit." Michael leans against a counter and stretches his neck to the side. "That woman must have been some kind of military sergeant in a past life."

"How's the place look?"

"Good as new, really. Des is considering opening tomorrow."

"That sounds a bit soon."

"You don't want to stay closed for too long," Carmen says. She carries her plate into the kitchen and leaves it by the sink. "Reopening sends a message to the community that everything is on track."

But nothing is on track, I think. After speaking to Amelia, I'm not sure sending the message we support Mom is the best move. She committed awful crimes. Whatever messages we want out there, it's only a matter of time until the truth is revealed.

My phone rings with a number I don't recognize. A week ago, I would have ignored such a call, assuming it was another sketchy operator calling about my car's extended warranty, but now there is no telling who it could be.

I answer.

"This is Doctor Raul at North Bay Hospital. May I speak with Marion Sams?"

"Just a minute," I say, already handing Ava over to Michael again. The guilt stays with me, knowing these constant interruptions keep her at a distance. I enter the guest bedroom down the hall, cracking the door so I can focus. "I'm here."

"Your mother had a second surgery this morning. It went well. The preliminary scans are promising."

I blink hard, warm tears in my eyes. Beneath my mounting anger, there is undeniable love for this woman. For Mom. Eileen. The woman who spent what little she had to give me the best life she could. She did an awful thing, but I'm not ready to let her go.

"When will she be allowed visitors?"

"We're keeping her sedated for the time being. The surgery was successful, but we need to make sure her body can withstand the healing process. Her oncologist has a series of tests he'd like to run—"

"Wait," I say, unsure I'm hearing correctly. "Oncologist?"

"Yes. We want to make sure the stress of surgery won't interfere with her ongoing chemotherapy."

Ongoing chemotherapy. My heart starts pounding faster, like I've balanced on a wave, only to be knocked down by another.

"You're calling about Eileen Sams, correct?"

"Yes. Your mother was brought to us after her attack in the county jail."

"Right. This is the first I'm hearing about chemotherapy."

"According to her medical records, she's been receiving treatments for the past three months. To combat the breast cancer."

I lean against the wall, resting my head back. My mouth is open, but it seems impossible to breathe. I'm stuck here, in this awful moment. The doctor continues talking, and I do my best to process what he is saying, but I keep returning to those words. *Oncologist. Chemotherapy. Cancer.*

"I understand. Thank you for the update."

The words, like so many I've spoken these past few days, don't sound like my own. They're not a true expression of what I'm feeling, more a cursory impulse of politeness. I hang up, sliding down the wall until I hit the floor.

After several minutes, I leave the bedroom. Carmen is now holding Ava, and Michael has joined the children outside. Such a normal, beautiful day for the Banks family, in their upscale house by the sea. What a shame my own world is falling apart against the same charming backdrop.

"How's Eileen?" Carmen asks.

"She has cancer."

She freezes, her eyes wide and blank, then she nods toward the closest armchair. "Maybe you should take a seat."

I remain standing. "She's had it for months. She's been undergoing chemotherapy. Has an oncologist. All of it."

"Did the surgery impact her—"

"I don't know. I don't know anything. Why wouldn't she tell me she was sick?"

Carmen sits, bouncing Ava on her knee. "Maybe she had her reasons."

"Her reasons?" I gasp, nervously. "Maybe Mom just has a reason for everything. I'm sure she had a reason to steal me as a child. A reason to lie about my entire childhood. A reason to hide her cancer diagnosis."

"She didn't come out and lie," Carmen says. She whispers, even though we are alone. "She just didn't tell you."

"No shit, Carmen. I didn't know you were supposed to ask people these things. Are you my real mother? Are we hiding from my biological family? Do you have cancer? I assumed, being as close as I thought we were, she wouldn't have a reason to be so deceptive."

I pop my knuckles. Carmen has been quick to defend Mom when it comes to the charges against her, but I assumed that was her acting as an attorney. I thought she would have been more taken aback by this latest news. She doesn't even seem surprised.

"Did you know about this?"

Carmen looks from me to Ava. "She was waiting to tell you until after Ava's party."

I take that seat Carmen said I might need. My knees could buckle, sending me straight to the floor otherwise.

"You knew Mom had cancer and you didn't tell me?"

"It wasn't my place—"

"You're my best friend! Of course it's your place."

"Like I said, she wanted to wait until after Ava's birthday. She knew how important it was to you. She didn't want you to be worrying about her condition."

"This is unbelievable," I say, leaning my forehead into my palm.

"It was a big year for you. Even before the party, you had your hands full with Ava. For the first time in ages, you seemed happy. When she got the news, the last thing she wanted to do was upset you."

"So she told you instead."

"Yes. Not right away. But between the restaurant and Ava, she needed help organizing everything—"

"She needed help hiding it from me," I correct. She enlisted the help of my best friend to deceive me. "And Des? Does she know?"

Carmen nods.

"Why wouldn't you two tell me any of this? Especially after her arrest."

"Believe it or not, it's not been the biggest thing on my mind. After the jail attack, I was just hoping she'd pull through. Every other moment I've been working on Eileen's case, trying my damnedest to get her back to us."

"That's not true. You were in court today, and it had nothing to do with Mom."

I know this is a low blow, but I don't care. I'm not about to let Carmen masquerade as some savior, not when she has withheld this from me. I'm reaching, searching for any type of reaction. Her betrayal dives that deep.

"Yes, I have other clients, Marion. But trust me, Eileen is my priority."

"What about me? Has everyone forgotten my role in all this? That I'm a victim here?"

Carmen opens, then closes her mouth. It's not like her to lack the appropriate response. I know she must feel conflicted, because while she loves Eileen, she is also my best friend. She knows Mom didn't do right by me.

I stand, flexing my fingers toward Ava. "We need to leave."

"Don't go this upset."

"I've been in a constant state of upset since the party. Just when I think it can't get worse, it does."

"Stay. Let's talk this out."

"The only person I want to speak with is Mom, and I can't." I laugh. "It's ironic. She didn't tell me about her cancer because she didn't want to ruin the party. Getting arrested was much more discreet."

Again, Carmen looks as though she wants to say something, but doesn't. She just watches me leave.

CHAPTER 20

Then

Eileen

Cliff's family planned the funeral. They made the cheapest, most detached decisions possible. It was obvious to everyone in attendance—to the dozen who did show up—that this was something they wanted to be over and done with. Like lancing a boil. Cliff's entire life had come to this: an annoying afternoon for those he left behind.

Of course, I didn't feel that way. I wanted to celebrate his life, mourn his loss. Cliff never introduced me to his family. After seeing the way they behaved at the funeral, I understood why he avoided them. They didn't seem interested in getting to know me. I wasn't his wife or his fiancé—just some sad, crying girl on the front row. No one even asked my name.

Jamie postponed her trip. Her old apartment—briefly, in my mind, the place I might live with Cliff—found a new tenant. She stayed with me in my dingy studio. Her place seemed like a palace by comparison, but she never commented on the leaky faucet or inconsistent electricity, the fact you had to flick on the kitchen light in order to get the living room fan to work. For two weeks, she slept on a futon, making sure I continued eating and did something during the day besides cry.

"I can stay longer if you'd like," she said, as the start date at her university approached.

"You can't. Your classes will begin soon."

"I'm already starting late. Pushing back a little longer won't be a problem."

"No. You have to go. I'm not going to let you give up college."

"I know, but you're—"

"I'm fine."

I was harsher with her than I should have been. Jamie had only ever tried to help me, but now she was leaving, abandoning me to my memories of Cliff. Even when I thought of something happy, my insides would clench with anger and... and guilt. His death, accidental and tragic as it was, wouldn't have happened had our lives never crossed paths. He might be alive if we weren't naively daydreaming about the future that day, if he wasn't helping my best friend move. I was nothing more than a screw-up, transferring my bad luck onto him, and now he was gone forever.

I had what some might call a breakdown. I quit going to work. It was too difficult to stand at the same counter where we'd once been together, to sit in the same alleyway where we first got to know one another. I locked myself away in my apartment, refusing to leave. The only person left in my life was Jamie, and she lived miles away.

"You have to get your life together," she'd say over the phone. "I'm worried about you."

"I don't know how I'm supposed to do any of this without him," I said, tissues sprinkled over my comforter, the curtains pulled tight to block out the sun. My room mirrored the darkness and claustrophobia I felt inside.

"He'd want you to get better," Jamie said. "Cliff would want you to move on with your life."

I'd been so close, it seemed, to having the life I'd always wanted. The family I felt I deserved. That same day—the very day he died!—we'd been imagining the future. They say when we plan, God laughs, but sometimes it's a cruel laugh, and it's like I could hear His merciless snickering when I tried to sleep at night.

*

I stopped going to my counseling sessions. That was a dumb move. If my probation officer wanted to be a stickler, a thing like that could get me thrown in jail. Thankfully, most probation officers have a bigger workload than they can handle. A few missed sessions barely beeped her radar. Still, I didn't want to run the chance of making my situation worse, so I returned to the center.

I sat as far away from the receptionist's desk as I could, away from the windows, away from anyone who might see me and want to strike up a conversation. A half hour with Ms. Lang was all I could stand in one day. I'd promised myself I wouldn't talk about Cliff—I'd stick to the same little details: job, apartment, bills. Hell, I'd even bring up my childhood to fill the time, anything to keep me from sharing my true feelings.

"Sarah?"

The woman standing in front of me wasn't Ms. Lang, but I recognized her.

"I'm Amelia Parker," she said. "We've spoken before."

"I remember."

For a moment, the heartache of the past month washed away. You'd think after everything I'd just gone through, seeing her again, this perfect woman who seemed to have everything, would make me bitter. But it didn't.

"Ms. Lang is no longer working at the center," she said, hugging a clipboard to her chest. "I'll be handling your session today. Is that okay?"

"Sure." I stood, almost too quickly. There was an eagerness inside I hadn't felt since—well, you know. Since Cliff was alive.

I followed her down the same hunter green hallways and entered a room similar in size and layout to that of Ms. Lang's office. And yet, the energy was clearer. Amelia must have been into feng shui, or something like that. I'd never given that stuff much thought, but I could feel the effects right where I stood. This was a place you wanted to stay, and Amelia was someone you wanted to speak to.

"Let me just glance at your file," she said.

Staring at her, I noticed her figure looked bigger than before. Was she pregnant? I wanted to ask, but knew it was rude. Instead, I focused on her face, expecting a judgmental flinch when she reached the details of the convenience store incident, waiting for her friendly expression to fall.

She placed the folder on her desk and smiled.

"It looks like you've been coming here over two years. Have you found counseling helpful?"

"Sort of."

"What's helpful about it?"

"I… um." I started looking around the room, as though I'd stepped on stage and forgotten my lines. Ms. Lang never asked questions like this. She barely made eye contact.

"Let me rephrase," Amelia said. "You said *sort of.* What doesn't work about it?"

"You know, we just kind of talk about what I did to get arrested, what I'm doing now. We don't really go beyond that."

Amelia nodded. Like she knew exactly what I meant.

"It's weird, isn't it? Talking to a total stranger."

"Yeah. Yeah, it is."

"Maybe if I tell you a little about me, you'll feel better opening up?"

I nodded.

Amelia talked about her family, her southern roots, her husband and the types of places they liked to go on vacation. Vacation. *Let's go to the city*, Cliff had said. This happened sometimes, where I'd hear his voice so clearly it felt like he was in the room with me, but of course he wasn't. Only Amelia was here, and she was talking to me like I was a human being, more than an appointment slot in her agenda.

"And that's about all there is to know about me," she said, finishing. She rested her palms on the desk and waited for me to speak.

"Have any kids?"

I'm not sure where that question came from, other than I'd been thinking about her stomach, trying to figure out if it had gotten any bigger since the last time we spoke. *Idiot*, I scolded myself. *Classless idiot.*

"Working on it." It was an eloquent way of dodging the question. She smiled, but this time there was a tightness around the corners of her mouth. Still, she didn't seem offended.

"I've always wanted children," I said, looking down, unsure why I couldn't shake this topic. It's not something I ever talked about with Ms. Lang. "Now I'm not so sure."

"How come?"

Amelia's eyes didn't look away. She wanted to know. She wanted to hear my answer.

"My boyfriend… um, Cliff… he just died."

"Oh, Sarah. I'm so sorry."

And just like that, the floodgates opened. I told her everything. About how we first got together, how he was the only person who made me feel loved. Like he needed me as much as I needed him. I told her how excited he was to build a future with me, that he wanted a family and all the other things I wanted too. I told her about the car. I explained what his body looked like, lying broken in the middle of the street. I told her how angry I was that the police showed little interest in finding out who killed some line cook from Buster's. I told her I'd stopped going to work and never left my apartment. I told her Jamie had left, hopped on a plane to start over. Something I'd never be able to do. I was stuck here, alone, not sure what my next step should be.

When I finished, it was like I'd surrendered all my strength, all my tears. But instead of feeling exhausted, I felt clean. Pure. I'd purged and was waiting to be filled with something new.

"I'm sorry. You must wonder why your life has unfolded like this. I wish I could provide you with answers." She reached across the table and held my hand. There were tears in her eyes. Ms. Lang never seemed to care. "All I can do is give you options."

"Options."

"Possible steps for what to do next." She opened a folder, taking out a series of brochures. "You're in this situation now, whether you like it or not. Only you are capable of deciding where to go from here."

I liked that phrasing. Even though it seemed everything had been taken from me, I might have some control left.

Amelia would show me the way.

CHAPTER 21

Now

Marion

Two Moms.

The woman who is always there for me, and the woman who keeps me in the dark. I want to see the best in her, but how can I do that when she continues to lie?

It's bad enough she committed these unspeakable acts years ago, ripping me away from my birth family and any opportunity I had at a better life. Even now, after all the years we've spent together, she's continuing her deception. She didn't tell me she had cancer. Worse, she enlisted the two people I trust most, Des and Carmen, to help hide it from me. With each passing day, the life I've known unravels, threads loosening around what once kept me together.

I try to focus only on Ava, on her needs and desires. *The days are long but the years are short*, they say. These days have been some of the longest, but I'm not going to let that ruin my time with my daughter. I don't want her to ever feel I put my own needs before hers. All she understands of this world is what I show her. I can choose to let her see me as an emotional mess, or I can let her see me smiling, enjoying the day.

I put my phone on Do Not Disturb mode for the rest of the evening. I don't anticipate hearing from the hospital until at least tomorrow and I have no desire to speak with Carmen or Des. I make sandwiches and stroll Ava down to the beach in front of our apartment. I wait until it's almost sunset, to be sure there are as few people around as possible.

At night, once Ava is tucked away in her crib, the despair returns. Like a heavy blanket covering me, wrapping around tighter, restricting my ability to breathe. I feel the anger toward Mom fighting against the hope I have that she'll pull through. I feel the sorrow Amelia must have carried all these years, living in a world without her daughter.

I find myself checking the baby monitor more often than I normally would. I squint at the tiny screen, confirming Ava is safe and asleep. I watch her chest rise and fall. The relief I have watching her is fleeting. More than ever, I'm aware of how dangerous and unfair this world can be. There are real monsters out there, some closer than you would prefer to admit.

It feels like I've only slept a half hour when I hear my phone ringing. I'm inclined to ignore it, but everything going on with Mom makes that impossible. I pull the comforter away, the brightness paining my eyes. It's been daylight for hours. Des' name is on the screen.

"You coming by the restaurant?" she asks.

"No," I croak. I reach for my bedside water but see it's not there. And I'm still wearing my clothes from yesterday.

"We're opening at eleven if you change your mind."

"Didn't you think I should have a say in when we reopen?"

"This is the best thing for the business, and for your mom. We're not going to let a little gossip tank the restaurant."

Except it's more than a little gossip. There's evidence Mom killed a man. She even admitted she's used a fake name all these years. I don't see how Des can continue with this blind faith. Surely, she feels equally deceived? She's trying to pretend we can move our lives back to where they were. But it's not that simple for me. Des is able to sweep the floors and polish the tables, act as though nothing happened, but Mom's actions wrecked my whole life.

"How long have you known about the cancer?"

I hear Des exhale on the other end of the line. I'm sure Carmen called her after I stormed out last night. "I was there when she received the diagnosis."

Sounds about right. Mom and Des have been best friends for decades. It's completely natural she would turn to her in a time of crisis, like she did when we moved here all those years ago. And yet, me—her adult daughter—deserves no explanation?

"Why didn't she tell me, Des? Why am I finding out all these things about my mother's life from strangers?"

"I told her to tell you about the cancer, if it makes any difference," she says, and I know she's being truthful. Des doesn't lie. "I can't speak for her on any of the other stuff. Hard to tell what's true, what's not."

This much is clear: Mom's actions all those years ago ruined lives, and the repercussions are now ruining mine. I'd like to think some of what they say isn't true. That she's not a murderer, not a kidnapper, but the more time passes, the more it becomes clear there aren't enough excuses in the world to justify what has been done.

"I need to go," I tell Des, ending the call. It's bad enough I'm worrying about Mom, but I no longer feel I can even count on Des and Carmen. With each passing day, it becomes harder to trust the people I love.

I wander into Ava's nursery. She's not yet awake, but she's rolling from side to side. Normally she'd already have been up a couple of hours by now. We're getting off schedule, a ritual that seemed of the utmost importance only a week ago. Breakfast by eight, a stroll along the sidewalk by nine. Taking Ava with me to the restaurant and preparing for the day. Attending Mommy and Me in the afternoons on Tuesdays and Thursdays. Bedtime at eight thirty on the dot.

None of that seems to matter anymore. Both our sleep schedules are disrupted, and I'm not sure I can face the participants at Mommy and Me ever again, not after they witnessed Mom's arrest. I tiptoe out of the room, shutting the door behind me.

I'm alone again. I wish there was someone I could talk to about this newest revelation. I can't speak to Mom, and I have no desire to talk to Carmen and Des. I consider calling Evan, but that's a can of worms I'm not willing to open at the moment. I'm still suspicious of his true motives for returning to North Bay. There's so much I've been keeping inside, wrestling with myself. All that does is tear me apart.

I pick up my phone, scrolling through my contacts. My thumb rests on Amelia's name.

After the third ring, she answers.

"Marion?"

"I was wondering if you could talk?"

"Sure." She sounds re-energized. "Should we meet at the pier again?"

"Ava is still sleeping. You could come by the condo, if it's not too much trouble."

"No trouble at all. I'll be there within the hour."

I boil a kettle of tea and set out cheese and crackers. Normally, I wouldn't put in so much effort, but I feel an unspoken need to accommodate Amelia. To impress her, even. There's still this awkward cloud hovering over us, a lot of pain lingering beneath our interactions. I want to make our time together as enjoyable as possible. Not only are we getting to know each other, it seems she's one of the few people in my life I can actually trust.

When Amelia arrives, she's impeccably dressed, as she was the last time I saw her. She's wearing coral capris and a black V-neck with pearl studs in her ears. I lead her into the kitchen. She stops in front of the bureau, leaning down to look at the pictures on display of Ava and myself. She smiles. Then her hand lands on the security baton. She lifts it up.

"What's this?"

I wince, rolling my eyes. "My lawyers left it here. They seem to think I should up my security in the wake of Eileen's arrest."

"You must have one heck of a lawyer," she says, placing it back on the dresser. "They do have a point. The press and the people following the case can be relentless. Some are a bit nutty."

"Better safe than sorry, right?" I force a smile. I resent being at the center of this case, which only a week ago I knew nothing about. Then again, I didn't know Amelia a week ago either. I'm happy to see her again. Something about her presence brings me peace.

We sit at the table in front of the living room window.

"Beautiful view," she says, looking ahead. The blinds are turned, otherwise the sun would envelop the entire room. "I could get used to waking up to this every morning."

I wonder what she must really think of my place. I've always thought it was nice, but Amelia Boone Parker must have higher standards. Her family's wealth makes Carmen and Michael look like middle-class.

"Tell me about your place in New Hutton."

"I have a house outside the city. It's far too big for just me, really. I spend most of my time outdoors in the garden."

"I wasn't blessed with a green thumb."

"Not everyone takes to it. I didn't at first. I guess you could say it's my happy place, like you said the beach is yours."

We lock eyes, both wondering where this conversation will take us. It's clear how important our meetings with one another are to her. She hears everything I say and commits it to memory. After all these years of imagining who her daughter might be, she finally gets the chance to know.

"I hope I didn't inconvenience you by calling."

"Not at all, Marion. I've waited half my life to hear your voice."

It's a forward comment, but it's honest. I flinch each time she says my name. It's the only name I've ever known, but to Amelia, and the rest of the world, I'm Baby Caroline. It must be strange calling your daughter something other than the name you gave her.

"The way you sounded on the phone, I thought you might be upset," Amelia says. "Is everything okay?"

I don't know how far I can take this. We've discussed parts of the case, but we've left Eileen in the present—Mom—off the table until now. More than anything, I want to be honest with her about what's happening, but the subject of Mom is a sore one. The hatred she must have felt for Sarah over the years contrasts with the woman I prefer to remember.

"Eileen was attacked in the jail not long after her arrest."

"My lawyers told me." Amelia takes a deep breath, flattening her hands against the table. "Despite what Eileen has done, I realize she's the only parent you've known. Those feelings can't dissipate overnight. I hope she pulls through, for your sake."

"Thanks."

"I'm also grateful she was able to provide you with a good life. If I couldn't have you with me, that's what I wanted. Someone to love you, care for you. My mind has considered so many ugly alternatives over the years."

I understand completely. I worry about it all the time. All the dangers that exist. All the ways I could lose Ava. I don't want to rub Amelia's face in the fact that, despite the trauma of being kidnapped, I've lived a decent life. I can't imagine anyone taking Ava from me, but if they did, I would hope she would be loved. I wouldn't want her life to be hard.

"But she also lied to me," I say, and it feels like a dam is breaking. "Everyone in my life wants me to stay strong for Eileen. They won't allow me to express what I'm feeling. She gave me a good life, and I'm grateful, but it wasn't my own. All of it was a lie. And now it's like all these little comments and stories that didn't make sense over the years are finally adding up."

"Like what?"

"Why she didn't want to take me on vacation. Or why there aren't any pictures of us before we moved here. Why I don't have any extended family, or a clear idea of what Eileen's childhood was even like."

Each lie plants a seed for a future one, sprouting another, then another. I'm caught in a wilderness of deception Mom created, and there's no one able to fetch me out of it.

Amelia puts her hand over mine. "What Eileen did wasn't fair. To either of us."

"And she's still lying to me. Her doctor told me she has been undergoing chemotherapy for months. She told our business partner, Des. She told my best friend. But she's still lying to me!"

Amelia sits back and crosses her arms. She looks out the window. The sun is shining in, making each crevice and imperfection of her skin more apparent, but she looks kind. Beautiful.

"I'm sorry this is how it is between you. You deserve so much more."

There's more she wants to say but won't. She must be considering the type of relationship she'd wished to have had with me, one built on honesty and respect.

"I don't know why I'm telling you any of this. I'm upset with my friends right now and just needed to vent. I needed—"

"You needed a mother," she says, her eyes back on me.

She finished the sentence more perfectly than I could. I still love Mom, but there's a hardness in me now I'm not sure will ever go away. She lied to me—continues to lie. Not to mention all the other hurt she inflicted. At least Amelia is willing to hear my honesty. She's what I need right now.

"It must be so hard for you being here. Having to relive all of this."

"I've relived it every day from the moment you were taken. It's hurtful, yes, thinking of Bruce and the way things could have been. The knowledge you're okay makes up for a big part of that hurt. I understand your anxiety stems from knowing so little. I can tell you stories about my life, about what your life might have been, but I can't give you any insight as to why Eileen took you from me. Only she can do that."

"I know, which is what makes the idea of losing her now so difficult. All I want is a conversation. The opportunity to ask her why and how. And now that she's in the hospital, the case against her is on hold. It's like I'm stuck without answers and don't know when I'll get them."

"We could always take things into our own hands."

"What do you mean?"

"This case is more than three decades in the making, but law enforcement's only had the last week or so to start building their case. That means they're going to take their time doing everything by the book. If you want confirmation, we could always do our own DNA test. No more sitting around waiting for answers."

The suggestion releases an immediate jolt of endorphins, the idea that at least part of this could be proven. But I remember what Carmen said. *Tests will come. Wait for them.* A DNA test would seal Mom's fate, at least on the kidnapping charges. As angry as I am with her, as bitter as I am, I still don't want to deliberately hurt her cause. Not when my hand will be forced eventually.

"Carmen says not to do anything like that. The police will organize their own test."

"My lawyers say the same thing. They want to do everything by the book. They don't understand what it's like to wait for answers. I wouldn't be doing it for them. Not for the police. Just for us. So we can know, and can move on. All I need is a cheek swab and I can sort everything out."

I open my mouth, then close it. I feel like a hypocrite, because as much as I've been begging for answers, a bigger part of me is afraid to know.

Amelia must read the unrest on my face. She holds up her hands. "It was only a suggestion. The last thing I want to do is put you under more pressure. You've got enough to deal with."

"Thank you," I say.

I can tell it goes against her desires, but at least she's willing to wait for me. She's putting my needs before her own, like all great mothers do.

CHAPTER 22

Now

Marion

As much as I'd like to avoid Carmen, she's still Mom's lawyer. After I dodged countless phone calls, she finally sent a text:

Updates in the case. I'm coming over at 5. Be there.

I can't stay mad at her forever, but it feels like every person in my life is lying to me. Everyone except Amelia, that is. Our visit this morning wasn't very long because I wanted her to leave before Ava woke up. Selfishly, I don't want to share Ava with her yet. And maybe I don't want to share Amelia, either. Amelia is everything a person aspires to be. Educated, classy, witty. She comes from a privileged background, but she doesn't use her upbringing as a crutch, like so many people in her position might. She's tried to make the world a better place. It's nice to be distracted from the world I know, to be transported to a completely different one, a life that could have been—should have been—mine.

Carmen arrives a little later. She's alone, which already makes this meeting feel more intimate. There's no Rick waiting in the corner, listening to our every word.

"What's the update?" I ask. I'm seated in front of the high chair, spooning food into Ava's mouth.

"We'll get to that in a second," she says, putting her satchel on the counter. "First, I need you to talk to me about the cancer diagnosis."

Typical Carmen. There might not even be an update, but she's determined to force a conversation. She doesn't like being ignored. I put down the spoon, wipe my hands and turn to face her.

"Less than a week ago, I watched my mother get arrested. Since then, all I've heard is that the life I've been living is a lie. That the woman I love more than anyone, the person I thought was my best friend, stole me from my real parents when I was younger than Ava is now. That she's been hiding me, lying to me, all this time. I don't want to believe any of it is true. More than anything, I want the police to admit they've got it wrong and that Mom did not do the horrible things they're saying she did—at least not all of it. But how am I supposed to have faith in her when she lied about her name? Her cancer? That you and Des—my other two best friends—knew about it and didn't tell me?"

Carmen doesn't break eye contact, but her bottom lip quivers, slightly.

"I hate that you're going through this. I do. I'm doing everything I can to help you and Eileen. But you have to understand, when she found out about the cancer, she had no way of knowing an arrest was imminent. She simply wanted to wait until Ava's party was over. I understand now it seems you're being hit with one blow after another, but, at the time, she was doing what she thought was right."

I know Carmen's talking about the cancer diagnosis, but the same logic applies to all my mother's poor decisions. She took me, hid me, raised me… because she thought it was right? Did she ever stop to think about what was wrong? No, she was more concerned with her own feelings. They were more important than mine. Or Amelia's.

"You said there was an update," I say, steering Carmen back toward the case.

"When they arrested Eileen, they took her fingerprints and ran them against what was found at the New Hutton crime scene. They also ran them against the fingerprints taken from Sarah Paxton when she was arrested. They all match, which means—"

"Which means Mom is definitely the person who attacked Bruce." My body closes in on itself. Ever since Mom admitted she was Sarah Paxton, I've feared this, but having it confirmed is another type of torture.

"Not necessarily. It means she was there. It doesn't mean she attacked anyone."

"What are you trying to prove, Carmen? I'm not a juror. I'm your friend. You don't have to try and spin this."

She sighs. "It's not good, that's for sure," she admits, painfully.

I lean over the table, propping my chin on my hand. "What else?"

"You know they've searched her apartment and the restaurant. They're also trying to track down people who might have known your mom as Sarah Paxton, which will be difficult considering how much time has passed."

"Okay."

"All this means they're getting closer to asking you for a DNA sample." She tilts her head down and looks up, waiting.

"How long?"

"Possibly a week. Maybe more. I've been trying to stall them while Eileen's in the hospital, but we knew this would happen eventually."

"When it shows I'm not her biological daughter—"

"Then we'll take it step by step."

"But what will happen?"

"Well, she's already been arrested. But obviously that will become the crux of their case. We'll have to try and prove Eileen was somehow granted permission to take you, or that she had just cause for doing so."

"Proving just cause for stealing an infant?" I look at Ava, who's smiling, globs of pureed sweet potatoes dribbling from her lips. "That's a stiff one, Carmen."

"Like I said, we'll take this one step at a time. If it comes to a conviction, our goal will be to get Eileen the lightest sentence possible."

"But if they can prove I'm not her daughter—"

"We'll show that she was still an adequate mother. That she supported you, loved you. You're Eileen's biggest defense."

Mom gave me a good life. Because of that, she should have my unbending devotion. A week ago, she would have. But I won't try to justify her crimes or help her avoid punishment. I won't be made to feel like an accessory after the fact to my own abduction.

"What about the Parkers?"

Carmen whips her head in my direction. "What about them?"

"Will they run my DNA against theirs? Try to prove I'm Baby Caroline?"

"Eventually, yes. But I'm not saying any of this to scare you. I'm simply preparing you for the inevitable."

"What if we just went ahead and volunteered a sample? We could get this over with."

"Like I said, you are Eileen's greatest defense. There's no sense in volunteering information that could jeopardize the case." Carmen's phone starts ringing from inside her bag. She grabs it, glances at the screen and holds up a finger. "This is Rick. Give me a second."

She walks down the hallway leading toward the bedrooms. I free Ava from her high chair and bring her into the living room. She begins contentedly playing with toys on the floor in her playpen.

I look outside, watching as a trio of seagulls fly past my window. Amelia's offer still lingers in my mind. How nice it would be to simply know the truth. Hard revelations are still to come, but I'd rather get this first one out of the way. Start recognizing who I really am. Start accepting the person I never got the chance to be.

"What the hell is this?"

Carmen's yell startles me. She walks into the living room, but her eyes are still staring at her phone.

"What is it? Is it Mom? Is she okay?"

"Now I know why you're asking questions about the Parkers," she says, holding out her phone for me to see a picture. It was taken by the pier, only a few steps away from Crabby's Coffee. "What the hell are you doing talking to Amelia Parker?"

CHAPTER 23

Now

Marion

Carmen's anger is building, threatening to spew. She shakes the phone in her hand, begging me to take it. I do.

The picture accompanies an article written by a national online news outlet. I'm sitting on the beach with Amelia. This was taken on the first day we met. I thought I'd been careful. I hadn't spotted any press.

"Again," Carmen says. "What the hell are you doing talking to Amelia Parker?"

"She came by the condo."

"When?"

"Yesterday."

"And you just let her right in? Made her a cup of tea? Let her change Ava's diapers?"

"She hasn't even met Ava," I say, handing over the phone. I'm careful enough to keep Ava at a distance, and I don't appreciate Carmen bringing her into this. "I'm not ready for that."

"So, when you left Ava with Des and Michael, was it so you could meet Amelia?"

"That was the first time she came over, yes. I asked her to meet me at the beach. I thought it would be harder for the press to catch sight of us there."

"Well, that didn't happen. The press is all over this. I've tried my best to keep them away from the condo, away from the restaurant, but anywhere else you go is open game. This case has circulated in the media for decades. You didn't think a public meeting with your biological mother after years of separation would grab people's attention?"

"I'm not used to being followed! She reached out to me, and, yes, I wanted to hear what she had to say. She's the only person who is willing to talk to me anymore without wanting something out of it."

Carmen looks as though she's about to address that dig, but she stops, narrowing her eyes. She circles back around to something I said earlier.

"You said the first time she came over. Have you seen her again?"

"She came over this morning."

"What was the reason this time?"

"I don't know," I say, shrugging. "Just to visit. Don't we have a right to get to know each other?"

"Of course you do." Carmen clears her throat. "But like I keep telling you, every action you take right now impacts Eileen's case. If you're cozying up to Amelia, or any of the Boones and Parkers, for that matter, it won't help your mother."

"I'm conflicted about helping Mom. Don't you get that? It's one thing to not actively hurt her case, but openly defending a kidnapper and murderer doesn't sit well, either. I can't base my every decision around a woman who made it a point to deceive me my entire life. I enjoy having Amelia around. It's nice to have someone else's perspective on all this."

"What do you two talk about?"

"She tells me about her life in New Hutton. What her life was like as a child. She tells me about what happened before I was born. Before Bruce died."

I can see Carmen feels sorry for me. No one should hear such details this late in life. Imagine a whole other world for themselves if they hadn't been kidnapped.

"I understand why you want to connect with Amelia, but she is clearly siding with the prosecution. You'll have time to get to know her. After the trial."

It's not a statement. It's an order.

"And how long could that take? Even if Mom does pull through, we could be fighting this battle for years. I'm just supposed to ignore Amelia that entire time?"

"It would be best for Eileen if you weren't in contact."

"What about me? Eileen made her choices. I didn't ask for any of this, and I shouldn't be responsible for helping her avoid punishment. Eileen didn't even care to tell me about her cancer, but I'm in the wrong for venting to Amelia about it?"

"Did you tell Amelia about the cancer?" Her tone is serious again.

"Yes."

Carmen exhales and presses two fingers against her temple. "That's a perfect example of something the prosecution could use against us. They'll make it look like Eileen is continuing to lie. Like she's dishonest."

"Maybe the prosecution doesn't have to make it *look* that way," I say. "Maybe that's just the way Mom is."

"But she's still *your* mom. She loves you. Gave you everything she had, even if that wasn't much."

I feel tears forming, but I don't want to cry in front of Carmen. In over a decade of friendship, I don't think we've had as many arguments as we have in the past week. I feel a sudden urge to be near Ava. She's the only one left innocent in all this, and I'm determined to find the truth about my life before it impacts hers. I lift her from her playpen, putting her in my lap. She sinks into me, still playing with a fabric doll in her hand.

"Anything else we need to discuss?" I ask.

"Did anything I say sink in?"

"What about what I've said? I appreciate everything you're doing for Mom. I do. But I really miss having you as my best friend."

Carmen winces. "I'm sorry for everything you're going through. I know it's hell. I'm trying to ignore the emotional aspects of this mess and stay practical. It's the only way I can help you. That's what you want, isn't it?"

I sling the diaper bag over my shoulder and carry Ava toward the door.

I'm not sure what I want anymore.

CHAPTER 24

Now

Marion

It's harder to stay mad at Des. Even though she also chose to hide Mom's cancer diagnosis, I can't forget all that she has done for us over the years. Who knows? If it weren't for her, we might have never stayed in North Bay. We might have continued the nomadic routine we had before settling here, during that mysterious portion of my early life. Des rented Mom the apartment I called home. She gave Mom a job in the restaurant, then invited her in as business partner years later. I know Mom couldn't have had much money; Des was acting on good faith. And she continued that charity when she allowed me to take over only a few years ago.

I stop by the restaurant. I wait until after eight o'clock, hoping there won't be many customers. There's a few media vans parked across the street, but they look as though they're packing up for the day. I don't give them a second glance as I cross the street to The Shack.

The front door is unlocked. Des jerks her head but relaxes when she sees me. She beams when she sees Ava.

"Finally acting as though you have a job?" she asks.

"Consider the past few days personal leave," I say, taking the diaper bag off my shoulder and resting it on a nearby chair. "Besides, I don't remember being consulted about reopening the place."

"Consider it an executive decision." She pats her hands with a washrag, then leans against the counter. "Can't say you missed much. Opening day was a disaster, so I'm closing up early. We maybe had ten customers all day, and half of them I suspect were some form of media."

"That's disappointing."

"I dipped into a big portion of our savings to replace what the police ruined. Business will have to pick up, otherwise we'll stay in the hole. And the other local businesses hanging us out to dry doesn't help." Des whips her head at me. "You talked to Holly Dale yet?"

"Not yet." I exhale, rubbing my forehead. "I will."

"I really thought people would have Eileen's back more. The people around here should know she's a good person, regardless of what lies the press cooks up."

Des is the only person convinced they are still lies. Everyone else, even Carmen, sees the mountains of evidence against Mom. They see how the timeline of Sarah Paxton fits perfectly with Mom's own mysterious past. I still don't know who tipped off the police in the first place, but it must have been someone convinced of Mom's guilt. I'm starting to wonder why Des continues to look the other way. Maybe she knows more about Mom's past than she's willing to admit.

"The customers, did they say anything about Mom? Or the arrest?"

"Not a word. That's a nod to their support. It shows some people still believe Eileen is a good person. It's amazing how easily some people forget."

I know that last comment was aimed to hurt me.

"Why didn't she tell me about the cancer, Des? I understand if she thought I couldn't handle the other stuff. She thought I was too young. She was trying to protect me. Whatever. But why wouldn't she tell me about the cancer?"

I watch as Des' shoulders tense then relax.

"Everything you just said remains true, Marion. She was going to tell you, but she was looking out for you. She didn't want everything to be about her."

"Everything *is* about her, isn't it? Ever since the party—the one she wanted so badly not to ruin—all we can talk about is Mom. Her lies. Her health. Her past."

Des turns, her face thick and red. "Be careful. You're sounding ungrateful."

"Ungrateful?"

"Yes, ungrateful. I understand you are confused and you want the truth. No matter what she might have done before you came along, that woman gave you a good life. I was there for it." She raises a shaky arm above her head, trying to stifle her anger. "I'm trying to support you just as much as I'm trying to remain loyal to her."

Des sits in a chair, her body practically collapsing. She's suffering in all this, too. My own grief has been so close, it makes me forget. If what the police are saying is true, I'm not the only person Mom has betrayed. And I'm not the only person having to sort out my allegiance to her.

"I came in to see if you need help with anything." I sit in front of her, holding out my hand to touch hers.

"What makes you think I need help?"

"You just reopened the place. Do you need help closing up? Setting up for tomorrow? I've been out for a few days, but I still know how this works."

Behind me, the door opens. I expect a straggler, but instead, see Evan.

"Marion," he says, as surprised as I am.

"What are you doing here?" I ask.

I instinctively pull Ava closer. This is the first time they've been in a room together. He's never met her before. Never asked.

"I invited him," Des says, standing.

"I've been helping Des here and there," he says. "You know, with the reopening."

"Why?" I ask him, then turn to Des. "I thought you had Michael to help?"

"Another set of hands doesn't hurt. Don't worry about it. You've been taking personal days, remember?"

Des begins gathering the empty mugs. "Excuse me." As she walks past, she nudges my shoulder. I take the hint, following her into the kitchen. Evan walks into the dining hall, staring at the television, which is muted, pretending not to listen to our conversation.

I lower my voice another octave. "What's he doing here? Don't you think I'm dealing with enough?"

"He might be your ex-boyfriend, but he's still my friend," she whispers, walking back toward the dining area.

I hear Evan's unmistakable chuckle behind me, and I feel my skin burn hot. The dynamic between Evan and Des always takes me back to my adolescence. It's like they are ganging up against me, even though there is no way Des could have predicted I'd be stopping by the restaurant tonight. It's just a coincidence.

As for why Evan has really returned to North Bay, I don't know. It goes against everything he told me at the time of our breakup. A degree from Sanderson would set him up for success anywhere. Why come back here? And why now?

"I'm happy to run into you," Evan says, stepping forward. "I've actually been wanting to talk."

"I'm sure you need to help Des—"

"Not much left to do," she volunteers.

"It's almost time for Ava to go to bed. I hadn't planned on staying long."

"Then don't," Des says. "Let her play out her energy. She'll sleep like a rock by the time you take her home."

"We could take a walk on the beach," Evan says, placing a hand on the back of his neck. He's smirking. He must enjoy the serendipitous way this evening has worked in his favor.

I turn to look at Des, but she is already turned away from me. She's holding a remote in her hand, turning up the volume on the television. Maybe I can finally figure out what it is Evan wants from me.

"A very short walk," I say, following him out the door.

CHAPTER 25

Now

Marion

This is my favorite time of night for viewing the seaside. Tonight, the sun is resting just above the water, casting orange beams through the steel-blue skies. Within twenty minutes, ten maybe, the entire sky will be gray, and another ten minutes after that, stars will blink in the distance. The heat of the day is gone, and a strong breeze cuts through the air between us.

Evan walks a safe distance away from me. Too close, it could be misinterpreted. Too far, we wouldn't be able to hear each other over the wind and waves. We leave our sandals by the ramp, walking closer to the water's edge. I always like to walk with my feet in the water, dying waves splashing at my shins. Evan prefers to stay in the sand at that precise point where the water recedes again.

We've walked several minutes, and still not said anything.

"What did you want to talk with me about?" I ask.

"I want to know if you're okay, you know, with everything."

"I'm fine," I say, brushing a strand of hair off my neck. "You must have had some reason for wanting to get in touch before my life went to hell."

"You're always so blunt."

"And you always take too long to say what's on your mind."

"You know I'm moving back." He rubs the back of his neck with his hand. "I guess I'm wondering how you feel about that, but I feel ridiculous bringing it up considering what's going on with Eileen."

"I hope you aren't moving back here because of me," I say, knowing that's a little too harsh. Evan is being open with me, and it's not technically his fault the timing sucks.

"I'm moving back here because I want to be here," he says. "North Bay is my home."

That's not what he said when we broke up. He talked about wanting to get as far away from North Bay as he could. He wanted to take me with him. Three years. He has been gone three years. And with everything that has happened during that time, we're still not sure where we stand with each other.

"We're not the same people we were before you left for Sanderson."

"Don't I know it."

I stop walking, my feet sinking into the mucky sand. "What's that supposed to mean?"

"You've just come a lot farther than I have, I guess."

"Come on, you have your degree now. I'm sure you've already got a job lined up."

"I'm opening up my own practice, actually."

"Does Carmen know that?" I ask. She's one of the few defense attorneys in the area.

"She's always complaining about her workload. I don't think she'll mind sharing the pot. She's even offered to help me get started."

The thought of not being in a relationship with Evan is a bearable one, as is the idea of him living halfway across the country without me. But swallowing the fact that he'll live mere minutes away from me, yet still not be in my life, irks me. I don't like the idea of bumping into him at the grocery store or at a restaurant, the likelihood of Des scheming to have us around each other, knowing Carmen is helping him navigate his new career. It's selfish, but life is easier having him away. At least then I don't have to confront my feelings.

Of course, as much as I like pretending North Bay is my town, it's his too. He has as many connections to this place as I do. And his sister, Cassie, still lives here. He's the doting uncle to her kids. I only wish it hadn't taken him so long to figure out where he belongs.

"Was it worth it?" I ask. "Going to Sanderson?"

"Going to Sanderson, yes. But I wish other things could have been different."

Is he referring to me? At times, I think the same thing. But I'm imagining a different Evan and a different Marion. A life before Ava existed. There's too much change now.

"Have you been happy since I left? Before everything that happened with Eileen, I mean."

"Yes."

It's true. A series of moments flash before my mind, almost all of them including Ava. She's been the prize in all this. The rainbow after the storm that was losing Evan.

"That's all I wanted to hear." He pauses. "She's beautiful, by the way. Des has shown me pictures but seeing her in person… it's unbelievable. She looks just like you."

I smile, thinking of Ava. Thinking of Evan. These thoughts are comforting, but I need to stay focused.

"It would be easier if you weren't dropping by all the time. I know you're just trying to help Des, but you know how she is. She's meddling. Mom's case is my biggest priority right now, after Ava, of course."

"I understand. Where do things stand with Eileen?"

Mom and Evan always got along. I can hear her now, celebrating the idea we're on this beach together. Of course, I'm thinking of the person I remember before I knew Sarah Paxton existed.

"Doesn't Des give you updates?"

"She does. But I'd rather hear it from you."

"Carmen says the police are looking into Mom's past. They're trying to find witnesses, anything that connects her to the Baby Caroline shitshow."

"It's good Carmen is on the case."

"Yeah, she's a good friend. She's pissed at me right now, though."

"How come?"

"How much have you followed the case?"

"Enough. It was a mystery to me until a few days ago. Never knew Baby Caroline was a thing."

"Yeah, me either. Anyway, Caroline's—my—parents were the Parkers. And Amelia Parker showed up at my house yesterday. She wanted to talk with me, so I did."

"What did she have to say?"

"She just wants to get to know me. I mean, think about what this woman has been through. Her daughter was taken. Her husband was murdered. And the police think Mom is to blame for all of that."

"That's just one side of the story."

"And Amelia has another side. I want to hear it. That's why I invited her over tomorrow."

"Does Carmen know that?"

"No, but only because I don't feel like listening to another one of her rants. I enjoy spending time with Amelia. She's being honest with me, which is more than I can say about other people right now."

"You should think twice before letting Amelia into your life."

"She's my mother."

This is the first time I've spoken those words. I pause, letting them percolate through my brain. On the one hand, it's true. On the other, I'm turning my back on the only mother I've known. I still can't decide whether she deserves that rejection or not.

"Eileen is your mother."

"Eileen is comatose in a hospital bed. Eileen stole me from my parents when I was a baby." My words are so bitter I can almost taste them. "And Eileen refused to answer any of my questions when she had the chance."

My phone pings with a message from Carmen.

Don't freak out. I'm giving you a head's up.

She attaches a link to an article written in the *New Hutton Star*.

"Oh no," I say, my stomach dropping before I even begin reading.

"What is it?" Evan asks, but I ignore him.

The article is titled "Baby Caroline Has a Baby of Her Own."

The woman believed to be at the center of the Baby Caroline mystery is now a mother herself...

"Oh no. Ava."

"What is it?" Evan asks, concerned. "Did something happen?"

"The *New Hutton Star* has written an article about us. It's talking about me being a single mother to Ava." My voice catches. "See the shit we're having to go through because of Eileen?"

"Just wait a minute. What does it say?"

My eyes scan the article. It's talking about my life in North Bay. About my decision to have Ava on my own. None of it is new information to me, but I hadn't planned on sharing the details with the rest of the world. And someone close to me must have passed on this story to the press. I don't know who would have betrayed me like this, but the newspaper wouldn't have access to this information otherwise.

"I'll send you the link," I say, my tone cynical. "I have to go."

I stuff the phone in my pocket and start jogging toward the dock.

"I'm sorry, Marion," Evan shouts after me.

Knowing Evan, he wants to say more. He won't. If anyone understands my stubborn nature, my reluctance to forgive, it's him.

CHAPTER 26

Now

Marion

Ava was never a guarantee. Now I'm replaying everything that happened in the years leading to my decision to have her, each milestone rolling into the next, like film on a reel.

I've always been a strategic planner. Maybe it's because so much of my life with Mom felt thrown together. If Des hadn't come along, our lives might have continued on that unpredictable trajectory. I always knew I wanted my life to be different. I wanted solid relationships. A dependable job. A stable place to call home.

That all changed after my breakup with Evan. After six years together, he was gone, off to pursue his new dream, the one that no longer included me. I'd spent my entire adult life creating my world with meticulous precision, and now I was abandoned in it.

I had my career. I owned a home. I tried dating, and yet it always felt forced. A relationship wasn't what I was after. I'd already found my compatible match, and he was living on the other side of the country. He'd chosen to leave, and I'd chosen to stay. Evan wasn't the type of person I could replace. And even if that had been my aim, North Bay didn't have much of a dating scene. Most of our peers had already been married a couple years, were starting to have children.

It hit me this might be my life. Sure, I could see what would happen if Evan ever made the decision to come back, but that was still years away, and so many things could happen during that time. It's the reason we'd agreed to break up in the first place. I had to adjust to this new version of life without him in it.

Mom was the only person I could fully share my feelings with. The only person I felt wouldn't label me as whiny or pathetic, but simply accept my fears for what they were.

"What's bothering you the most?" she asked. "Is it Evan you miss?"

We were sitting in my newly decorated living room. This space was meant to reflect my independence, a place I could call my own; instead it seemed to echo the loneliness aching inside, an isolation that felt unending.

"I don't know."

Of course, I missed Evan. A part of me always would, I thought. He'd been gone over a year at that point. My feelings for him had faded, yet at the same time, nothing had really glimmered since he left. "I guess I just feel like I've put all this work into building the life I want, and it still might not happen."

"What might not happen?"

"Starting a family. Having kids. I'm in my thirties. That's still young, but it feels a lot older when you consider I'm not even seeing anyone. If the guy of my dreams walked into my life tomorrow, it would be years before we'd even consider settling down and having children. Time is not on my side, and it sucks. I don't want to be one of those girls who marries a guy simply because she's running out of options. That never turns out well for anybody."

It was an honesty I could only manage with my mother. I'd just revealed so many of the secret thoughts I felt I couldn't share with anyone else. Mom sat there, watching me cry into a throw pillow. She didn't speak until I'd let it all out.

"So, you're worried about not having a child?"

"Mostly. Love can come around at any age. Motherhood, not so much. And I really want that experience. I never imagined my life without it."

"And you feel like you're ready for that? To be a mother?"

"In all the other areas of my life, sure. I've set myself up for success, but what has that left me with? Jack shit."

She sat there, lost in her thoughts. I'd seen her like this many times over the years. Contemplating. Like she was on the verge of confession, wrestling with whether her words would add value or pressure.

"If you think you're ready, why not just go for it?"

"Go for what?"

She scooted closer and smiled. "Have a baby."

Have a baby. Like it was an add-on service you could select at the spa. Something you could throw in the grocery cart alongside your carton of eggs and jug of milk.

"It doesn't work like that. You can't just decide to have a baby."

"Nowadays you can. There are all types of procedures. You can freeze your eggs. Explore insemination. Surrogacy. You can have a child right now, if that's what you want. Like you said, you're ready in all the other ways."

"What are you saying? That I should just get pregnant on my own. Choose to become a single mother?" My voice lacked the calm tone Mom used. The idea seemed ludicrous. Yes, it was possible. Women took their fertility into their own hands, but that wasn't what I wanted to do, was it?

"I'm more progressive than you think." She chuckled, like this was some joke between us. "Several women in your position have decided they want a child and they aren't willing to wait for a potential partner to show up. I've always believed if you want something in life you have every right to get it. Besides, I did it."

"I could never handle raising a child on my own."

"You wouldn't be on your own. You've got a strong support system. That baby would be surrounded by love. Romance could always come, but at least you wouldn't be sitting around waiting for it. You're my daughter. I would never make the suggestion if I didn't believe you could handle it."

"I don't know. I know women do this, but it's different trying to think of myself making a decision like that. It's scary."

She looked down, rolling the words around in her head before sharing them aloud.

"Sometimes you have this idea in your head of what life should be. Call it a dream, a fantasy. It doesn't work out. You find a new dream, but this time it's not a fantasy. You make it your reality, and it's like that other life you thought you wanted never existed. That's how you live. It's how we all live."

That was the first time the idea of a child—beautiful baby Ava—started to become a reality. It would be another year before I went through with my decision. Countless doctor's visits. Painful shots and medications that pushed me to the edge of giving up. Spending thousands of dollars I'd spent the latter half of my twenties trying to save. And limitless more moments of doubt, wondering if what I was doing was right at all. And in those moments, I'd turn to Mom. She'd remind me I was enough.

Now, even that memory is tarnished because the same woman who raised me, uplifted me, convinced me I was capable of being a mother myself… has done nothing but lie to me about her own experience. I used to feel empowered by Mom's decision to raise me on my own. I didn't realize she had to kidnap me and murder Bruce in order to get the life she always wanted.

CHAPTER 27

Then

Eileen

Over the next month, every time I went to the center, I spoke with Amelia. I had a connection with her I never managed with Ms. Lang.

Amelia, for some reason, seemed to enjoy talking to me as much as I did her. Maybe it was because we had so much in common. Among other things, we enjoyed the same music and movies. We both liked horses, too, although I knew them only from pictures. In Amelia's line of work you're supposed to remain impartial, but I think she couldn't help but feel a connection to me. I'd opened up with her in a way I hadn't with anyone else. She understood how drastically my life had changed in recent months.

I was standing to leave after one of our sessions when she asked me to sit back down.

"There's something I need to tell you," she said, her face hard to read. "This will be our last session together."

I failed to contain my disappointment. My body lurched to the edge of my seat. "I don't understand. We've made such progress—"

"I promise it has nothing to do with you," Amelia said, raising her hands. "I'm leaving the center for a while. I've been experiencing some medical issues."

"I see." My eyes fell on her stomach. I looked away, trying to choke down my emotions. I felt robbed.

"I'll arrange for another counselor to take over your case."

"I don't want another counselor," I said, defiantly. Amelia was the only person with whom I felt comfortable discussing my problems. "You're the first person I've opened up to about any of this. You're the only one who is making it better."

"I'll miss you too, Sarah. I've enjoyed our time together. You have so much potential waiting to be unlocked."

"Then don't just leave me!" I hadn't meant to say the words out loud, but it's exactly how I felt. First, Cliff left. Then, Jamie. Now Amelia was leaving too. "Maybe we could still find a way to stay in contact. Maybe we could meet up outside of the center?"

It was a weak suggestion, but I was desperate to find a way to keep Amelia in my life. She was one of the only people I trusted.

Amelia sighed, her eyes cutting to her office door. "I'm not really supposed to do this sort of thing. Can you keep a secret?"

"Yeah."

I liked that Amelia was willing to bend rules. I guess she was allowed to do that sort of thing since she was a sponsor. Amelia was here by choice. She wanted to help people. She cared.

"We own two horses. The stables are only a twenty-minute drive outside the city. If you want, you could join me this weekend."

"Are you serious?"

"Very serious. I thought it might… I don't know." Amelia pursed her lips and exhaled, like she too was afraid of looking like a fool. That was how I always felt around her. "I understand if you are busy. I thought you might just like to look at them."

"I'd love to, Amelia. Thank you."

"Our little secret?"

"Our little secret."

Amelia picked me up outside my apartment the following afternoon. Now that I was no longer working at Buster's, I had no plans on the weekend. I was trying to stretch out what little money Cliff and I had saved before he died, at least until I was ready to find another job. I tried not to think about any of that as I rode further and further away from the city. I was just happy I had someone who wanted to spend the afternoon with me, and that that person was as perfect as Amelia.

The stables weren't very crowded. Most people who could afford to buy a horse lacked the space and time required for upkeep, which is why owners hired someone else to look after them. Some of the owners, like Amelia, allowed their horses to be used for riding lessons.

The short walk from the car to the track left my sneakers covered in dirt. I'd worn some thick socks over my leggings, but even they were smattered in beige dust. Amelia was wearing slim pants tucked inside riding boots. She looked like she belonged in an equestrian magazine, and I felt a small tingle of envy.

"Are you riding?" I asked.

"Not today. It's nice to visit, though. I thought you'd like to meet Daisy."

Daisy was a black horse. Her coat was thick and shiny, like she had been varnished in ink. Horses are beautiful creatures, but it was my first time being around one up close. I was nervous.

"Don't be afraid," Amelia said, running a gloved hand across Daisy's back. "They can sense that sort of thing."

I took a deep breath and exhaled. My hand was bare, which allowed me to feel the straw-like fibers of Daisy's coat. Coarser than I thought she'd be.

"She's beautiful."

"Yes, she is. Special too. Have you ever heard of equine-assisted therapy?"

I shook my head.

"Some people use these horses to help them grieve. Heal. It's therapeutic. Like I told you, the horse can sense what you're feeling. You can just leave it here on the track, and the horse will comfort you."

For a second, I felt disappointment. I'd tricked myself into thinking Amelia invited me here because she actually liked me. I hadn't thought it was an extension of our counseling sessions. She continued speaking.

"Daisy has helped me a lot over the years. Bruce bought her as a gift, not long after we got married. A year or so later, we started trying for a baby. And we tried. And we tried. Sometimes we'd find out we were pregnant, but then…"

She looked away, across the other side of the track, where a young girl was being helped on top of another horse. For several seconds, Amelia didn't say anything. She kept rubbing Daisy's back, transferring her grief to the horse, or however she put it. Leaving it on the track.

"When I find out I'm pregnant, I can never be truly happy. I'm so used to things not working out. All I can hope is this time it will be different. It's the one thing in life I don't have, really, and it's what I want more than anything."

Everything clicked. Why her paunch never grew any bigger, but stayed visible, like a continuous case of bloat that wouldn't shrink. Why this woman, always smiling, had days where she looked like she might be on the verge of breaking. She had everything, yes, except the one thing she really wanted.

"I never knew, Amelia."

Normally, Amelia was the one listening to my problems. In all the times I'd been around her, envied her for everything she had, I'd never considered her own struggles. I'd never seen her pain.

She looked down, rubbing a hand over her stomach. "We think this time it might work. That's why I'm leaving the center. My doctor has suggested I stay off my feet as much as possible. It's not necessarily how I'd envisioned my pregnancy playing out, but if bed rest gets me a healthy baby, hell, I'd do anything for that." Her eyes filled with tears. "So, when I talk to you about options, I want you to understand you can't ever be sure what life will give you. Cliff dying. My infertility. None of that is under our control.

That's why it's important to handle what we can, make deliberate decisions. Life is hard enough without all the chaos."

We stayed at the track for hours. Amelia told me more than she ever had about herself, and I opened up, too. We'd shed the roles of counselor and patient; we were just two women, sharing our greatest fears and grandest desires. Amelia and I differed at almost every turn, but we each wanted the same thing out of life: a real family. The more time I spent with her, the more it felt possible.

Once again, I felt like I'd found some type of acceptance. Amelia was there for me, filling in the absence left by Cliff and Jamie. Selfishly, I feared Amelia's responsibilities would eventually outweigh the bond we had formed, and I'd be left alone all over again. Things always worked out for people like Amelia Parker. Eventually, she would get the family she'd always desired, and I'd be left with... nothing.

As I went to bed that night, all sorts of ideas went through my mind. Daisy the Miracle Horse. Amelia and her babies. My own future. What I really wanted out of life, and whether I was going to sit around waiting, waiting for things to get better, or whether I was going to actually do something about it.

That's when I first started thinking of a plan.

CHAPTER 28

Now

Marion

By morning, I've slept only three hours and read the *New Hutton Star* article twice that amount. I'm a private person, a trait I no doubt inherited from my mother. The fact all the intimate details surrounding my pregnancy with Ava are out there for people to read upsets me. I resent the fact that Ava, still a small child, is already being thrust beneath a grueling spotlight.

And when I say intimate details, I mean it. There were facts in that article the journalist wouldn't have gotten from a mere acquaintance. The fact I went through two rounds of IU before getting pregnant. The fact I drained my personal savings account to pay for the procedures. Sure, I guess a person doing enough research into the process could make assumptions, but reading the article felt more personal than that. These weren't inferences. These were facts delivered by someone close to me.

I don't believe Des and Carmen would sell me out; they're my closest friends. They hid Mom's cancer, but that seems more well-intentioned than sharing details about my life with the press. Besides, they'd never do that to Ava. Still, that paranoid part of my brain wonders, how far would Carmen be willing to go in order to create a distraction? Does Des have other reasons for wanting to defend Mom so fiercely?

And then there's Evan. Some might consider his sudden return to North Bay suspicious. Worse than that, he's back in my head, his words haunting me long after our conversation at the beach ended. There's always been a part of me that hoped we might one day reconnect, even as friends. My decision to have Ava changed that, and Mom's arrest has changed everything since then. I wonder if his return to North Bay is too coincidental. He was here, what, a day before Mom was arrested? And he's been trying to contact me ever since. Maybe he still cares about me and wants to make sure I'm okay. But that paranoid part of my brain wonders.

I'm not only thinking about what Evan said concerning his return to North Bay. I'm equally bothered by what he said about Amelia. Evan, Des, Carmen—they all have their reasons for telling me to keep my distance from her, but none of them could even begin to imagine the dilemma I'm in. This woman—a stranger until last week—is my biological mother, and she's suffered more than any person should. The fact we know so little about each other rules her out as the source; I've not told Amelia the circumstances of Ava's birth.

Today will mark the first meeting between them.

I've made cucumber and cream cheese sandwiches for lunch. I've also made pasta salad using Mom's recipe. I don't realize until I'm arranging the place settings how bizarre that is. I've invited Amelia, my mother, over for lunch and am serving a recipe given to me by Mom, the woman who raised me. I'm not sure when, whether in my mind or otherwise, I'll begin to separate these two women. If I ever will.

The doorbell rings just as I'm pulling a yellow dress over Ava's head. I leave her in her crib to open the front door. Amelia stands on the porch holding a gift bag.

"I hope you don't mind," she says. "I wanted to give Ava a little something, seeing as I'm meeting her for the first time."

"That's so kind," I say, taking a step back. "Come on in."

Amelia walks inside, her eyes scanning the room just as she did last time. She's still not comfortable around me, and it shows.

"I probably should have asked before buying a gift. I know some parents can be particular about that sort of thing. Don't want their children being spoiled."

"Really, it's fine. I think it's nice you thought of her."

Amelia and I are still getting to know one another, but Ava is her granddaughter. It makes me happy that despite all the loss this woman has suffered in her life, perhaps she can begin a happier relationship with Ava and me. I understand why she is cautious of boundaries, but we can define those at our own pace.

"Should I go get Ava?"

Amelia nods and takes a seat on the living room sofa. Her breathing is controlled. She must be so happy to finally see Ava—a bonus after finding out I was still alive—but there is no way to prepare for something like this.

"Ava, there's someone I'd like you to meet," I whisper, talking to her in that way parents do, with no expectation of response. Ava's gnawing at her fist when we turn the corner, not even taking in the stranger sitting on our couch.

Amelia stands and slowly walks toward us. "She's absolutely beautiful."

"Thank you." I shift my body forward, a silent signal to Ava it's okay to be comfortable. We're all friends here. Family, really.

"I see the resemblance," Amelia says, reaching out and caressing the fabric of Ava's dress. "She has your eyes."

"That's what everyone says."

Ava's still looking away, not actively avoiding Amelia, but also not engaging. Babies can be temperamental, especially Ava. It takes her time to warm up to people before she's playful the way she is with Des and Carmen.

"Are you hungry? I made some sandwiches."

We sit at the table, and I put Ava in her high chair. I can see how happy it makes Amelia to simply be close to her. I imagine, despite her worldly travels and grand experiences, this is the happiest she's been in a long time. I feel happiness in return, knowing I've provided this for her.

"I must admit, when I first arrived in North Bay, it was a bit of a culture shock. The pace here is much slower than it is in the city. After this week, it's starting to grow on me."

"I know. I love it here. The beach. The people." Although the community has certainly had better days. I try not to think about how quickly we've been shunned as outcasts. "Where is it you're staying again?"

"Emerald Shores Resort," she says, picking up a sandwich. "It's one of the biggest ones here."

"Yeah, it is. I know the hotel manager."

That's Holly Dale's hotel. I didn't realize Amelia was staying there, and I find it odd Holly hasn't mentioned it in all the times she's tried contacting me this week. She's usually on the gossip frontlines, and I'm sure she's been eating up every detail of the Baby Caroline saga since Mom's arrest. Des told me she's been reaching out, claiming to want to know about this summer's advertising, but I wonder if she's simply on a hunt for more information. I make a mental note to get in touch with her.

"And what about you?" Amelia asks, after taking a bite of her sandwich. "I'd like to hear more about your life, if you feel comfortable."

I clear my throat. Amelia has certainly shared more than I have, but that's only because I hate rubbing my own life in her face. It was a good one, even if I was never meant to have it.

"You know, I grew up in North Bay. Lived here my entire life, except for when I went to college."

I tell her some memorable moments from that time, stories I imagine most mothers would want to hear from their daughters. Stories Eileen already knows. I tell her about my role as a small business owner, what it's like working with customers on a daily basis. And I tell her about Ava, memorable stories from her first year.

She smiles and nods along, and in some ways, with each shared experience we're becoming less like strangers.

"And what about Ava's father?" Amelia looks at Ava, then me. I can tell she's hoping she hasn't overstepped. "Is he in the picture?"

"I'm guessing you didn't see the article in the *New Hutton Star*?"

Amelia narrows her eyes and shakes her head. "You'll have to forgive me. The media has left me jaded over the years."

"I'm a single parent by choice," I explain. "Ava was conceived through artificial insemination, so there's no father in the picture. I prefer it that way, really. Even in this day and age, it's hard for some to accept. People always say it takes two people to make a baby, but that's not really true anymore."

"That took a lot of bravery, making the decision to become a parent on your own."

"It did." I straighten my posture, a subconscious tic. "I was at a point in my life where I felt secure, and I was tired of waiting. I knew I wanted to be a mother, but, unfortunately, we don't always have as much time as we should to make that decision."

"I understand completely." Amelia purses her lips. "Women have more options now than they did in the eighties. You were just starting to hear about all those things that are commonplace now. In vitro. Sperm donation. Surrogacy. I always wonder if we might have explored those options. If we'd had more time."

It feels like I'm holding my breath again, watching her speak. Unfortunate timing. Not just for us, but for so many women then, who didn't have the medical marvels we do now. I look at Ava, fully grasping the painful reality that I might not have her if this were a different decade.

"I know I'm lucky. Some people may not see it that way. Being a single parent certainly has its challenges, but I hated the idea of waiting around and missing out on this experience."

"It's certainly one that shouldn't be taken for granted." Amelia looks at Ava, then me. "What does this have to do with the newspaper again?"

I exhale. "Someone wrote an article about us. They're trying to spin this whole Baby Caroline is a mommy angle. The decision I made comes with judgments, I just didn't expect for it to happen on such a large scale."

"I'm so sorry, Marion. The media has been a thorn in my side for years. I wish I could have protected you."

"I shouldn't even be bothering you with this—"

"Please." Amelia raises her hand. "Don't feel you have to hold back on account of me. There are so few people that understand what it's like to be in our situation. To be at the center of such a salacious tragedy. People read about it and write about it and watch the specials on television. We live it. Sometimes the only way to make sense of it is to lean on each other."

"I guess I just feel like you've been through enough."

"Whether it's a week of your life or three decades, it doesn't get easier. Don't worry about tiptoeing around my feelings."

"You're right about no one else understanding. And I feel guilty about Ava being brought into any of this. Someone close to me must have talked to the paper, so it makes it feel like my fault." I prop my elbows on the table, letting my head dangle between them. "And then there's the business. I've worked my entire adult life to try and turn The Shack into a profitable restaurant. Now all that's about to go under."

"How so?"

"The police left a lot of damage after their search. We had to dip into our savings before reopening. And business has been at a standstill since the arrest. People are wanting to distance themselves from Eileen and The Shack—which I understand completely," I say, careful to let Amelia know that I'm not complaining about Eileen's treatment. "That doesn't change the fact that this is my livelihood. It's the only business I've ever known, and if I lose it, I'm not sure where I'll go from here."

"I'm sorry you're losing so much. It's not fair."

"At least I'm gaining something out of this mess." I place my hand over hers and squeeze. "You."

Amelia can't hide her satisfaction. She smiles and her eyes fill with tears. "It means so much to hear you say that."

"You've lost much more than I have, Amelia. I don't want to sound ungracious."

"I don't think you are for a second. In fact, I'd like to help you any way I can."

"You're helping me just by being here. By listening. I need that more than you know."

"But the business. You and Ava don't deserve to lose the roof over your heads because of Eileen's mistakes." She looks at Ava, then me. "Let me help you pay for the damage the police caused."

"Amelia, that's generous, but it's not your place. Or your responsibility."

"I have no one else to spend it on. When I die, this money goes with me. The least I can do is help you out. You're my daughter, Marion."

It's the first time she's said those words directly. Hearing them steals the breath from within my lungs. *I'm her daughter*. It's a realization I've been struggling to accept, but for the first time, it feels right.

Beside us, Ava lets out a squeal. We both laugh, wiping away tears.

"May I hold her?"

I nod, standing to take away the tray holding Ava in.

"Hello, beautiful girl," Amelia says, holding out her arms.

Ava stares at her, remaining still, then she leans forward. Amelia scoops her up, holding Ava close against her chest. I'm afraid Ava will squirm or reach for me, denying Amelia this moment she so desperately wants. But she doesn't. She leans her little head on Amelia's shoulder, raising her fist to her mouth.

"It looks like she's warming up to you," I say, offering my encouragement.

Amelia sways her weight from side to side, syncing into that tempo so many mothers master over the years.

"She's a very sweet baby."

Amelia closes her eyes and smiles, as though she's trying to memorize this moment, hold onto it tight, so that the next time she's confronted with a bad memory, a flashback to her own daughter being taken, she can switch it out for this.

CHAPTER 29

Now

Marion

After a few hours, Amelia leaves. She has a late afternoon meeting with her lawyers, and another conversation with investigators in the morning. Our brief reunions are interspersed with the harsh reality of our circumstances.

Throughout all this, I've felt like no one understands what I'm going through, but Amelia does. She too must balance the fine line between the justice system and her own emotional needs. What is protocol and procedure to investigators is so much more to her. So much more to me. Although she has dealt with these annoying elements of the case much longer than I have—the interviews and the press and the community badgering—at least now she is getting something of a happy ending. Getting to know us doesn't erase the pain of these past three decades, but I'd like to think it eases the blows. It's a far happier outcome than most parents of missing children ever receive.

Similarly, my life has been torn to pieces, all in a matter of days. I've been forced to re-examine every element of my past, everything that made me who I am today. It's not something I would wish on anyone else, having to accept that the person you love most in the world is capable of a monstrous act. What Mom did is exactly that. Monstrous. Selfish. Unforgivable.

Two moms.

And yet, getting to know Amelia has eased my pain. We are both being forced into these nightmarish situations, yet we can cling to each other. It's a small escape from the outside world that could never understand what we've been through, both together and separate. In this new, bleak reality, I somehow feel full. I feel, for possibly the first time in my life, entirely seen. Amelia has managed to make sense of things in a way my mother never could.

And yet, there's a part of me that feels like I'm pretending, dabbling in a life to which I can't yet commit. I'm beginning to feel like I can connect with Amelia, include her in our lives moving forward. But I need certainty before I can start living that truth, something that still seems beyond my grasp.

Ava's covered up with a blanket in her pack-and-play, watching a cartoon. Her lazy eyes and shallow breathing suggest she'll be asleep within the hour. I return to the kitchen, cleaning up after my lunch with Amelia. I keep thinking of our time together, how good it feels to simply be around her. I stare at Amelia's plate. Her utensils and drinking glass are on the table, right where she left them.

An idea comes to me.

Maybe I could be sure of the truth, without getting others involved.

An hour later, there's a knock on the front door.

I open it, welcoming Rick inside. I called him, requested he stop by the condo. He doesn't falter when I tell him to keep our meeting a secret from Carmen.

Rick's brute stature doesn't fit with the relaxed décor in my living room. He looks over the furniture, trying to find the best place to sit. He peers over the top of the pack-and-play and sees Ava sleeping.

"Cute," he says, then settles on the loveseat, his back to the window. "Press giving you a hard time?"

"No," I say, sitting in the seat across from him, my hands on my knees. "They've not been around the complex since Carmen intervened."

"I thought maybe that's why you'd called me over." He gives the room another inspection. "Doesn't look like you're in any kind of trouble."

"What would I need in order to submit a DNA test?"

He crosses his legs, cradling one knee with both hands. Rick doesn't seem fazed by the question. I don't imagine many requests bother him.

"About anyone can get one these days. You just go to one of those walk-in clinics."

"The last thing I need is a photo of me outside a testing facility."

"You're right. So what did you have in mind?"

He doesn't ask who the test is for, but I suppose he doesn't need to.

"Has Carmen said anything about me meeting Amelia Parker?" I know he was the person who told her about the picture at the pier.

"She might have some opinions." The way he says this makes me think she addressed the topic with heavy disdain at a high volume.

"Amelia's the one who suggested we get a test. She thinks we should get the whole knowing/not knowing out of the way."

"Do you agree with her?"

"I'm growing impatient," I say, my eyes fixed on his.

"All I need are samples. One from you, one from her. I can take the samples to a lab. No one would have to know you were involved."

"What would work as a sample?"

"Anything containing saliva, or even hair follicles."

"So, like a drinking glass?"

"Sure, if the sample is big enough."

In my mind, I picture Amelia's glass. I've stored it in a Ziploc bag and left it underneath my bathroom sink, but I don't tell Rick yet. Not until I'm sure I want him to go through with it. Deep down, even though I'm longing for answers, I'm wondering if I can handle the results.

"How long would it take?"

"Most labs around here ship off their tests. Usually takes a day or so."

"And they're accurate?"

"As accurate as can be. You don't have to share the outcome, if that's what you're worried about. The state will run their own tests. It would just give you peace of mind until then. Or not."

In all the years I've known Rick, this is the most I've ever heard him speak. He's not a big talker, but he gets things done. He's effective. That's why I reached out to him. I thought my biggest obstacle would be whether he'd give Carmen a head's up about my plans.

"Give me a minute?" I stand.

"Take your time."

Rick pulls out his phone and starts scrolling. He doesn't seem concerned with what my decision will be.

I walk down the hallway leading to my room and sit on the bed, contemplating. A voice inside screams for me to go through with it, get it over with, but I'm still dreading what I might find out. Having concrete proof Mom isn't my biological mother will destroy her case, but even that seems like an afterthought. I'm more worried about these results eliminating what little trust remains between us.

The pearl ring Mom gave me the day of Ava's party sits in a little white bowl on my nightstand. I pick it up, twirling the jewelry between my fingers. Each pearl is so distinct, so unique, like the three of us—Mom, Ava and me. This symbol of unity now exists as a declaration of our differences moving forward. Our relationships, if not completely severed, will be forever changed based on what I decide.

As I walk into the bathroom, I catch sight of my reflection in the mirror. I don't look like myself. My ashen skin and disheveled hair remind me of how I looked when Ava was a newborn. My appearance, like my mental well-being, is withering away. I might not like the results. They might break me. But maybe that brokenness can lead to healing. Besides, it's only a matter of time before the police force my hand. I'll eventually have to confront it. What's the point in dragging things out a bit longer? Nothing can be worse than the waiting.

I bend down and open the sink cabinet. My eyes scan the clutter, landing on the Ziploc bag in the corner. This is it. Only days away from knowing the truth and beginning to deal with the aftermath. And maybe I need this, to accept these results without the watchful eyes of so many around me. I'm deceiving everyone, it seems. Carmen. Amelia. Mom.

I must follow my intuition, the guide that led me to Ava and so many other monumental moments in my life. It's never failed me before, and I'm relying on it now, as I walk into the living room and give Rick what he needs to submit the test.

CHAPTER 30

Now

Marion

I have to take my mind off the results. Rick says it will be at least twenty-four hours before he has any information, a timeline that seems excruciating.

I drive over to The Shack. According to Des, the place hasn't been very busy, but I can at least show support by being there. As I pull into the parking lot, I can tell something is wrong. The windows at the front of the restaurant are streaked in red and black. I pull into a parking space. I lift Ava in her carrier as I move closer to investigate.

"What the hell?"

It looks like something was written on the glass, but the first layer has already been smudged. What remains are rivulets of paint and soapy water, pink suds on the base of the windowpane.

"Don't worry. It will be gone before you open."

Evan comes walking up behind me. He is carrying a bucket of water in one hand, a mop with the other.

"What happened?"

"Someone vandalized The Shack last night. Des called me this morning," Evan says, resting the fresh bucket of water by the door. "I told her I'd clean it off."

"What did it say?"

"Does it matter?" He hoists the mop into the water and begins scrubbing the glass. "I'll have it cleaned before customers show up."

I look around the parking lot. Beach towns tend to start early; people have likely already seen the damage. Not to mention the media parked across the street. It's embarrassing, invasive and certainly doesn't cast the business in the best light.

"Let me help you," I say.

"It's really a one-person job. If I were you, I'd check on Des. She's upset."

"We should be able to check the security cameras—"

"I already asked her about that. She says she's not hooked them back up since the police search. Said something about paying the security company." He looks over his shoulder at Ava in her carrier. There's a perceptible glimmer in his eyes, then he looks at me. "Like I said, I think Des needs a friend right now more than she needs someone to blame."

I lift Ava off the ground, taking one more look at the muddied windows. Inside, the restaurant is dark and quiet. Des is sitting in a corner, scrolling through her phone. She puts it down on the table when she sees us.

"I guess you saw our latest art project?"

"I'm so sorry, Des. I wish you'd called me."

"You haven't been much of a talker the past few days."

Des lifts her coffee mug to her lips. She takes a sip, winces, then lets out a sob.

"Des, are you okay?" I move quickly, pulling out the chair by her side.

"It's just all hitting me, you know?" Her eyes are glossy, puckered skin beneath them. She makes another scowl. "What am I doing? Anything I'm going through is hitting you ten times worse."

"That doesn't mean you can't talk about it," I say, looking down. I've been upset with Des because she didn't tell me about Mom's cancer diagnosis, but now I feel guilty. She has been struggling through all this, too. "I'm here. Let me listen."

Des exhales, and I catch a whiff of alcohol on her breath.

"People think I'm naïve, but I still don't think your mother is capable of what they're saying. I mean, she's my best friend! Don't you think I would have been able to pick up on the fact she was a liar? A killer?"

"I know how you feel," I say, my voice low. Truth is, I didn't pick up on it either. I place my hand on her shoulder.

"The more time that passes, I guess it makes sense, doesn't it? The police wouldn't have arrested her if she wasn't guilty. And now they've confirmed the fingerprints match. Thinking about what she did to the Parkers all those years ago makes me sick, but I'm mad because she fooled me, too. I thought she was better than that.

"All I've been trying to do is keep myself busy. Think positively. But I can't even come to work without some dipshit vandalizing my building. My regulars haven't stepped foot in here since the arrest. It's bad enough I've lost my best friend, but now I'm about to lose my business, too."

Even if we have enough money to bail us out, neither of us wants to start over. The Shack is at the center of both our lives. To think all that hard work could be gone overnight is devastating.

"We won't lose the business."

"Won't we?" She makes a face. "This isn't the type of industry where you can start over again from scratch, and it's all I've known."

"We won't lose the business," I repeat. "Trust me, okay?"

I give Des a hug. She rarely shows emotion like this, but I'm glad she has. I need to know I'm not the only person devastated. Mom betrayed us, something Des is only beginning to admit.

Des snorts and wipes her cheeks with the back of her hand. "I need more coffee."

"Just coffee?"

"Yes." She stands, her jovial nature returning. "This time, it's just coffee."

Des walks to the back. I unload Ava from her carrier and put her in the playpen. From behind, the front door opens, and Evan walks inside.

"I think one more wash is all it needs." He looks around the room, seeing I'm alone with Ava. "Where's Des?"

"She's fixing herself up."

"Is she okay?"

"I think she will be." I cross my arms, walking closer to him. "I appreciate you cleaning up the mess. You didn't have to do that."

"Des is my friend. I'm just happy she can lean on me when she's feeling overwhelmed."

My phone pings with a text from Amelia: *Are you home? I was thinking of stopping by.*

I've not spoken to her since yesterday, which was before I reached out to Rick about the DNA test. Now I'm the one harboring secrets, and I don't like it.

I'll be there in ten, I type back.

"Could you do me another favor?" I ask Evan.

"Sure," he says, leaning the mop in the corner.

"I need to run by the condo for a second. Can you stay here with Des? Help her keep an eye on Ava?"

"No problem."

"Thanks."

I take my wallet and keys out of the diaper bag and start heading for the front door.

"You know, I'm here if you need me."

I stare back at him, pushing the door open with my back. "The window looks great. Thanks again."

*

Amelia is sitting on the front porch of the condo when I pull up.

"Out and about today?" she asks as I approach.

"We have some work to do at The Shack."

Emerald Shores Hotel is right across the street from the restaurant. I wonder if Amelia drove by there earlier and saw the graffiti on the front windows. If she did, at least she is being polite by not bringing it up.

She looks over my shoulder into the back seat of the car. "Where's baby Ava?"

"I left her at the restaurant. I can't stay long. Anything in particular you wanted to meet about?"

Already, I can feel this barrier between us. The barrier of the DNA test she doesn't know I'm submitting. Part of me wants to tell her, but I'm afraid of what other problems that might cause. I need to come to terms with the results on my own, then I can start involving others. Still, it doesn't feel right holding onto this secret.

"I wanted to give you this."

She pulls a folded paper out of her pocket and places it in my hand. It's a check.

"Amelia, I already told you—"

"You need this right now. So does Ava. Please, let me help you."

I unfold the paper and look at the amount. My mouth falls agape.

"It's too much. I couldn't possibly take this from you. I mean, we're still just getting to know each other."

Amelia holds both her hands together and smiles. "Listening to you talk about the business the other day bothered me. Like I told you then, you shouldn't lose your career because of someone else's mistakes. This amount should be enough to get the place running again. You could use that, couldn't you?"

Less than an hour ago, Des was crying about the state of the restaurant. Des could use this as much as I could. But something about taking Amelia's money, especially when I've not been upfront about the DNA test, doesn't sit well. I don't want Amelia to feel like she has to buy my friendship or respect.

"Promise me you'll think about it," Amelia says, placing her hand over mine. She leans in and kisses my cheek. I smile, appreciating her kindness, still conflicted about how to react.

CHAPTER 31

Now

Marion

Other than the graffiti incident at The Shack, the past two days have been normal, whatever that means.

I've worked my regular shifts, trying to raise Des' spirits. I've taken Carmen's calls concerning the case. There still aren't many updates from the hospital because Mom is under sedation. I'm resting on the couch, having just put Ava to bed. The room is dark except for the blue glow of the television.

My phone pings with another text message from Holly Dale: *I've been trying to reach you.*

No shit, she's been trying to reach me. If she's not pestering me with text messages, she's calling Des at The Shack. I've been dodging her, but I can't avoid her much longer. I dial her number.

"Is this a bad time?" Holly asks when she answers the phone. She knows what the past week has been like; she was at the party when Mom was arrested.

"As good a time as ever," I say, punctuating my response with a deep exhale.

"It's a business matter," she says, her voice artificially nice. "We're about to send the hotel's promotional offers out to the printer. I didn't know if you wanted us to include The Shack, like we did last year."

"I can't think why you wouldn't. We've partnered with your hotel for the last several years."

Holly is fishing for an excuse to exclude us. If Mom's case continues to garner the attention it has in the past week, any association between the hotel and the restaurant would be bad press. They're not the only local business that will reconsider their partnership with us, but Holly is the most irritating. I'm not willing to give her an easy out. If she wants to cut ties, she's going to have to say so.

"I just thought you might have other things on your mind right now." She pauses. "Maybe this isn't the best time to be promoting."

"It's almost summer. That's always the best time to start promoting." I tear open a potato chip bag with my teeth and dig in. My first meal all day. "We'll keep the same placement we had last year. I'll send over a check by the end of the week."

"That's, well…" Holly pauses again, trying to process her reaction at lightning speed. "That's fine, Marion. I'll put you down."

An easy forfeit, which isn't very much like Holly. I hope other businesses will continue to work with us, that Mom's newly tarnished reputation won't destroy the business I've worked so hard to build.

"Everything else okay with you?" she asks.

"Yep."

"What about your mom?"

This is the real price I pay. In exchange for not losing our advertisement, Holly will demand some fresh gossip.

"I'm not sure if you heard, but she's in the hospital. We're hoping she'll recover soon."

"I'm very sorry to hear that. I'm sorry about all this." She sounds sincere. "How's Ava holding up?"

"Ava is one, Holly. She doesn't even know what's happening."

As I say the words, I'm not sure that's true. She must sense some of my anxiety, she must sense that her grandmother isn't around. But even if she has these realizations, they're fleeting. Even now, she's sleeping peacefully in her crib. She doesn't have to deal with the reactions from other people.

"Do you think they'll take this thing to trial?"

"I don't know." At least, I don't want to think about it. I remember what Amelia said about staying at the Emerald Shores Hotel. Holly must have noticed the other woman at the center of this tragedy. "Don't you hear enough about the case from your guests?"

"I try not to interfere with their business," she says, curtly.

Just mine, I think. The line beeps, letting me know there's another incoming call. I pull the phone away from my face to check the screen. It's Rick.

"Holly, I have to go."

"Let me know if you—"

I end the call before she can finish. I've been anticipating his call for days, and I'm hoping he's reaching out to share the results of the DNA test.

"You're home, right?" he asks after I answer.

I look out the window. In the parking lot, a dark car sits a few spaces away with its headlights on.

"Are you watching me?"

"Carmen wants me to keep an eye on you. And I have your results."

"Okay. Tell me."

"I haven't read them. I'll leave them in your mailbox. I just didn't want to leave them for someone else to find."

Still peering through the window, I watch as Rick exits his car. He walks over to the shared mail station at the center of the complex. He holds up an envelope, waves it for me to see, then slides it in my box.

"Thank you, Rick."

He returns to his car and drives away. His job is done, and he's as impartial about the outcome as he was about the task.

Ava's in her crib. She'll be fine long enough for me to run across the street. I take the monitor with me, just in case. I jog to the mail station, unlock my box and pull out the lone envelope.

Once inside, I close the door and lock it. The place is silent, like it's waiting. The past weeks' turmoil all comes down to this moment. All these pent-up emotions will finally have reason to break free. I'll know the truth about what my mother did, without ever having to hear her utter the words.

She stole me. She wanted a child so badly—she wanted me so extremely—she abandoned all sense of right and wrong. When Bruce Parker tried to interfere, my father, she murdered him. And even though she did her best to repent for those sins by giving me a decent life, it can't make up for everything she's taken away. If it weren't for this decision, my entire life could have been different. I could have been a Parker. With a fancy house and an enviable education. I could have had two parents who loved me, and not just one who wanted to hoard that love for herself.

I tear open the envelope and unfold the paper inside. I scan the words until I reach the results.

Positive match.

I drop the paper, letting it float to the floor.

The patchwork of my life as I knew it is gone. I'm bare. Confronted by cold, unforgiving truth.

It's a positive match.

But I didn't use Amelia's DNA. I submitted Eileen's.

That means Eileen is my real mother.

CHAPTER 32

Then

Eileen

I've waited until now to tell you this part because I wanted you to see me as a complete person, not solely as your mother.

The world doesn't do that, does it? Once you're a mother, you are bound to a certain set of standards. Wear this, not that. Go here, not there. A mother would never act that way, say that word, do that thing. You're held to an almost impossible set of guidelines, something you might well understand one day, if you choose to become a parent.

And I say *choose* because motherhood is a choice. And sometimes you're acting as a mother even when you are choosing to let that child go. When you realize that your situation isn't one this child deserves. When you realize all the indecision you've felt up until this point is a mound no bigger than an anthill compared to the decisions you'll face afterward.

Don't ever think you weren't loved. Don't ever think you weren't wanted. Letting you go doesn't make me any less of a mother. Some might say it makes me a stronger one. I had more responsibility than simply granting you life. I wanted your life to prosper, and if I couldn't do that for you, the most brave and honest thing I could do was admit it. People wouldn't know I was already a mother, living without you. They wouldn't know that their comments, even the unintentional ones, would hurt me. It would become my private pain to carry but suffering in secret doesn't lessen the sting.

I am your mother. Cliff is your father. You grew inside my body, and I gave birth to you. I was four months pregnant when Cliff died. We were on the cusp of having the family we'd wanted, before my entire world changed.

It took fourteen hours of labor to bring you into this world. They wrapped you in a thin blanket and put you on my chest. The young girl inside me was terrified of seeing you. I'd never held anything so small, so fragile, so important. The most miraculous thing happened: you stopped crying instantly, snuggled into my chest, and became calm. *We did it*, you seemed to say. *We can get through this together.* That's my first memory of you. It was the most amazing experience of my life, our reaction to each other.

I think back to that moment. To feeling your flesh against mine. That burst of love that seemed to travel at lightning speed throughout my body, pulsing all the more with each second I looked at you. Which made it all so heartbreaking that I had to let you go.

I was your mother. I am your mother. But I had to choose what was best for you, and that's what I did.

If you can think back on what I've told you to this point. All the problems and issues I had to overcome. It seemed difficult for any young woman, but impossible for a pregnant one. I thought I could give motherhood a shot, but that was before Cliff died, taking with him any hope and confidence I'd harvested.

That's why Amelia gravitated toward me. She saw a young girl drowning in her own misfortune, overwhelmed by the choices in front of her. Jamie was gone. Your father was dead. And I was left to make all these difficult decisions on my own. Amelia stepped in. Those numerous visits to the horse stables became the only thing that ever gave me any optimism.

On our fourth trip to the track, Amelia told me she'd lost her baby. Despite all the sacrifices—the bed rest and the doctors, quitting her job—her body wasn't capable of carrying a baby to term. I listened to her cry and vent, all the while thinking of a way I could help her, ease her pain and fix my broken situation all at the same time.

Although I loved you more than I even knew how to express, I wasn't capable of giving you the life you deserved. Of giving you the life I'd always hoped my little girl might have. Amelia, on the other hand, was more than capable. And she had already told me of her struggles to conceive. The treatments that didn't work. The pregnancies that never made it past the second trimester. It took a while for me to connect the dots, but when I did, I knew I could solve both our problems.

"Would you consider adopting her?" I asked Amelia. We were at the track, eating Key lime pie to celebrate the beginning of my third trimester. Amelia had never made it that far.

She froze, her eyes drifting to my growing stomach.

"You want me to adopt your baby?"

"Why not?"

"Sarah, we've already contacted agencies. We're supposed to be meeting with families this month."

In addition to my counseling, Amelia had helped me seek out adoption services. Those were the options Amelia had presented that day back at her office. I always knew the best thing I could do for you was leave you in the hands of prepared parents; I'd never considered the most eligible person was in front of my face the entire time.

"I'm willing to meet with them," I said, watching the horses as they galloped down the track. I had to look away, in case she declined. "But I already know you. I know you would be a perfect mother. And I know how much you want a baby."

Amelia was silent for several seconds. I could feel her staring at me, but I didn't want to look. I didn't want my suggestion to ruin the friendship we'd built. It's not like I was asking to borrow a sweater, or even a car. I was asking her to raise you, my child.

"Have you and Bruce considered adoption?"

"We have," she said, looking away. "I guess I never thought it would be a situation like this."

"I understand if you don't want to—"

"I didn't say I don't want to. I care about you deeply, Sarah. But I don't want you to feel pressured."

"I've been set on adoption since the first time we met in your office. I've known that's what I needed to do since Cliff died."

I looked down at my belly, at this hardened mushroom that contained a child who was half me, half him. How I wish things had been different. Parenting with Cliff would have been a struggle. We had little money, very few opportunities, but we had so much love, and we could have given you a foundation that neither of us got from our own families.

We used to talk about it all the time. Eventually, we'd get a place and paint a nursery. Cliff never knew whether you were a boy or a girl, but funnily enough, he'd talk about painting the nursery pink. And he said he'd paint bunnies and ducks above the trim. And fill a shelf with books so we could read to you every night. He loved the idea of being a father, which made the idea of being a mother a little less scary.

Once he died, I didn't trust my judgment enough to be a mother. Although it was hard to admit, I was easily manipulated by my first boyfriend, Albert. And while I vowed to never be so foolish again, I feared the pressures of being a single mother might lead to bad decisions. I had screw-up written all over me, and I wanted so much better for you.

I thought of all the times I'd watched Amelia. Before I even knew her, I'd thought she was the perfect woman. Everything I wanted to be. After getting to know her, I knew she'd be even more suited to provide you with everything I couldn't. And I knew she was as desperate to raise a child as I was to find you a healthy home. If only she would agree to my request.

"Sometimes, when you know the adoptive parents, it makes things harder," Amelia said. She looked at me, and this time I didn't flinch under her gaze.

"That wouldn't happen with us. I've not wavered on this decision once. I know I want Caroline to have a better life, and nothing would make me feel more secure than if you were the one to raise her."

She wrapped her arms around me, and for several seconds we embraced and cried. I felt safe knowing I was leaving you in good hands. The best hands.

"I'll need to talk with Bruce, of course," she said. "And I'd have to talk to the agency, see what kind of legalities are involved."

"We have time," I said, both hands on my stomach. On you.

"And if at any point you change your mind—"

"I won't," I said, placing my hand on her arm. "I've never felt more sure about anything in my life."

And that's how it started.

CHAPTER 33

Now

Marion

I called Carmen and Des, begging them to come over. I didn't want to wake Ava, and my nerves were too jumbled to drive.

These weren't the results I was expecting. I'd anticipated a negative result. I'd predicted I'd spend the rest of the night crying, another few endless days sorrowing over this revelation. This was meant to be my final confirmation that everything I knew about my background was a lie. I'd thought the test would prove my mother—Eileen—was never my mother at all. But it didn't. Which makes me wonder what the basis of these charges really is.

Carmen walks into the living room first. I can tell I interrupted her nightly routine because she's wearing no makeup and her hair is pulled away from her face. She looks like she hastily threw on a pair of sweats, but she's still clutching a designer tote in her hand.

"What's wrong?" she asks, her eyes wide.

"I submitted a DNA test."

"You did what?" She drops her bag on the sofa and takes a step closer, her hands on her hips. "After everything I've told you. I've tried to be understanding about what you're going through, but you're deliberately hurting Eileen's case."

Behind her, the front door opens. Des walks inside wearing cloth shorts and a hoodie. Her eyebrows are arched at Carmen's yelling.

"What the hell is going on?" she asks, her stare ricocheting between us.

"Marion did the one thing I specifically told her not to do," Carmen says. "She is trying to sabotage Eileen's case—"

"Keep it down or you'll wake Ava," Des says, coming closer and sitting directly in front of me. Her tone sounds like she is gearing up for a lecture of her own. "Tell us what's going on."

"I submitted the test using Mom's DNA," I say, holding up the paper. "It's a positive match. Eileen is my biological mother."

Carmen's anger doesn't completely leave her face, but she now looks a bit unbalanced. As does Des. Like everyone, they assumed that any test would eventually prove Amelia was my biological mother, or at the very least, that Eileen wasn't.

Carmen reaches for the paper. Her eyes move wildly, scanning every word.

"I knew it." Des is smiling, gently rocking back on her heels. "I knew Eileen wouldn't have done all those things they were saying."

"When did you do this?" Carmen asks.

"Two days ago. I just received the results."

"You submitted the test?"

"No. Rick did."

Her head jerks, another hint at annoyance, then she goes back to examining the paper.

"You'd warned me not to do it, but I couldn't stand not knowing anymore," I tell Carmen, feeling the need to explain. "I couldn't stand the waiting. Who knows when Mom will be able to talk about any of this? I had to come to terms with the results, but I wasn't expecting this. This changes a lot."

"This changes everything." Carmen looks at me, and I can tell she's trying hard not to smile. "If Eileen is your biological mother, we might be able to get the kidnapping charges dropped. Or even better, the police might have the wrong person after all."

"Might?" Des turns around to get a better look at Carmen.

"If the Parkers were your legal guardians, say through adoption, she could still be charged. But there's never been anything in court records about the Parkers being adoptive parents."

There's been nothing in the media, either. For decades, Amelia Parker has been cast as the woman whose child was stolen from her. Now it appears I wasn't that child. A victory for me, but it means Amelia's child is still out there.

"Do you think maybe I'm not Baby Caroline after all?"

"I don't know. They could have the wrong person, but all the evidence that's been gathered thus far suggests Eileen definitely went by the name Sarah Paxton," Carmen says. "It seems most likely the police have the wrong suspect entirely, which means Baby Caroline is probably still out there."

"What if they still have something proving Eileen attacked Bruce Parker?" Des asks.

"You said Mom's fingerprints were found at the scene," I add.

"There's still more we need to understand, but this is a huge first step. I'm sure the prosecution assumed a DNA test would connect you to Amelia, not Eileen." She sits down, crossing her legs, but continues to hold the paper as though it's a winning ticket she refuses to let out of sight. "You said Rick ran the test. How did you get a sample of Eileen's DNA?"

"She leaves an overnight bag at the house for when she watches Ava. I took her toothbrush and ran it against mine."

It was right there, sitting next to Amelia's drinking glass in the cabinet. I think I'd forgotten about it until that moment.

"Why didn't you submit a test with Amelia's DNA? She's the one who has been pressuring you to take one."

"I don't know," I say, considering what I'd contemplated while Rick was sitting in the other room.

It would have been easy to call Amelia and tell her my intentions, but another part of me, the loyal part, thought I needed to resolve this situation with Mom first. I needed to know she wasn't my biological mother before I could fully open up to Amelia, accept that she was. And I thought receiving the news that I wasn't related to Mom would be easier to swallow in private, whereas Amelia would have been elated by the results.

My stomach churns when I think of Amelia now. This will be catastrophic for her. Somewhere along the line, a mistake has been made. Her hopes have been catapulted higher than ever before. She has accepted the fact that I'm her daughter. That she has a granddaughter, even. She has given me her time, offered me money. When she finds out the truth, that Baby Caroline is still out there, all that hope will come crashing down. I'm heartbroken for her.

My phone rings, pulling me away from my thoughts and ending the conversation between Carmen and Des. They watch me, waiting.

"It's the hospital," I say.

"Answer it," Des says, waving her hand.

I answer and listen to what the nurse on the other end is telling me. I nod along, saying "Okay" when appropriate. The excitement and grief in my chest rise and fall as I follow her words. I hang up.

"We need to go to the hospital."

"Why?" Des and Carmen ask in unison.

"Mom is awake."

CHAPTER 34

Then

Eileen

Do you know how unprepared I was to be a mother? I never even went to the doctor until after I'd made my proposition to Amelia. I'd taken the store-bought pregnancy test as gospel and was taking daily vitamins, but I was too scared to admit your existence to anyone outside of Jamie or the women at the center.

After we started talking about adoption, Amelia insisted I see someone and offered her own personal doctor. She accompanied me to his private clinic and made sure to pay all the medical expenses. You weren't even born yet, but she was giving you the best care.

I met Bruce once for lunch, and he seemed thrilled about the prospect of being a father. After so many years of trying, parenthood was happening for them. And I was proud to be a part of that. Amelia's lawyers got the paperwork in order. By the time you arrived—three days late, mind you—everything was set.

Jamie had returned for your birth, even though it meant missing a midterm exam. I'm not sure what I would have done without her. She held my hand the entire time. She rubbed my back when the contractions became overwhelming, but she couldn't stand to watch me hand you over to Amelia. She said she respected the decision I made, but it was all too sad for her to witness. I couldn't help wondering if she felt like I was giving a part of Cliff away.

I was sad, too, of course. But I knew the risks of being raised by an unprepared parent. I was a product of two. At that point in my life, the best thing I could do was give you the opportunities I was never given. I was being a mother, even as I placed you in Amelia's arms and kissed you goodbye.

"You'll let me know if you need anything?" Amelia asked, preparing to leave.

It's funny. I should have been asking them. They were the ones headed home with a newborn. Even if I had offered, I didn't have anything left to give. I'd given them you, my whole heart.

"I'll be fine," I said, weakly. Jamie was staying for the rest of the week. If I needed something, I'd lean on her, not them. I didn't want to become their burden.

Amelia hugged me tight, holding me for several seconds. When she pulled away, my cheeks were wet from her tears.

"I'll never be able to repay you for this." That was a funny statement coming from the richest woman I knew.

I went back inside the hospital and waited. I was still crying when Jamie returned to drive me home.

Amelia had told me I could stay in touch, but the truth is, I couldn't. I didn't want updates of how you were doing or pictures of what you looked like. Teases that only made me want you more. It's hard to describe exactly what I felt. I never regretted my decision to give you away, and yet, I wished the woman caring for you could have been me. I wished I could have been rocking you to sleep and showering you with kisses.

And yet, as the weeks passed, my life reverted back to normal. Jamie returned to New York. I returned to my job at Buster's; most of the staff hadn't seen me since Cliff died. They didn't even know I'd been pregnant. At night, I stayed in my apartment alone.

My neighbor in the unit next door had a baby, too, and every time I heard him cry, I longed for you. I felt a burning ache in my breasts, a more ravenous one in my chest. You were out there in the world, absent from my life, yet hovering around the periphery. Haunting me, in a sense.

I'd told Amelia time and time again I didn't need anything in return. I'd wanted to place you up for adoption. It had been my choice. And yet, she'd said she wanted to repay me. I was blown away by what she'd done. She'd put me in touch with a financial aid advisor, and only three weeks after you were born, I was enrolled in college in another state. The second-best part was that the campus was only ninety minutes away from where Jamie currently lived. The best part: Bruce and Amelia had paid for my first year's tuition.

"It's too much," I said to her over the phone. I was still holding the letter in my hand that informed me of the payment.

"It's nothing to us," she said. "Besides, that's why we put you in touch with an advisor. She can help you take out loans to pay for the rest of the time. You've given us so much. Please, let us help you in return."

I cried, because already this letter had given me more than I'd ever thought my life could hold. I would be going to school. College. If any of my relatives heard this, they'd faint from the shock. *Not a screw-up anymore, huh?* For the first time since Cliff's death, I thought I might have a shot at a real life. More than that, I might have a shot at happiness.

"I hope you know how much this means to me," I said to Amelia over the phone. "I'm going to go and—"

I stopped talking when I heard you cry in the background. A low, guttural whimpering. Instinctively, I wanted to reach out and hold you. My body started aching, a gravitational force pulling me closer to you.

"Sarah, are you okay?"

I'd been quiet too long, and Amelia sounded worried.

"Yes, I'm fine. I just wanted to say thank you. I won't let you down."

And I hung up the phone.

Finally, the time had come for me to leave. I used the money from my last shift at Buster's to rent a car for the drive up north. I didn't need anything big, as I only had a few boxes of belongings.

It was harder leaving the apartment than I expected. As usual, I felt like I was leaving a piece of Cliff behind. I thought of all the times he'd slept here, of all the memories we shared. It's like his spirit would stay lost in this place forever, but I promised I wouldn't let that happen. Moving on with my life didn't mean ignoring his. I'd talk about him and keep him alive, in my heart. At least I would no longer have to pass the same street where I had seen him die.

Amelia had suggested meeting before I left, but I thought it would be too hard. It would be easier to see pictures once I got settled in my new place but seeing you in person would have been too difficult. I would want to hold you, take you with me, and I knew I couldn't do that.

And yet, as I sat in the driver's seat, my hand on the steering wheel, it felt impossible to move. I couldn't just leave New Hutton without seeing you. Although I'd look like some foolish young girl again for changing my mind at the last minute, I knew I couldn't leave without saying goodbye.

I got out of the car and ran across the street. I fed coins into a pay phone and dialed Amelia's office number. It felt like a punch to the stomach when they told me she still hadn't returned, that she wasn't working at the center at all. I'd missed my chance, and who knew when I'd get to see you again. Would I even recognize you?

I walked back to my car, defeated. The handwritten directions for my journey were sitting in the passenger seat. I was trying to muster the determination to put the car in drive. Then I thought of something. What if I simply drove to Amelia's house? Maybe she would be there when I arrived, and I could see you.

It would be unexpected, but Amelia would understand. Like she said, she would never be able to repay me. And yet she could. By letting me hold you one last time.

CHAPTER 35

Now

Marion

Mom is awake, but she's not exactly lucid. By the time I arrived at the hospital, she was already out again. Carmen is waiting in the lobby. Des stayed back at the condo with Ava.

"How long was she awake?" I ask the nurse. A name tag attached to his green scrubs reads, Roy.

"Only a few minutes."

"How was she? Did she say anything? Ask for me?"

"She was pretty out of it because of the drugs. That's to be expected. It might take another day or two until she's ready for any conversation."

Great. As though I haven't waited long enough. All I've wanted to do is talk to her. When I received the phone call saying she was awake, I thought this was finally my chance. I need her now, more than ever, to make sense of everything.

"Is there anything I can do?"

"You're free to visit. There's always a chance she could wake up again, but I wouldn't count on her being coherent. Sorry the call got your hopes up."

"No, it's okay. I'll stay a while."

"It might be good for you. Her too, in some way."

Now I'm sitting here. Waiting. For what? I don't know. It's not like she is going to start a conversation. I was foolish to think otherwise. And yet, this visit feels necessary. It is my first time seeing her after learning the truth. She's my mother.

Mom doesn't look like the person I remember from a week ago. Her skin is dull, fixed, not unlike a corpse. Every time she inhales the machine to her left makes a loud wheezing noise, reminding me she is still alive, even if her mind is elsewhere. There are a series of tubes attached to her body, at her elbow and mouth. Beneath her gown, I can see the top of what looks like a long line of staples, souvenirs from surgery. How I wish I didn't have to see this person. I want the woman I remember, the woman I love. I want my mom back.

There's a knock at the door and Nurse Roy pokes his head inside.

"Your name is Marion Sams, right?"

"Yes."

"You have a phone call at the receptionist's desk."

I look in my lap at my cell phone. There is full service and no missed calls or messages. Carmen is still in the waiting room. Des, still at the condo, wouldn't have called the hospital line unless there was some sort of problem with Ava.

"Do you know who it is?"

He shakes his head. "I'm just passing along the message."

I stand, taking another look at Mom. She's not moved since I've been here, and yet there's that worry that she'll wake up the moment I'm out of the room. I follow Roy into the hallway. Beside the door, sits the police officer I've seen during each visit. He's reading a newspaper, only raising his head once to scan my face.

Roy leads me in the opposite direction from the lobby to a small nurse's station. There's a woman behind the counter shuffling paperwork. When she sees me, she hands over a portable receiver and gets back to her work.

"This is Marion Sams."

A few seconds of silence, and then, "It's good to hear your voice."

The voice is female, but I don't recognize it. It's definitely not Amelia or anyone else I know.

"Who is this?"

"Do you have a pen and paper?"

On the counter, there is a cup full of pens and a writing pad. I take one, surprised that the voice on the other end ignored my question.

"Yes, but who is—"

"Write down this address: 127 Greenfield Drive. There's a storage facility there. You need to go to Unit 308 and press in this code." She gives me a six-digit combination. I write down everything she says, even though it feels like I'm doing something wrong. "That's all you need to get inside. You'll find a green folder. There's something you need to read."

Something about this, the secrecy of the phone call, feels wrong. I think of the press, of Carmen's rage if she were to discover I was continuing to correspond with people without her permission. "Tell me who this is."

"Just do what I say. It's to help Sarah."

The line goes dead. I pull back, staring at the useless receiver in my hands. Who was it that just called me? How would they know I'm at the hospital, and why would they wait until this moment to give me such muddled instructions? No one—other than the police and Amelia—has referred to my mother as Sarah. Could this be someone from her old life? Someone who knows something? Of course, if that's the case, I wonder why they wouldn't have already come forward. If this woman is doing this to help Mom, why wait until now?

"Excuse me," I say to the woman at the desk. Her back is turned. "Excuse me?"

She faces me. The dark circles beneath her eyes and heavy sigh suggest she will be less helpful than Nurse Roy.

"Do you have any idea who called this number?"

"No clue."

"Is it possible to trace the call?"

She makes a dramatic turn and exhales again. "This is a hospital, not a directory center."

I leave the phone on the counter and stuff the written instructions into my pocket.

When I return to Mom's room, it doesn't look like she has moved. She's still sleeping, her body fighting to regain consciousness. I sit with her a little longer, hoping against reason she will open her eyes.

CHAPTER 36

Then

Eileen

Bruce opened the door.

I'd only met him twice. Once before the adoption paperwork was finalized, and again at the hospital when they came to take you home. Amelia showed me dozens of family photos during our outings to the horse track. He seemed smaller in person, less powerful. Being a Parker or a Boone meant a ribbon of aristocracy was tied to whatever you did, but Bruce appeared normal, even boring. The type of dorky father you would want raising your child.

"May I help you?"

Our meetings were so brief he didn't recognize me at first. I'd already shrunk back to my pre-baby weight. The most notable change in my appearance were the dark bags beneath my eyes, badges of too little sleep.

Then, his face changed. He remembered.

"I'm sorry. Are you—"

"Sarah. I'm Sarah. I should have called."

"No, no. It's fine. I, um, it's nice to see you again." He started a handshake but pulled me in for a hug instead. I think he was embarrassed at not recognizing me immediately. "My God, what am I thinking? Would you like to come inside?"

As you would expect, their home was beautiful. I was seized with fear I might break something; everything looked too delicate to touch. The far wall was made entirely of glass, overlooking the backyard pool. I was too afraid to speak at first, but Bruce kept looking at me, waiting for an explanation.

"I'm just making a late afternoon snack," he said, walking into the kitchen. I followed him. The room was bigger than my entire studio apartment. There was a large island in the center complete with a second sink. He pulled out a chopping block and started slicing small rectangles of cheese.

"Amelia might have told you," I began. "I'm leaving town soon."

"She did. Starting school, right?"

"That's the plan."

I sat at one of the barstools pulled up to the island. It felt awkward, being alone with this man I knew nothing about. Amelia was an old friend by now, but Bruce was something different. Neither of us was sure what to do in her absence.

"Any idea what you'd like to study?"

"I was thinking about being a teacher. Younger kids. You know, like preschool age."

"I worked in education for years myself, but my students were older." He unfolded his arms now, getting more comfortable in his seat. "I taught at Phillips Academy."

The name sounded familiar, but I couldn't figure why. Suddenly, I was thinking about Cliff, about all those stories he used to tell about the kids passing through his neighborhood. *Khaki pant pricks*, he'd called them. As with most memories of Cliff, part of me wanted to laugh, while another part wanted to cry. I still hadn't accepted his loss, and I was resentful he never got the opportunity to meet you, to hold you in his arms.

"I'm leaving town today," I said. "Everything is packed and ready, but... I don't know." I started to lose my confidence, afraid, for some reason, that Bruce would deny my request to see you one more time. "It doesn't feel right leaving her like this. I've not even held her since she was born. I'd like to see her just one more time, if that's okay."

Bruce stopped what he was doing, crossing his arms. "Have you talked to Amelia?"

"I tried calling, but the center said she no longer works there. I guess I assumed she'd return after Caroline was born. I decided to come here instead."

"I'm glad you did. Caroline should be up from her nap soon."

"I can wait."

I leaned back, finally at ease. I'd get to hold you one more time, and then I would be off to start my life, and you would stay here to continue yours. I'm not sure why I was nervous, hung up on the idea they wouldn't let me see you. We had an amicable relationship, always putting your best interests ahead of anything else. For the rest of time, you would be theirs.

He walked to the other counter and retrieved a bundle of fruit. He pulled the twigs apart, dropping the dried stems into a separate bowl. After several seconds of silence, he rolled up his sleeves, folding them just below the elbow. On his left forearm, there was a long gash, now smooth and silver. It looked out of place compared to the rest of his neat look.

"What's that?" I asked, pointing at his arm. "Looks like that was a bad cut back in the day."

He stopped, looked down at his arm, then up at me.

"A reminder of my misspent youth."

I forced a laugh.

"No, really," he said, looking away. He arranged the food on the wooden slab. "Just a bad cut I got when I went on this camping trip with my brothers. I hope Caroline will be into that sort of thing."

I hoped so, too. I hoped you would have all the experiences I couldn't give you.

"Would you like something to drink?" he asked.

I cleared my throat. "I'll take some wat—"

"I know," he said, cutting me off and raising his hand. "I'll be right back."

He walked out of the kitchen, disappearing down a hallway. It sounded like he was going downstairs.

I wandered into the living room, daring myself to look around. I thought back to all the times I'd watched Amelia, analyzing my life through her lens. Now my analysis was different. This wasn't Amelia's home, but yours. The place where you would grow up, take your first steps, never go without a need or want. Walking around the room, envisioning what your future might be, I knew I'd made the right choice.

My eyes stopped on a bookcase. There were six shelves, reaching from the floor to just a few inches below the ceiling. The top and bottom rows held books. More books than I'd ever read. Most people don't read all the books they have on display, but I'd bet anything Bruce and Amelia had read them all. They were reliable in that way. They didn't pretend to be perfect; they just were.

The two middle rows held a collection of vases and frames. I reached out and touched the speckled glass, wondering if it was Venetian. Amelia had told me all about their honeymoon there, how they toured Murano and Burano, even took a day trip to Verona. All these experiences would be impossible for me to give you, and yet, in a way, I had. Because I'd given you to Amelia, and she could compensate for everything I lacked.

One of the pictures was of a group of people standing in front of a building. The fine print indicated it was taken at Phillips Academy. Students and teachers crowded the steps. I spotted Bruce standing on the back row, wearing the same kind of navy vest as his co-workers.

Then, out of nowhere, something familiar. A face. A face I'd missed so much, it hurt to suddenly be confronted by it again.

Jamie. She was standing in the second row, sandwiched in with the other disinterested pupils.

My mouth felt dry, and that lump in my throat returned, but this time, instead of sadness, I felt sick. Jamie. I scanned the years written at the bottom. This was her high school. Phillips Academy. That's why it had sounded familiar when Bruce mentioned it. It wasn't Cliff's story I'd remembered, but Jamie's. In the photograph, she stared back at me with those sad eyes. And there, only a few rows away, was Bruce, beaming at the camera.

"Are you a wine drinker?"

I jumped, realizing he'd re-entered the room. The frame was still in my hand, and I clutched it tighter. "What?"

"I've been dying to try this new red wine. You should have a glass."

"No." I turned quickly, putting the frame back in its place. Before I could step away, I felt the heat of someone standing behind me. "I'm really not a big drinker."

"That was my last year at Phillips," he said, staring at the picture before us. "I taught there for ten years."

"Why'd you quit?" I asked, trying to ignore the warmth of his breath on my neck.

"I started working for Amelia's father. Longer hours, but a bit more flexibility than the academy offered. Better pay, too. I quit right around the time we started trying for a baby, but, well, you know how that turned out."

I did. Amelia had detailed every false positive, every heartbreaking loss. I turned to face him, and could see he was looking down, no doubt thinking over the same awful history. Then he looked at me.

"Of course, thanks to you, we finally have the family we always wanted. You'll never know how much this has meant to us." He smiled. For the first time, I noticed the faint gray line on his gums.

Fuzzy Sweater Gray Gums.

I took a step back. "Do you have a restroom I could use?"

"Sure."

His brow furrowed. He'd picked up on my sudden change in attitude. He pointed me toward the hallway. I walked quickly, gently closing the door and locking it behind me.

Think, think, I chanted to myself. This idea had struck me from nowhere, but it would be too coincidental, wouldn't it? What were the odds Jamie's attacker would be your adoptive father? Amelia's husband?

I tried to remember everything Jamie had ever told me about what happened at her school. She didn't talk about it often, and it had been well over a year since the topic had been mentioned. I closed my eyes, trying to remember her exact words.

He had a reputation at the school, I remembered her saying. *He'd gotten away with it with other girls. He followed me into the bathroom, but I fought him off. Left a nice scar on his forearm.*

Bruce had said that picture was taken his last year at Phillips Academy. And he, I realized with a twisting sickness, fit Jamie's juvenile description. *Fuzzy Sweater Gray Gums.* That was the name girls around school had called him. He had the scar on his arm. But could it be true?

Maybe I was simply tricking myself into thinking these things. Maybe this was a last-ditch effort to convince myself not to leave you behind. It was the hardest thing I'd ever done, giving you away. I did it for your benefit. If Bruce Parker was the man who attacked Jamie, I wouldn't be leaving you in loving hands. I'd be leaving you in danger.

"Everything okay in there?" Bruce asked from the other side of the door.

"Be out in a sec."

I took a deep breath, staring at my own reflection in the mirror. I wished, more than anything, I could reach out to Jamie and ask her the name of the person who attacked her. What I would have given for the mundane ease of sending a text message or making a direct call, but it was the late eighties, and no such luxury existed. I took a deep breath, and exited the bathroom, determined not to leave New Hutton until I knew the truth for myself.

CHAPTER 37

Now

Marion

I haven't gone to the address written on that slip of paper, mainly because I haven't had the time. I'm not willing to take Ava anywhere with me, for fear there could be a sinister reason the person was calling. And I don't want to tell Carmen and Des I received a phone call while at the hospital. I'm not sure why, but something inside begs me to keep quiet.

"She's going to be fine," Des says, sliding a cardboard pizza box across the counter toward me. "Try not to worry about it."

"I know," I say, my hands grazing the box's smooth surface. I'm trying to stay focused, but that's difficult. Des is right. Mom is on my mind, but ever since I left the hospital last night, I've been thinking more about that phone call.

"Have you heard anything? From the hospital, I mean."

Des puts on a better front, but she is anxious, too. Mom has been her best friend for years, and I know she must miss having her around.

"No. They said they'd call when she wakes up again, but she hasn't yet."

Des nods and unloads another large pizza into a takeout box. This is my first day back at the restaurant. It's not been busy, but there have been more customers than I would have predicted. Mostly tourists, and part of me wonders if they're here because they're completely oblivious to Mom's arrest, or if they came as part of some morbid spectacle.

Normally, Ava would spend most of the afternoon in the back room, but neither of us are willing to take our eyes off her. I wonder if this paranoia will ever go away. The DNA test proves Mom is my biological mother, that somewhere along this path the police have gotten something wrong, but this whole ordeal is still frightening. It's clear there are manipulative people out there, willing to kidnap children. I'm just thankful Mom is no longer considered one of them, at least in my mind.

Between the DNA test results and my time at the hospital, I've had little time to think about Amelia. When I do think of her, my body seizes in sorrow. This woman—a perfectly nice and respectable woman—still believes I'm her daughter. She believes that the infant stolen from her all those years ago has been found. I know I'll need to see her again, but it weighs on me, knowing she'll eventually learn the truth. That I'm not Baby Caroline, and the police are no closer to learning what happened to her daughter.

"Martinez!" Des yells from behind, startling me.

A young woman walks to the counter. I hand over her pizza, and she pays. As she leaves, I look around the dining room. Lunch rush is officially over, and there's only a few customers left. This might be the only chance I'll get to find out what's inside that storage facility.

"I'm thinking of grabbing lunch," I say to Des, untying the apron around my waist. "Will you keep an eye on Ava for me?"

"I can make you something here," Des offers.

"I could use a minute alone, really."

"Take your time," Des says, looking over at Ava in the corner of the room. She's playing with a stack of blocks inside her playpen.

I bend down to kiss the top of her head before I leave.

*

The storage facility is almost forty-five minutes away. I'm not sure why I was expecting it to be closer. Perhaps I'm used to the convenience of North Bay, everything being exactly where you need it to be. I know I'll be gone too long if I go now, but I'm not sure when I'll get the opportunity to return. I'm not comfortable taking Ava with me.

I drive in silence, enjoying the gentle whir of passing cars on the highway. I'm about five minutes away from my destination when the phone rings. I fear it's Des, already irritated that I'm taking this long to "go get lunch", but it's not. Amelia is calling.

"Are you busy?" she asks when I answer the phone.

"No. Just on my lunch break."

"I'm never sure whether it's a good time to call. I'm afraid of pestering you too much."

"It's not a problem, Amelia." I'm uncomfortable talking to her now that I know the results of the DNA test, but I don't want to ignore her. I'm hoping when the news does break, it can be done gently. "Everything okay?"

"Just fine. I only wanted to tell you how much I enjoyed having lunch with you this week. Ava is an absolute doll."

"It was my pleasure."

Even thinking back to that lunch makes my stomach ache. When she left that day, a big part of me believed she was my mother. That we were three generations spending time together, getting to know each other. It's part of the reason I felt so compelled to seek out the DNA test on my own. I feel guilty, knowing I know the truth and she doesn't.

"Are you free for dinner tonight? I know we're trying to avoid being seen in public, what with the press and all. My hotel has an impressive room service menu. I thought maybe you and Ava would like to come over."

"Oh, Amelia, that sounds lovely. I'm afraid I can't tonight. It's been a busy day. We've just reopened the restaurant since, well… you know. Maybe another day?"

I can't ghost this woman, but I'm not ready to tell her the truth either. At some point we'll have this conversation. I'll make sure Amelia knows whatever horrible ideas she's had about Mom are unfounded. That Mom was not the woman who stole her child, murdered her husband. But it's tragic to know that person is still out there.

"Yes, yes. That's perfectly fine. Are you sure everything is okay?"

There's that fear in Amelia's voice. She's been so careful whenever we're together, afraid of pushing me away. That's probably what she thinks is happening now.

"I've loved getting to know you, Amelia. I'm just trying to get us back to our normal routine. We'll see you later in the week. Is that okay?"

"Completely fine. You'll let me know if you need help with anything, won't you?"

"Of course," I say, pulling into the storage facility complex. "I'll call you soon."

I sit in the car for several minutes, staring at the series of buildings in front of me. It's a cement L-shape with a series of red garage doors in front of each unit. There must be dozens.

I step outside, looking behind me. It appears I'm the only person at the unit. I start walking forward, following the numbers until I find 308. I can tell we're farther away from the sea here. The air is muggy, lacking the soothing breeze I'm so accustomed to in North Bay.

I reach my unit and plug in the code. For a brief moment, I hope the numbers won't work. I hope this is a wild goose chase, mainly because I'm afraid of what I might find inside. No such luck. The screen above the lock turns green, and when I try the handle, the door pushes open with ease.

I remember Evan used to watch a show about these places. People who don't pay their monthly fee get their units, and all their possessions, taken away from them. The contents are usually auctioned, and you never know what you might find inside. A stack of old newspapers. Boxes of clothes, misshapen and stained. Or you might find an old record signed by The Beatles or a mason jar full of gold coins. A $200 bid could result in thousands of dollars in profit, if you're lucky.

This unit wouldn't have gone for very much. There's barely anything inside. Only four plastic containers, each about four feet long. I sift through the boxes. Nothing miraculous. Clothes and papers and notebooks. Then, at the bottom of one, I find the green folder the caller mentioned on the phone.

I open the folder, holding my breath in fear that something disastrous might lie within. I look at the first page. It's addressed to me.

Dear Marion,

I'm writing this letter in the hope you never have to read it…

It's Mom's handwriting. I flip through the pages. There is a series of handwritten notes, front and back. They're all addressed to me, from Mom.

My phone beeps with a text message from Des. I don't have to read it to know she's probably bitching at me for being gone too long, and I still have close to an hour to get back. Even though all I want to do is read the letters, I know I need to go. Besides, that paranoid part of me doesn't want to stay in this place one second longer than I must. I don't know who told me to come here in the first place, or who might be watching me now.

I make sure all the papers are secured inside the folder, stuffing the packet under my arms. I lock the facility back up using the code, get in my car and leave.

CHAPTER 38

Now

Marion

As expected, Des complained from the moment I got back. I ignored her, mostly, focusing instead on the normality of being around customers again. And, of course, monitoring Ava in the back corner of the restaurant. But it was difficult pretending I wasn't fazed by her or anything else, when all I could think about were those notes.

Handwritten by Mom.

Addressed to me.

More than once, I thought about sneaking into the bathroom and reading them, or coming up with another excuse to leave. But there's no telling what those letters might contain, and what my reaction to reading them might be. So I waited.

Now, I've finished giving Ava her bath and put her to bed. It didn't take long to rock her to sleep, and I'm hoping she'll stay down the remainder of the night. Another annoying consequence of my lie earlier in the day is I'm starving. I scarf down the leftover sandwiches I made when Amelia visited, pour a glass of white wine and settle in on the living room sofa.

Alone in the corner of the living room, the overhead light shining down on me like a spotlight, I open the folder. I read the opening lines again.

Dear Marion,

I'm writing this letter in the hope you never have to read it...

Of course, that's what she'd hoped. There's been so much Mom has hidden from me over the years. She was concealing parts of my life—parts of her life. For almost two weeks, I've been comparing the mom I know against the person the police describe her to be. Comparing Eileen to Sarah Paxton, all the while thinking of every odd occurrence in my childhood, every bizarre story that didn't add up. My father. My birthplace. The real reason she decided to stay here. The DNA test provided some answers, but there's still a heavy mystery surrounding all of this, isn't there? And despite my greatest desires, I've not been able to talk about any of this with Mom.

At first, she shut me out with a hysterical outburst in the jailhouse visiting room. Since then, she has been comatose, recovering from her attack. Alive, and yet, not really there.

Dear Marion...

Part of me is afraid to go beyond those words. For over a week I've been preparing myself for the truth, knowing on the other side of it, I might be left devastated. But heartache or relief, whatever new mysteries this letter might reveal, I have to know. I'm ready.

I begin to read.

CHAPTER 39

Then

Eileen

By the time I exited the bathroom, I'd analyzed every possible way to handle the situation. If Bruce was dangerous, would he try to keep me here? Harm me? I even considered making an excuse to leave, call Jamie, and return, but I didn't want to leave you alone with him if my suspicions were correct.

I didn't want to start a confrontation. I doubted I would have the ability to fight him off. Instead, I decided I'd favor him with some more small talk. After a few minutes, I'd ask to use their telephone. I'd say I was calling someone from the rental company, when in reality I'd call the police. I didn't have any evidence to support my claims, but at least then I could voice my suspicions to someone and not feel so vulnerable.

When I walked back into the living room, Bruce was sitting on the sofa in the room's center. He held a wine glass in his hand. My glass, the one I'd said I didn't want, sat on the coffee table. I took a seat on the sofa across from him.

"You know, you really look like her," he said, getting up and picking up the glass to bring it closer to me. He sat down beside me. "You both have beautiful eyes."

"Thank you."

I'd come there to see you, but in that moment, I tried to push your image away. Thinking of you would only distract me, and I needed to know if my suspicions about Bruce were correct.

"What time will Amelia be home?"

"It's unpredictable. She's just recently started working for her father. We try to take turns, allowing one of us to stay with the baby. Hopefully she'll be home soon."

I wondered if that was true. What if she wasn't coming home at all? What if Bruce was just telling me that? Jamie told me this man was dangerous; I hoped he wouldn't be reckless enough to attack me in their own home, but I couldn't be sure.

"Is she a good baby?"

I thought maybe talking about you would keep him distracted. It worked. He had that goofy smile most dads get when talking about their children.

"She loves bath time. Most kids hate it that young. I know my nephews were never big fans of the water, but Caroline loves it. Did you have any brothers or sisters?" he asked.

"No."

"I'm one of five. Big family. I'm the last one to have kids, so it's like I've been waiting on this a long time. You should drink your wine," he said, nodding at me. He took a sip and continued his story. "It's funny we ended up with a daughter. My family has been dominated by boys for the longest time. Caroline changes things. It's true what they say, too. I feel like Caroline has turned me into a big softie."

The man sitting beside me might be talking about his hopes for his child, my daughter, you... but it was all a smokescreen. I believed he was the man who had attacked Jamie, and each minute I was left alone with him felt dangerous.

"That's funny," I said, forcing a smile. "Say, do you think I could use your tele—"

Across the way, I heard a heavy door sliding across the floor, then a lock being clicked.

"Bruce?"

It was Amelia's voice, followed moments later by the sound of her heels clacking against the floors. She stopped walking when she saw me sitting beside her husband. I still wonder if she could detect the look of fear on my face. The terror, thickening, spreading throughout my entire body.

She scrunched her face in confusion. "Sarah, what are you doing here?"

Amelia didn't seem particularly happy to see me. In all the times we had spent together—at the center, at the hospital, at the stables—this was my first time in her house, and I had arrived uninvited. And now, I was holding on to this secret that her husband, your appointed father, might have attacked my best friend.

He definitely attacked her, I told myself. The scar. Phillips Academy. Everything was too coincidental.

I stood quickly. "I'm on my way out of town. I tried calling you at the center, but…" The adrenaline coursing through my body made it hard to focus.

She looked to Bruce. "Where's Caroline?"

Bruce stood. His hand rubbing the back of his neck. His gaze remained downward, avoiding Amelia and me. "Still sleeping." He walked into the kitchen and held up the charcuterie board like it was a prize. "I thought we'd snack on some of this until she wakes up."

"You're staying?" Amelia asked, her attention back to me.

"I'm leaving town this afternoon," I said. "I just wanted to see Caroline one last time."

Amelia eased at this and smiled. "You must be so excited about your classes."

"Yeah, I am."

"Let's sit outside," Bruce said, carrying the tray toward the patio doors. "It's such perfect weather."

I looked back at Amelia. She was watching me the way I was watching Bruce. I wondered if she was afraid I would change my mind about you. She might have been worried I'd cause a scene.

"Set up the table outside," Amelia told Bruce.

He obeyed, stepping into the backyard and shutting the door behind him.

Amelia stepped closer to me. "Are you sure everything is all right? You look upset."

She'd been around me enough to sense when I was acting off. Even though I still felt conflicted about what I needed to do, I felt safer knowing she was here. And I felt an overwhelming need to tell her the truth about what I was thinking.

"I think… I think I know something."

There I was again, sounding like the idiot girl I was when I first met Amelia. Before we became friends and she led me toward greater opportunities. I was back to falling over my words like a buffoon.

And yet, Amelia acted as though what I'd just said made complete sense. She seemed startled. She nodded. "What do you think you know?"

"Something about Bruce," I said. It felt like I was running out of breath.

At this, she looked surprised. "What about Bruce?"

"He used to work at Phillips Academy, right? I had a friend who went to that school. And she…" I failed to find the best phrasing. I closed my eyes. I had to just say it. Leave no room for misunderstanding. "She was attacked by one of her teachers."

Amelia raised her chin. She wasn't expecting to hear me make such an accusation, but she didn't look completely disgusted either. "Just because he taught there doesn't mean—"

"He has a scar. On his forearm. My friend fought this teacher off."

Amelia had a pained look on her face. "When did you come up with all of this?"

"Just now. When I met him again."

"It doesn't… he couldn't…" Amelia stopped talking, raising a hand to her forehead. She looked like she might faint. She gave her head a little shake and took a deep breath. "Are you sure?"

"I'm not sure if it's him, but everything in my friend's story adds up. I'm sick to my stomach. I know he's your husband, but… he could be dangerous. I think we should leave with Caroline. Together. Just until we find out if my suspicions are correct."

Amelia's face turned to the closed door. She looked like she might be ill. "I'll tell him to leave. We'll get him out of the house, long enough for us to decide what we need to do. Maybe we could reach out to your friend. Ask her for a name."

I nodded hurriedly. I knew she was taking a huge leap of faith, believing my outlandish accusation, but then again, he was her husband. Maybe a portion of the story I'd told her registered, made sense in some way. Maybe she already had suspicions. She certainly didn't look happy when she had returned home to find the two of us alone in a room together.

"I'll be right back," she said, squeezing my hand. She walked to the patio door and stepped outside.

When I arrived at their house, I believed I was making peace before my departure. Now, in the light of what I had uncovered about Amelia's husband, I had a new purpose. If Bruce was dangerous, I couldn't allow you to grow up under the same roof. *He'd done it to other girls*, Jamie's voice rang in my ears. I paced through the living room, nibbling at my nails. The patio door opened, and I stopped, eager to hear what Amelia would say.

But it wasn't Amelia. Bruce walked inside, locking the door behind him.

"Sarah, I think we should talk."

A hot flame of fear climbed my spine. For a few seconds, I stood there, mouth open, unable to speak.

"Amelia seems to think you have me confused with someone else," he said.

"Why did you leave Phillips Academy?" I asked, wanting to focus on the few facts I knew.

Bruce stiffened. "I told you. I started working for my father-in-law—"

"Why did you *really* leave?"

"That's the truth," he said, a bit too breathy.

"What if I told you I know how you got that scar on your arm? And it wasn't from a camping trip."

"That's a lie," he said.

Wouldn't a normal person ask questions, want to know more? An innocent person wouldn't immediately dismiss the threat. He took a step back and an ugly cloud shadowed his features.

"What is this? Some kind of a shakedown? Do you want money? A free ride to college isn't enough for you, eh?"

He raised his hand. In one forceful push, I was down on the couch.

"What's this about?" Bruce asked, standing over me. "Why are you really here?"

"I'm here to see Caroline," I said, scooting farther away from him, trying to create distance. "I'm calling the police."

I rolled my body, trying to squirm to the other end of the couch. Bruce grabbed my arm, his grip leaving white indentations on my arm, and pulled me back. He climbed on top of me, straddling me.

"I can't let you do that."

"Let go of me."

But he squeezed harder. I tried to wriggle away, but his weight was too much. Horror pulsed throughout my body, my mind conjuring sickening images of what he might do next. Of what he'd already done before. In this moment, there was no doubt in my mind he was the same predator who had traumatized Jamie all those years ago.

"Stop moving," Bruce yelled, his voice a deep roar. Gone was the polite socialite, and in his place was a monster.

I kneed his groin. The jolt delivered enough pain to make him hunch forward, sinking more of his weight on top of me.

My hand, now free, reached aimlessly for the side table. I felt the heavy stem of a lamp. With what little strength I had, I whacked him over the head with it. It was enough to get him off me. Now standing, I hit him again, waiting another second to make sure he wouldn't move.

I raced to the front door, but when I jiggled the handle, it wouldn't budge. The door was locked. My breath quickened and I could feel a cool line of sweat developing on the back of my neck as I debated what to do. I still didn't want to leave you, and I was unsure how to get out.

I ran through the living room, making sure Bruce was still passed out on the floor. I opened the back door, clicking the lock behind me in case Bruce regained consciousness and came after me.

A bean-shaped pool sat in the center of the concrete, and beyond that, was a perfect view of the setting sun. How wonderful it must be to spend long afternoons like this, relaxing as the day turned to night. I imagined you one day having holidays and parties at this very spot. I imagined you taking swimming lessons in this very pool. It all felt so useless now, an expensive varnish with no durability.

"Bruce?" I heard Amelia's voice before I saw her. "What happened? Did you get her to—"

Amelia came around the corner. She froze when she saw me instead of her husband.

"Sarah, where is Bruce?"

"You said you were going to make him leave. I told you he was dangerous."

"I think what you're doing right now is projecting. You have this story about Phillips Academy in your head, and now you're using that to make yourself feel less guilty about leaving Caroline behind. You're trying to make yourself feel better."

"No, that's not what I'm doing. I really did come here to say goodbye. But I can't just leave her—"

"What do you mean you can't leave her?"

"I can't leave her around a man like that. And you! You let him go back inside. You waited out here so he could attack me."

"I know my husband. What you are alleging is ridiculous." But something in the way she said it made me wonder if she really thought that. She didn't seem offended, the way I would be if someone were to make such a suggestion about Cliff, or someone else in my life. She seemed nervous.

"Amelia, I'm sorry. This has all been a horrible mistake. I'm leaving and taking her with me. She's my daughter."

"Caroline is my daughter," Amelia corrected me. Her eyebrows arched. "There's no evidence you ever gave birth to her. Her birth certificate lists me as her mother."

"But the hospital—"

"New Hutton delivers dozens of babies a day. I'd be willing to bet they won't be able to remember you."

"People know you didn't give birth—"

"People know I left the center for maternity leave. They know I had a private physician. They believe Caroline was born at home."

"But the adoption—"

"That's what I'm trying to tell you," she said, calmly. "There is no adoption. On paper, Caroline is our daughter. You're nothing to her. And you sure as hell aren't leaving with her."

We both turned when we heard the patio door shaking madly. Bruce was awake, and he was trying to get outside.

Amelia ran toward me. We fell on top of each other. She was trying to hold me down long enough for Bruce to break down the door. I pulled back my foot and kicked her in the chest. She stumbled, hitting her head hard against the ground.

By the time I made it to my feet, Bruce was coming after me. One hand was holding his injured head, but the other stretched away from his body, his fingers splayed. I knew he would grab me, strangle me, hurt me. Dozens of possibilities, but he'd never let me leave.

I grabbed the wooden tray from the table and aimed for the other side of his head.

He blocked my hit with his forearm. "You bitch!"

This time, I held the board as high as I could, slamming it down on his shoulder, then the bridge of his nose. The pain sent him to his knees. Even then, he kept trying to grab at my ankles, his body squirming to gain even an inch in distance.

I kept hitting him, closing my eyes, trying not to look. He cried out, calling me names and making threats, but I didn't pay attention. In my mind, I was lost, unable to do anything but repeat that same physical action. Slamming the board into Bruce. Slamming the board into my father. Slamming the board into Albert. Slamming into every person who had taken advantage of me, determined never to be made a victim again, much like Cliff overpowered those bullies that day in the alley. I didn't stop, until I noticed the lack of resistance.

Cicadas buzzed around me, hurting my head. I looked down at Bruce, seeing what damage had been done. I had to turn immediately to prevent myself from throwing up. There was blood seeping from the wound in his head, stretching across the concrete toward Amelia. She was unconscious, but her shallow breathing warned me I didn't have long.

She would be awake soon, whether it was another hour, or in the next thirty seconds. And I didn't have it in me to harm her. Bruce had been an accident. It didn't feel like a choice.

I rushed back inside, startled by the cool temperature indoors. And the quiet. I ran upstairs, not even knowing which room was yours. When I pushed the far door, I saw your crib beside the open window, white curtains fastened at either side like something you'd see in a picture book. Yes, they'd succeeded in giving you a picturesque life, but what else would they give you? What nightmares lived behind the dream? You weren't safe, and maybe deep down I had known that all along.

I rushed to you. You were still sleeping, your head turned to the side, your chest pumping up and down. You still felt so fragile in my arms. And when I saw there were patches of blood on my sleeve, I felt immediate regret that I'd already brought you into a mess you didn't deserve. I'd screwed up again. Whether I'd caused this mess or not, it was my duty to get you out of it. I had to, as quickly as possible. You began to cry, which only heightened my anxiety. How was I supposed to protect you and comfort you all at the same time?

I grabbed a blanket from your crib and a handful of diapers I saw sitting on a dresser. Did you drink formula? Milk? Again, all this was foreign to me at the time, but I knew the most important thing was getting you out of the house and away.

I had almost reached the front door when it hit me: I didn't have a car seat. I couldn't very well drive down the road with you in my lap. Not only would it be unsafe, if anyone spotted me, I'd be pulled over in a second. And then the officer would notice the blood… I stopped myself from imagining all the ways this could go wrong and forced myself to think rationally.

I ran all through the downstairs, poking my head into rooms and coming up empty. Finally, I tried a door by the kitchen. It led to a four-car garage. I exhaled in relief. I spotted your carrier in the backseat of one of the cars. I tried my best to unhook it while holding you at the same time.

By this point, you'd stopped crying. Maybe my mad dash to get you out of the house stunned you. I strapped you in and turned to go back the way I came, then remembered the front door was locked. I looked around until I found the garage button, waited impatiently for the door to raise. It felt like I'd been standing there for hours, but it couldn't have been more than a few seconds. Had I done the right thing? Would I live to regret my actions?

You made a tiny grunt, which reminded me the clock was ticking, coming dangerously close to running out of time. I needed to get you out of there.

And that's what I did.

CHAPTER 40

Now

Marion

By the time I stop reading, it's nearing one in the morning. I didn't think it would take this long, but I also took several breaks along the way. With each passing word, it feels like I'm meeting Mom for the first time, at least a part of her. I'm meeting Sarah, the woman she was before me. Before all of this.

My emotions boomeranged as I read each section, trying to process everything she had written. The truth about her traumatic childhood. The truth about my father, Cliff—a name I've waited so long to hear. They were young. So very young. I remember those years of early adulthood. Thinking I was completely capable of taking on the world, trying to combat that voice in my head telling me I wasn't enough.

I can only imagine facing the decisions Mom had to make, and the sacrifices. The grief! To think her future would be one thing, whether she was truly ready for it or not, only to have it swiped away by something as cruel and unforgiving as death. To think—yet again, during this horrendous week—what my life might have been like if Cliff lived, if they had been able to start their life together. To imagine having a father, a young one, an impulsive one, but one who would have loved me. I have found him and lost him all in the same sitting.

And of course, those letters held something else: the truth about Amelia Parker.

I think back to everything she told me. She never once mentioned an adoption, or the truth about her relationship with Mom before my abduction. She even told me about being pregnant. She pushed for a DNA test, knowing what the results would be. Of course, she also offered to arrange it. I wonder, knowing the lengths she took back then, if she had some way of altering the results. This woman, who on the surface exceeds every ideal, can't be so manipulative, can she? I'd prefer to think she treated Mom the way she did because she was acting on her own maternal instincts, that she wasn't trying to intentionally deceive her. Maybe she was in denial about how dangerous Bruce could be.

Really, Amelia's motives don't matter. What matters is that Mom is my protector. Always has been. She gave me to the Parkers because she believed she was making the best decision for me. When she realized how dangerous Bruce was, she fought like hell to get me back. We have been hiding ever since. Not because she wanted to control me, but because she wanted to shield me. Every decision, every lie has been a form of defense.

Mom admitted she didn't want me to know any of this. I would have been saved a mountain of heartache if I had never found out, but now that I know the truth, the clarity I have is more monumental than the pain I've experienced this past week; it takes away the uncertainties I've carried about Mom and myself throughout my life.

I creep down the hallway to Ava's room. I push open the door and peek into her crib. She sleeps peacefully. I think about how much I love her. How I would do anything in my power to keep her safe. I realize, now, that is all Mom ever wanted to do for me.

And I shudder when I think of how I let Amelia get so close.

Desperation pushed me toward Amelia more than anything. After Mom's arrest, I was untethered, isolated in a lonely world. I was convinced Mom was a liar, a kidnapper, a murderer. Amelia's presence stabilized me, provided the hope and optimism Mom wasn't capable of giving. Now I see Amelia was trying to stay in control of the Baby Caroline narrative she had written years ago. She never came forward with her true connection to Mom, never admitted she agreed to an adoption. She is using the same tricks to manipulate me now that she used on Mom back then.

The silence in the living room bothers me. I've just uncovered all this information, everything I've ever wanted to know about my past, and there's no one I can share these new discoveries with.

Carmen needs to read these letters. It's only my mother's version of events, secrets she's spent an entire lifetime guarding, but there is a possibility this information could help her case. If she is believed, that is. Identifying the person who called the hospital would help. I can't know for sure, but I wonder if Mom's friend Jamie might have tipped me off. Maybe she saw the media circus and knew it was time the truth came out.

Yes, Carmen will have to know, and I'm sure she'll instruct Rick to start digging. Des also deserves the truth. She's respected Mom's boundaries to this point and been nothing but loyal since the arrest. In the morning, I'll call them both.

Tonight, I need to do more than simply plan Mom's next step. I'm still absorbing the information I've been given, and I need someone who is willing to let me do that. Be still with these shaky thoughts.

I think of Evan.

I'm here if you need me, he told me after he finished cleaning graffiti off The Shack's windows.

I need him tonight. I really do.

CHAPTER 41

Now

Marion

Evan pretends I didn't wake him, but his appearance gives him away.

He sits beside me on the living room sofa wearing maroon sweatpants and a top with a Sanderson logo. His hair sits on one side of his head, like it was brushed hurriedly, and he's wearing thick-rimmed glasses. He only takes his contacts out right before bed, and sometimes he forgets and sleeps with them in, or so I remember.

Even if he was asleep when I called, he's attentive now. He listens to my every word, as I tell him about finding the letters, sneaking behind Des' back earlier today to retrieve them. I tell him about Mom's life before me, about the choices she was faced with making. I tell him about my father, this young man I never got the chance to know. And I tell him how Bruce and Amelia Parker play into all of this.

"It's unbelievable," he says, after several seconds of silence. He has been thinking, his gaze deliberately avoiding mine. "And yet, it makes sense of everything, doesn't it?"

I've thought the same thing. Mom's protectiveness, her paranoia. It wasn't because she was afraid of what dangers might be out in the world—she had already been confronted by them. She knew Amelia was still out there and possessed more credibility than a twenty-something convicted criminal ever would. She must have lived in constant fear that one day Amelia would return for me.

"Do you remember me telling you about my eighteenth birthday party?" I ask. He nods, smiling. "That's why she finally loosened up. Became a different person. She knew I couldn't be taken away from her anymore."

"She knew you were safe."

"And I keep thinking about all those times I asked her questions about my father. A part of me hated her for never telling me who he was. It made me think he was some dirtbag. That he decided to walk away from us. From the sounds of this," I say, lifting the letter, "he was a decent person. Why didn't she ever tell me that?"

"Given the circumstances, she probably wanted to put as much distance between you and her past as possible. If she had told you the truth about him, even his name, and you looked into it, someone might have tracked the two of you down much sooner. Whatever happened in New Hutton back then, it must have been traumatic. I doubt her letters accurately portray the terror she felt."

I look down, the words on the paper blurring together.

"You're a lawyer now," I say, with a nervous laugh. "Will any of this help Mom? Or is her case still a lost cause?"

He looks away again, raising his hand to his chin. He used to do this back when we were together, whenever he had to think through something intensely. The longer I sit with him, the more I feel like I'm back in the past.

"The DNA test helps, but Bruce Parker's murder is still her biggest hurdle. These letters provide more insight to what happened on that day. His death very well could have resulted from an act of self-defense. We have the truth, the problem is proving it."

"What if we were able to track down Jamie? I think she might be the person who called me at the hospital in the first place. Maybe she would corroborate Mom's story. Admit that Bruce attacked her."

"It could help, sure. It's still going to be Eileen's word against everyone else's. And the time gap is hard, too."

I feel defeated, an intense welling in my chest that won't ease. "Mom doesn't deserve to spend the rest of her life in prison, not after reading this."

Evan squeezes my shoulder, rocking me closer to him. "Look at it this way, she has a better chance now than she did a week ago. If we're able to back up her account, it at least gives her a shot. Carmen's a pro. She'll do the best she can."

"She was happy enough with the DNA test results. When she reads these letters, her mind will really be blown."

"You've not told her yet?" He pulls both feet onto the couch, resting his arms across his knees. "I figured she would have been the first person you called."

"She wasn't."

We are quiet now, letting the room fill with whatever unresolved emotions remain between us. Evan has always been there for me, until he wasn't. The trauma of this situation has erased the last few years. Evan is the first to speak.

"When I moved back here, there were things I'd planned on telling you. But with Eileen's arrest, I've been trying to hold off. I don't want you to feel like I'm taking advantage of you at your most vulnerable moment."

"Like what?"

"I guess there was a part of me that was hoping we might be able to give our relationship another shot. Now that we're both settled."

He's said it, the words that have been going through my mind for years. Even with all the time that has passed, I'm not sure how to respond.

"The first few months I was at Sanderson made me realize I'd made a mistake leaving you behind. I knew it was the best school for me, but the idea of living another two and half years without you was almost too much to bear," he continues. "As time went on, neither of us had dated anyone else. I started to think maybe there was a chance, at the end of all this, that we'd get back together. Then bam. My sister said you were having a baby. There was a part of me that was happy for you, but I'd be lying if I said I wasn't hurt."

"How were you hurt? You're the one who chose Sanderson."

"And I asked you to come with me. I understood why you didn't. I knew it was a huge sacrifice, and when you said no, I accepted it. It even made me love you more, really. You've always been so determined to do things your own way, but then you just completely moved on."

"Isn't that what you're supposed to do after a breakup?"

"Yes, it is. But it still hurt. And you didn't move on with some other guy. You had a child, Marion. It's like you just carried on life without me."

"And you'd rather I'd waited?"

"No, of course not. But I'm trying to be honest right now about what I have been feeling since I moved away."

"You said you weren't ready to settle down here."

"And I wasn't, but it doesn't mean I didn't want all of those things with you eventually. It's like you just went on without me. You're the one who left me behind."

My cheeks are warm, and I'm grinding my teeth together. Why does he have to do this now? Why does he have to do this ever? We both made our decisions years ago and rehashing them accomplishes nothing.

"I was ready for Ava."

"I'm glad." The smile on his face is full of sincerity, even pride. It's clear Evan wants me to be happy. He lifts his head, and we lock eyes. "All I'm saying, is I hope one day you'll be ready to give me another chance, too."

The reality is, I've never fully given up on the idea that one day we might be together. Even when it didn't make sense, geographically or otherwise. When I decided to have Ava, I thought maybe that was what I was choosing—her over him. And yet I don't feel that way now. In my heart, there's room for both of them. That is why I called him tonight, in my darkest moment.

All the reasons I fell in love with him come rushing back. His loyalty. His patience. Maybe it's the wine, or the time of night, or the emotional exhaustion. Whatever it is, I can't stop myself from leaning in for a kiss.

CHAPTER 42

Now

Marion

I wake up on the sofa. Evan is sleeping on the opposite end, his feet halfway off the couch. He is still wearing that shirt, his glasses askew over the bridge of his nose. Nothing happened beyond the kiss. I don't think either of us wanted to look back and think we made a decision based on weakness. And yet, he was vulnerable in telling me how he felt. That's not easy for Evan to do.

It feels nice waking up beside him again. It's a feeling I could get used to.

My phone rings, which causes Evan to stir. I pat around the sofa, trying to find the source of the ringing.

"Who is it?" Evan asks.

Finally, I find it, stuffed between two cushions.

"It's the hospital."

I quickly answer, stumbling to the kitchen. I listen, nodding my head as the person on the other end speaks. Then I place the phone on the counter.

"Everything okay?"

"Mom is awake again," I say, trying to process what the rest of the day might look like. "The nurse says she has been up for hours. She wants me to visit."

It's time.

*

From the moment I saw Mom in handcuffs, I've been waiting for this. Days that felt like a prison sentence, with the answers she couldn't provide the only way to freedom. Now that the time has come, I'm nervous, my stomach tangled in knots.

Carmen is talking to her first. I gave her a call before leaving the condo, giving her a head start. She opens the door, and nods for me to come in.

Mom is lying in the bed. She looks as weak as the last time I saw her, but there aren't as many tubes and bandages, it seems. She doesn't appear frightened, like she did that day at the jailhouse. When she sees me, her eyes fill with tears. It's like she's just been given the most wonderful gift in the world.

All the stoicism and calm falls away, and I rush to her side. I lean over the bed, hugging her. At the end of the day, she's my mother. The woman who loved me, and that's what matters most. I'm thankful I have the opportunity to see her again, and I don't think I ever fully understood how devastated I would be if I'd lost that chance.

"Where's Ava?" she asks.

Again, a wave of guilt. For a few moments, I'd forgotten about her, so lost in this emotional reunion. And I'd forgotten about Carmen standing in the corner of the room. It's like the only two people in the entire world are my mother and me.

"Des is with her in the waiting room," I say.

"When can you bring her to see me?"

"Soon," I say, not quite capable of deciding whether or not this is the right environment for a one-year-old. "I need to know you're okay first."

"I'm awake. That's a start."

Carmen steps closer. "I'm heading outside. Take all the time you need."

She leaves, and the door closes. Not only is she giving us time alone, she is reading the letters I gave her. I'm hoping, praying, there will be enough in there to help Mom's case.

Now it really is just the two of us. I sit beside her, too afraid to speak, waiting for my mother to make sense of everything that has happened these past two weeks.

"I'm sorry for how I acted when you came to visit me at the county jail," she begins. "You have to understand how long I've kept all of this hidden. I thought maybe it would never come to light, and when it did, I wasn't ready to face you. It was selfish of me to leave you in the dark."

"I've been in the dark longer than this past week." The deceptions and half-truths didn't originate from her arrest; I've been hassling her for answers my entire life. I want to hear Mom's version of events before bringing up the letters. After all the deception, I suppose it's a test of sorts. "Tell me everything."

"Let's start at the beginning."

CHAPTER 43

Now

Marion

She begins.

"I was so young."

For a moment, Mom appears younger, like she is reverting to her prime, leaving behind the frail woman in her bed fighting to heal. Memories are an elixir in their own way, relieving the hardness of time, transporting a person back to a place, to see that familiar face, inhale that familiar smell.

"My childhood wasn't the best, I've told you that much. When your father and I learned we were pregnant—Cliff was his name— we weren't sure how we would manage."

"My father."

I'd read about him in the letters but hearing her say his name makes him feel solid. Almost tangible, even though I've forever lost the opportunity to reach out and touch him. He was this person who really existed, who really wanted me.

"He had a good heart and a wicked sense of humor." She smiles. "He had his demons, too. We all did back then, it seemed. He would have been a good father, with a little more time. He died before you were born. It was his death that made me decide to put you up for adoption."

"Why didn't you ever tell me about him? I've asked you so many times."

"I wanted to tell you. I've felt like I betrayed him the most in all this. You deserved to know all about him, how wonderful he was, but I couldn't run the risk of anything linking back to what I'd done. So I had to keep it all a secret."

There are more questions I want to ask, but I wait, allowing her the chance to speak in her own time.

"I met Amelia first," she says. "She worked at a counseling center I went to. All I saw was this nice woman, so put-together, so helpful. After a while, she told me about her own struggles. She couldn't get pregnant. Had tried a few times. She wanted a child more than anything, and I was searching for a family that would give you all the love and support I couldn't. It seemed like it was meant to be. Amelia wanted to handle the adoption privately. I agreed. She was a counselor, after all. She'd helped countless young girls do this sort of thing over the years, or so I thought."

"And then you had second thoughts?"

"I constantly had second thoughts. If I had made the decision with my heart, I'd never have let you go. You were always wanted. It was just the timing, and so soon after Cliff's death, I knew I wasn't ready. Not like Amelia was. And yet, there was this nagging feeling that I couldn't let you go. Moving away without saying goodbye felt wrong. I went to the Parkers' home in the hopes of seeing you one last time."

She continues her story, echoing her letters. She talks about her friend Jamie and about the secret she'd shared with her all those years ago. And she tells me about the confrontation with Bruce, about the terror she felt in those moments.

Finally, I've heard the true story in her own words. It doesn't make it any less shocking. I try to imagine my mother when she was younger, in the few pictures I've seen. I try to see her scrambling through the Parkers' house, strapping a crying baby into the car and driving away—where to, still a mystery.

"What did you do after you left with me?"

"I reached out to Jamie and told her everything. She helped me get out of New Hutton. I still didn't know what to do. To be honest, the fact I was going to be your mother didn't sink in until weeks later. All I wanted was to protect you. I guess it's one and the same when you think about it, really."

"Why didn't you tell the police about Bruce? About what he'd done to your friend?"

"He was dead! I thought I might have a shot at self-defense, but I was afraid coming forward would risk losing you. The story was in the media overnight. People talking about this missing baby and this murdered father, this grieving widow who was determined to find her child. Everyone was searching for the deranged madwoman Sarah Paxton. No one mentioned an adoption. Amelia knew what happened, but it seemed we were the only two. It was her word against mine, and I wasn't convinced anyone would believe me."

"That's why we stayed hidden?"

"We stayed in hotels the first year, mostly. It was a stressful time. Not only was I juggling a newborn, but I was also afraid every night I'd get a knock on the door. That the police would find me, take you away. Lord knows the case was in the news enough. I'm sure the Parkers' money helped with that. But people never asked any questions. They just saw a young mother and her child. If they thought we were running from anyone, they probably assumed it was some custody nonsense. No one ever suspected anything, and I didn't stick around one place long enough to give them the chance.

"It took some time, but Jamie was able to provide us with everything we'd need to start over. A driver's license, birth certificates, social security cards. Her family had connections for that sort of thing, and they didn't much care about asking questions. You had just turned two when we came here. I didn't plan on staying, of course. I'd been living on what little money Jamie could give me and the jobs I could get in between moves. I thought North Bay would be a nice place to stay for the summer. Of course, that's when I met Des, and the rest is history."

"You never told her the truth?"

"She never asked. I could tell she liked me, and she was smitten with you. A few weeks turned into a few months, then that turned into years. Before I realized it, this place was home, and I didn't worry as much about the police finding us. There were a few close calls, but nothing ever came of it."

"That's why you never wanted to let me go anywhere. You never let me out of your sight."

"It's not that I didn't want you to have those experiences. Every time you would come to me with that eager smile and I had to tell you no, it killed me inside, but I was doing what was best for us. Best for you. I knew Amelia would never stop looking."

"Is that why you were so happy when I turned eighteen? You knew there was no chance I could be taken away?"

"That was a big part of it, yes. Before you were born, my only concern was giving you the best life possible. After my confrontation with the Parkers, I realized my priority was to keep you safe. I tried to provide what I could, of course. But nothing was more important than keeping you out of harm's way." She pauses, averts eye contact. "I hope you know I tried my best, and I'm sorry for everything else."

Yes, I deserved the truth. Yes, I'm an adult in search of answers. But I'm also a mother. I understand the overwhelming need to keep your child safe, even if that goes against their best interests at times. It's an irrational compulsion rooted in rationalism. Is there anything I wouldn't do for Ava? Even if it meant she might be angry with me later?

"Your friend. Jamie. Do you still talk to her?"

"She was instrumental during those early years. We would have never made it a month without her help. Once we were settled in North Bay, we lost contact. It was safer for her that way."

I look down.

"I think I might have spoken to her, actually."

"Jamie? She reached out to you?" Mom sits up straighter in her bed. "She should know better. She doesn't need to get involved with any of this. I never would have made it out of New Hutton without Jamie's help. She doesn't deserve punishment for that."

"I can't be certain. Earlier this week, when I was visiting you in the hospital, I received a phone call. It was a woman, but she didn't give me her name. She told me about a storage facility about an hour away from town."

Mom leans back on the pillow and closes her eyes.

"She told me there were letters there. Letters for me."

"Have you read them?"

"Yes."

"So you already knew all of this?"

"I knew everything that was written in the letters, but I wanted to hear you tell it." I look down again. "I'm guessing Jamie is the only person who would have known about them."

"Yes. I told her I wrote everything down. I told her where they were in case… well, I suppose in case anything like this ever happened. The fear of punishment has never bothered me. What I feared most was losing you, then losing your respect. I can't say I've acted very respectably, but I had hoped you would at least understand why I made the choices I made."

"I understand. I do." I squeeze her hand. It feels like we are on the cusp of full transparency. "There's something else I need to ask you about. The cancer."

Mom closes her eyes again and lets out a long sigh. "Who broke first? Carmen or Des?"

"The doctors, actually. It came out when they were telling me about your condition."

I look around the room, at the bizarre setting for this emotional heart-to-heart. There very well could be a HIPAA violation in there somewhere, but the information is out now, so it doesn't seem to matter whether I learned about it in the right way or not.

"Why didn't you tell me?"

"I had a routine screening that didn't go in my favor, let's say. That same week, you'd been going on and on about Ava's party. I just didn't want to ruin it for you. I thought, let's have one more celebration before everything starts being about me. Obviously, I couldn't have predicted any of this would happen."

None of us could have. Even though I understand, the worry is now there, embedded deeply within me. She's recovered from her attack, but her life is still at risk.

"How bad is it?"

"Could be better, could be worse. Isn't that how most cases go?"

"I need you to start being honest with me. I need you to tell me everything that's going on in your life, regardless of how you think I might react. Whatever it is, I can handle it. Okay?"

She nods. "Okay. I know how capable you are, but even as an adult, I feel this need to protect you. You'll understand, when Ava is older. All I wanted was to enjoy the time I have left. If I'm lucky, I'll spend it with my girls."

She squeezes my hand as a tear rolls down my cheek.

I'm not sure she'll be that lucky. Even if she receives a small sentence for Bruce Parker's murder, she is likely to spend the rest of the years she has left in a prison cell. It doesn't seem fair. After everything she has done for me, hiding away from the world all those years, she still might end up alone.

CHAPTER 44

Then

Amelia

She has it all.

That's what people thought when they looked at Amelia Boone Parker. Sometimes they said it, openly complimented her looks or accomplishments. Sometimes she could tell they were thinking it. She recognized the way eyes would dance around her body, at her expensive shoes, her immaculate ensemble, her delicate string of pearls.

They thought she was perfect. Hell, maybe they were right. But what they didn't know was that the things Amelia wanted most in this world always eluded her. She had experienced her fair share of loss, but she didn't feel capable of admitting that to anyone without sounding like a spoiled brat. That's the difficult part about being a member of the elite—the pool of like-minded peers is small.

From the first time she begged her father to postpone a business trip, and he denied her, she had understood what it felt like to not get her way. It was an icky feeling. Making her feel full and empty all at once. Amelia's deprivation wasn't the same as others—she still dined at five-star restaurants and visited illustrious resorts, but her emotional needs always came last. Does it really matter what is dangled in front of your face? Whether it's a necessity—a warm meal, shelter, a father's hug—or some frivolous thing? Amelia didn't think so. She felt as unfortunate as any young child would, being surrounded by a world of luxury where she could never find fulfillment.

When she got married, it wasn't Amelia's Big Day… it was the Boone heiress tying the knot. No one wanted to celebrate with Amelia for her sake. They wanted to say they had attended the event. An outsider watching the affair unfold would have assumed she was lucky to marry Bruce Parker, even if he wasn't her first choice, or second, or third. He possessed the necessary qualifications: good family, handsome smile, decent degree, even if he was wasting it as a teacher at some private school.

It was enough, sure. He was the type of man most of her peers aspired to marry, of course. But to Amelia, like everything else in her glass house of a life, it wasn't quite right. *Wasn't quite right* was not enough to do anything about it, though. Not when you were a Boone. Not when you were a Parker. No, she'd been raised to persevere, march through the difficult times in life with her chin high, her shoulders back. She would arrive on the other side, shining.

That's why she didn't react the first time a young woman made a complaint about Bruce. This woman, a colleague, alleged he'd groped her—a completely ridiculous claim considering he wasn't particularly lustful with his own wife. He ended up taking a job at Phillips Academy, which was the solution to that—all the teachers there were male. Only the students were female, far too young to grab his attention.

When the first complaint came in, she knew it was nonsense. Not only would her husband never be attracted to a teenager, but the allegation had come from the girl's lawyer. The family offered to be discreet about the matter, as long as the Parkers could agree upon a certain sum. Complete money grab. Amelia had seen this before, had overheard her father handling scandals of his own. People hear Boone or Parker, they get all sorts of greedy ideas.

The second complaint came from a known friend of the first girl. What were the odds? Did they really think her husband would be so stupid? No, it was clearly another attempt to rob them blind. Amelia had wanted to fight them on that one, show people they weren't to be fooled, but Bruce and the lawyers had assured her it would be in their best interest to avoid scandal. And really, the amount the accuser was asking for might have made a difference in her pitiful life, but barely dented the Boone-Parker trust.

Besides, Amelia had bigger things that required her focus. She was unable to get pregnant. Had never been, actually. They kept trying; after a few months of inaction, they would try a different doctor, a newer drug.

As the years passed, Bruce was becoming less engrossed with her. Less interested in babies. When she mentioned adoption, he would get antsy. Wasn't his thing, he said. *Don't we do enough charity?* He had no desire to prove himself to a bunch of strangers. Beg them to choose him. And if those sexual misconduct allegations kept being raised against him, it would be impossible for even a Boone or Parker to adopt.

Amelia realized Bruce wasn't going to try anymore; if she wanted a family, she would have to make it happen herself. And if she couldn't get pregnant, something would need to fall into their laps. That's what she was thinking that day at the center as she stared out the window, watching the falling rain.

That's when she saw her. Young. Modest. Pregnant? It was hard to tell.

"Yucky day today," she'd said. "Sarah, right?"

The girl was all too eager to respond.

CHAPTER 45

Now

Marion

Carmen knocks on the door before opening it. Mom and I both turn in her direction.

"Sorry to interrupt," she says. "Marion, do you have a minute?"

"Sure." I give Mom another smile before exiting the room. I follow Carmen to the lobby, where I find Des waiting with Ava. She wanted to join us on the off-chance Mom would be allowed other visitors.

"Have you read the letters?" I ask Carmen.

"Yes. I'll have to dig into them a bit more. Is that okay?"

"Do what you need."

"She filled me in on the big parts," Des says, balancing Ava on her knee. "One hell of a story."

"Do you think these letters can help Mom's case?"

"They could. I was hoping to talk with Eileen about them," Carmen replies.

"That Amelia sure is something," Des says, staring ahead at nothing. It's like she's working something out in her own head, not fully tuned in to our chatter.

"I know." I've not fully acknowledged my anger toward Amelia. "Given what we know now, why do you think Amelia was pushing for a DNA test?"

"After all this time, I think they found Sarah Paxton and Baby Caroline and she couldn't just act like none of it mattered," Carmen says. "What exactly did she say to you about taking a test?"

"She told me all she needed was a cheek swab, and she'd be able to sort everything out."

"*Sort everything out.* She wanted you to hand over a sample," Des says. "She never asked you to join her at the facility?"

"No."

"Amelia Boone Parker has enough money to fabricate results," Carmen says. "She wanted to be the one to run the test so she could alter the findings."

"What about the police test?" I ask. "At some point they'd find out I wasn't her biological daughter. She must have thought of that."

"I'm sure she did, and she has enough money to tinker with the system, too. That must be why there is no mention of an adoption anywhere. We have to remember the bulk of this crime took place in the eighties. It was a lot easier to fudge paperwork back then."

"But hiding a birth? An entire pregnancy?"

"Eileen wrote in the letters she didn't tell anyone else about the pregnancy. She quit working after Cliff died. She didn't even go to a doctor until late on, and that was arranged by Amelia."

Carmen is chasing theories; it's what she's paid to do. What she's saying makes sense on the surface, but I still don't fully understand Amelia's motive now, all these years later.

"We'll figure it out," Des says, looking down at Ava. "All that matters is Eileen is awake and she's safe. And we finally have a shot at proving her innocent. She's not the monster people are making her out to be."

The monster I thought she was, I think, a guilty knot writhing in my stomach.

"Do you think she's up for a quick conversation?" Carmen asks me. "She didn't have the best reaction the last time we tried to bring up the case."

"Yeah. I think she can handle it now."

My phone pings with a message.

It's Amelia. Reading her name on the screen sends a shiver down my spine.

"What is it?" Des asks. She must notice the strange look on my face.

"Amelia texted me. She wants to meet up again. She called yesterday, too."

"Tell her she can go to—"

"Wait," Carmen interrupts Des before she can go into a rant. "You don't want to say anything disruptive. Does she know about the DNA test?"

"No, I never told her."

"Good. Make up an excuse. Tell her you're having company over or something. Make her think you still want to meet with her later in the week. It's better for us if she doesn't know we're on to her."

I nod, typing out a response. I punctuate my message with emojis, hoping she'll continue to think all is well. I slide the phone into my pocket.

"Let's talk to Mom."

I bend down, giving Ava a quick kiss on the cheek. It feels, in some ways, like the hardest part is almost over, although there is still a long road ahead. Before leaving the waiting room, my heart fills with gratitude for both Carmen and Des. That they've stood by me, and Mom, through all of this. They are my pillars, lifting me, providing stability. Mom who raised me. Des as backup. Carmen, my defender. I realize how lucky I am to have been surrounded by strong women my entire life.

When we enter Mom's recovery room, she is sitting upright, fiddling with the television remote. She presses mute. We let her know that Carmen has read the letters.

"All we have to do is validate your claims about Bruce and Amelia," Carmen explains. "There might be someone willing to support what you say. Maybe if Jamie—"

"No," Mom says, trying to sit up straighter. "I don't want her getting involved."

"Maybe she wants to get involved," I say. "That's why she told me about the letters in the first place."

"I never wanted any of this to come out," Mom says.

"It's out there now," Carmen says. "If you haven't realized, you're a victim in all this. All we have to do is present your side, and people will see that."

Mom looks back to me. "I want to make sure you're all right."

"I'll be better when I know you're not going to prison."

Which, I realize, is still a long shot. Warranted or not, Mom committed several crimes. It's hard to think they'll all be swept under the rug. Still, I have to cling to some small morsel of hope.

"I don't care about that," Mom says. "I made my mistakes, and if I'm punished for them, so be it. You know the truth, and you don't hate me. That's what matters."

"I could never hate you," I say. "Knowing Amelia, she's not going to let this go. She's going to support her own story, and the sooner we start denying her claims, the better."

Mom tilts her head to the side, her eyes bouncing between me and Carmen. "*Knowing Amelia*. You haven't talked to her, have you?"

I look at Carmen. Her shoulders are scrunched, her eyes wide, awaiting my response.

"She reached out to me shortly after your arrest," I say, cowardly. "She's staying in North Bay."

Mom makes more movement on the bed, struggling to sit upright. "No, Marion. You can't be in contact with her."

"She reached out to me. I was struggling to make sense of things—"

"No, you can't," Mom says. And there isn't jealousy or hurt in her voice. There's fear. Uncontrollable fear. "You can't let her around you. Or Ava."

"I won't, Mom. I won't."

This seems to calm her. Mom rests back onto the mattress, exhaling several quick breaths.

"Promise me you'll stay away from her, Marion. Please."

"I promise."

We talk a little bit longer about the case, about Jamie and her likeliest whereabouts. The visit lasts the majority of the day. I speak with doctors about Mom's condition. They are hopeful she'll be discharged by the end of the week, although she'll be sent back to the county jail. In light of recent events, I'm hoping she won't be there long, but there are no guarantees. Carmen assures me she'll try her best to set her free. She insists these letters are our best shot to make that happen.

Before we leave the hospital, Evan calls.

"How is she?"

"Better," I say, peering into the lobby, where Des is helping pack up Ava's things. "We're about to head out for the night. Des and I are going to run by The Shack, make sure everything gets closed up properly."

"Good." He pauses. "Did you get to talk with Eileen about the letters?"

"Yeah. She opened up a lot." I check the time, trying to predict how long we'll spend at The Shack. "You could stop by tonight, if you'd like. I'll fill you in on everything."

I hold my breath. I'm not sure if we're in the best place for a reconciliation. All I can think about is how good it felt to talk over everything with him last night, how it grounded me. I want that feeling again.

"Sounds great. Text me when you leave The Shack, okay?"

I hang up the phone and place it in my bag. As I'm zipping up compartments, making sure I have everything, my fingers brush against a sheet of paper. I unfold it, realizing it's the check Amelia gave me. For a few seconds, I stare at it. The amount. Her signature. Then I tear it in half and dispose of the pieces in a nearby trashcan.

I look out the visiting room window. The skies are darker than they should be this time of the evening, which means a storm is settling in. And yet, I smile. For the first time since Mom's arrest, I feel like everything is shifting back into place.

CHAPTER 46

Then

Amelia

Sarah. She was young, pretty. Amelia could sniff the girl's eagerness during their first conversation. She admired Amelia, like so many others did. How extraordinary it was that this quiet girl might be the answer to Amelia's problems.

The two sparked a conversation, a short one. It wasn't until later, when Amelia looked in Ms. Lang's file, that she confirmed her initial suspicion. Sarah was pregnant. At first, she felt a hot rage. Why did this girl, who was in no position to be a parent at all, get to have a child? She wasn't even married. The file listed the unborn child's father as Cliff, a boyfriend.

The next time Amelia saw Sarah at the center, she didn't speak to her. Afterward, she followed her, trying to get a glimpse into this girl's life. She saw the paltry restaurant where she worked. The young man who was always laughing and bouncing about, like he'd just told the best joke. The tiny brunette girl who smoked like a chimney. And there was Sarah between them, that ignorant smile on her face. She envisioned what Sarah's life must be like. Poor. Uneducated. But with a child? Resentment filled Amelia, hardening her bones and souring her soul.

At dark, Amelia would return to her massive house in one of the wealthiest neighborhoods of New Hutton. She would park her expensive car in the garage. Whatever she desired for dinner, she could have. Whatever she wanted to drink was available in the cellar. Before bed, she'd change out of her designer clothes and into satin pajamas.

And she'd spend the rest of the night sleeping beside a husband who refused to touch her. Love had left their marriage long ago; perhaps it had never been there. Regardless, the Parkers were civilized people. Sure, Bruce and Amelia sought different things in life, had different dreams, but they were stuck on this journey together. Amelia desired a child more than anything, and even though Bruce was no longer interested in doing his part to make that happen, she knew he wouldn't deny her the opportunity if she could create one.

Amelia arranged for Ms. Lang to take a job at another counseling center across town. It wasn't hard convincing her to leave; Ms. Lang never cared much about her work, could not remember which of her patients were pregnant or not. Amelia shredded any files Ms. Lang had kept on Sarah, any documented proof of the pregnancy torn to shreds. The girl was so overwhelmed she hadn't even gone to a doctor. Amelia knew she could arrange one when the time was right. Then she became Sarah's new counselor.

Sarah opened up faster than Amelia ever expected. It was obvious how lonely and insecure she felt, especially after the boyfriend died. Amelia pitied her, becoming increasingly convinced she was doing what was best for both of them. And of course, she was doing what was best for the baby. As she listened to the girl babble about her future desires for her child—Caroline, she might call her—the wheels in Amelia's mind turned. When she first suggested the possibility of adoption, she was surprised to hear Sarah had already considered it. Maybe this girl knew she wasn't fit to be a mother, which only strengthened Amelia's resolve to continue with her plan.

Once they started visiting the horse track, the two were more like friends. Of course, Amelia had to open up about her life, too. She told her about her struggle to conceive. The details in her story might have been fudged, but the crux of the story remained: Amelia wanted a child more than anything, and Sarah just might be the person to make that happen at last.

Then, finally, Sarah said it.

"Would you consider adopting her?"

All the months of planning and sacrifice had finally paid off. Sarah could see what Amelia always knew about herself: she would make the perfect mother.

Maybe she could finally get the life she always wanted. She deserved it, didn't she? She deserved happiness. She deserved peace. She deserved Caroline.

CHAPTER 47

Now

Marion

The rain is heavy. The droplets have banded together and are plummeting down in thick gushes. I drive slower than normal on the way home, my windshield wipers operating like twigs against a flood.

The sound, however, is peaceful. I've always enjoyed falling asleep to the sound of rain. Ava must agree. She is out by the time we arrive back to the condo.

I do my best to unfasten the buckles of her car seat without disturbing her. I pull my jacket over as far as it will go, trying to shield her from the falling rain. I skip up the walkway, avoiding the puddles starting to pool along the curb, and quickly unlock the front door. I rush straight to her room, feeling that her clothes are not too damp and her diaper not too heavy beneath her jumper. I place her in the crib, and she exhales a breath of relief as she turns her head to the left, still deep in slumber.

I too exhale. She is asleep. She is safe. And this horrendous ordeal is almost over.

I wander back to the living room, which is still dark due to my hasty trek into the house. And yet, not so dark. The door, which I could have sworn I kicked closed, is cracked, a sliver of moonlight peeking inside.

"I thought you were having company."

The voice behind me startles me so much I leap forward, closer to the door and light switch on the wall. I flick it, illuminating the room. Amelia stands in the kitchen. Her shoulders and hair are damp, as though she too just came in from the rain.

"Amelia? What are you doing here?"

"You said you had company. I didn't want to interrupt you, but when I arrived, the house was dark. Then I saw you pull up, so I followed you in."

"You really shouldn't be here."

"Why? It's clear I'm not interrupting anything. We're alone." She takes another step closer. "Are you trying to avoid me?"

"No, but… it doesn't matter. You don't have the right to walk into my home."

"Have you been to the hospital?"

"It's none of your business where I've been. It's late, and it would be best if you left."

"Is Sarah awake?" She asks the question calmly, ignoring my demands.

"My mother's name is Eileen."

"So, she is awake?" A smile. "Have you spoken with her about me?"

"If you don't leave, I'm going to call—"

"You might know her as Eileen. Mom. To me, she'll always be Sarah. That poor girl in over her head. I tried to help her, you know."

"Yes, actually. I know everything that happened back then. Most importantly, that you are not my mother. And really, I'm not convinced you were ever a victim in any of this. You need to leave."

"I didn't ask for this, Caroline. All I ever wanted was a child. I wanted you. And Sarah promised she'd do right by you, do right by me—"

"You didn't help her! You weren't forthcoming about anything, especially Bruce."

"All we ever wanted was a child." She looks down the hallway leading toward Ava's room. "You're a mother now, too. How can you not understand? Is there anything you wouldn't do to protect your child?"

"You weren't trying to protect me, Amelia. You tried to take me. There's a difference."

"Sarah is the one who took you. She's the one who promised you a better life and stole it away. Gave herself a little pat on the back for making a responsible decision once in her miserable life, only to change her mind."

"She did that because she realized you were a liar. That your husband was a pervert who attacked her friend. He attacked other students."

"Children lie, don't you understand? Women lie. They wanted a pay day, a little attention."

"Do you seriously believe that?"

It's hard to read her reaction. After all these years, she must have at least considered that Bruce was guilty. Mom wouldn't have fought so hard to take me otherwise.

"Bruce was a good man, and Sarah murdered him right in front of me." Her voice trembles.

"I know my mother. She wouldn't have acted violently unless she felt a need to protect herself or me."

"I am your mother!"

She stomps forward, stopping just inches in front of my body. She slaps me hard across the face. I step back, slamming into the door and pushing it shut. A trickle of terror climbs my spine. I need to run away, but I can't do that with Ava sleeping in the next room. I realize I'm in real danger. Ava is in real danger. The anger I have toward Amelia halts, and I try to focus all my energy into keeping her calm.

"I'm sorry," I say. "You're right. I shouldn't pass judgment without hearing your side of the story."

These words are a complete lie. Amelia has had over a week to tell me her version of what happened all those years ago. Instead, she tried to keep up the charade she has created for the police and press all these years. That she's a victim.

"I've told you my side," she says, without hesitation. "Sarah was in trouble. She had no business raising a child. Me? I was ready. I had every resource available and then some. It was supposed to be the answer to both our problems. I would have you, and she'd have the opportunity to stop screwing up her life."

Her words anger me. She was convinced Mom would be an inadequate parent, but she's wrong. I'm the living proof. Who is she to deem who is worthy and who is not? No one's ever completely ready to become a parent, but you adapt. You don't try to take control of another person. I try not to let my emotions cloud my thinking. I need to find a way to get Amelia on my side.

"Why didn't you just move on? Try to adopt another child? Why continue to support this lie for so long?"

"Because it was never a lie. You are my child. I couldn't replace you like some lost item. And even if I'd wanted to, Bruce was dead. And the media, everything else… there weren't as many options back then. You were my one shot, and then you were gone." She covers her mouth with a palm, her voice trembling. "But things are different now. You have Ava. We could still have a future together, the three of us. And I could give her everything I never had the opportunity to give you."

The idea of this woman being around my child leaves a twisting knot in my stomach, but I need to be careful. "That's very kind of you."

"It's meant to be, isn't it? You don't have a husband. Ava doesn't have a father. Between the three of us, she doesn't need one. We can be a family."

She takes a step toward the hallway leading to Ava's room. I step forward, blocking her.

"Ava is sleeping, Amelia. It's the middle of the night, and there's a storm. It's not safe to take her out in this."

"She'll be fine." Amelia looks down, frisking her hands against her clothes. "If we leave now, we can be in New Hutton by sunrise."

New Hutton? In what world would this woman think I'd be willing to take my child anywhere with her? Just as Mom described in her letters, her selfishness is frightening. All I want is to make her leave my house.

"It's not safe." I deepen my voice and take a step forward, forcing her to walk back toward the kitchen. She must see that I'm serious. We're not leaving.

"Fine." She looks at me blankly. "I'll get her."

On the bureau to her right, rests the baton Rick gave me. She picks it up in one quick movement, swinging it in my direction. I take a step back, but trip, landing hard on my hip just by the front door. I raise my hand to block her next blow, but I'm too late.

The baton lands hard on the top of my head. I close my eyes, seeing nothing but bright blasts of light. I feel another hit, then…

"Just close your eyes," Amelia whispers.

I do, and the world turns black.

CHAPTER 48

Now

Amelia

Many years had passed since that cool summer evening when Caroline was taken, but Amelia could remember each moment with total clarity. Finding Bruce's body. Finding the empty crib.

What happened after.

The press seemed to stalk her from that moment forward. Amelia had to be careful about what she said. She had to know who she could trust. She believed her own story would be more credible than Sarah's, which is why she didn't hesitate to give them her name. More than that, she knew it was her best shot at ever finding Caroline.

She never could have predicted it would take so long.

There had been several times over the years when she thought she had found them. A mother and daughter living in California, celebrating a third birthday. Another time, on vacation, someone swore a woman accompanying a ten-year-old girl was Sarah. And yet, all those were false leads.

Amelia never knew her daughter would be over thirty before she saw her again. Gone was the baby she had so desperately wanted, gone was the little girl she had worked so hard to find. But all wasn't lost, she realized. Caroline—Marion—now had a daughter of her own. Maybe Amelia's fate wasn't yet set. Maybe she still had a shot at having the family she'd always wanted.

And yet, with everything that had changed over the years, the same obstacle remained: Sarah. Although she was called Eileen now. Stupid name.

Amelia couldn't believe they had lived right under her nose all this time, but she tried not to let the bitterness consume her. Not when she finally had the opportunity to make things right, and even more than that, get revenge.

But she had to get Sarah out of the way. That's why she didn't rush to North Bay the minute she learned about Marion's existence. She had waited long enough, what would another month hurt? Instead, she used her resources to find out as much as she could about the Sams. She had to make sure everything was in place before she tipped off the police, and the information came in handy later when she needed the media to put pressure on Marion.

Before arriving in North Bay, Amelia made sure she had a connection in the jail, someone capable of stabbing an unsuspecting Sarah in her cell. And she had to make sure the guard on duty could be paid to look the other way. Everything worked according to plan, except Sarah survived the attack.

That's why she had to make a break for Marion when she did. Whether or not Sarah would pull through was out of her control, but none of that would matter if she could win back the daughter stolen from her all those years ago.

And who could forget precious Ava? Yes, the three of them would make a better family than even Amelia could have dreamed. No undependable Bruce. No screw-up Sarah. She knew then, after all the heartache, after all the sacrifice, some things were worth the wait.

CHAPTER 49

Now

Marion

Minutes.

I must have only been out for minutes, and yet my entire life might have been ruined in that short amount of time.

I feel drops of water falling on my face and neck. That's what wakes me. When I open my eyes, I see Evan standing over me.

"Marion, what happened?"

He's still wearing his jacket from outside, and it is dripping on me. The front door is wide open, letting in powerful gusts of wind.

"Ava." I move, struggling to stand.

"Tell me what happened." Evan sounds rushed, afraid.

"Amelia was here," I say, pulling on his arm to find my balance. "She wants to take Ava."

Now standing, I dart down the hallway, Evan fast on my heels. Each footstep seems to span its own moment in time. Reality has slowed, like I'm reliving a moment from the past. But it's not my past, it's Amelia's. As I push open the door, look around the room, rush to the crib.

It's empty.

I fall backward, Evan holding me up.

"She took her," I say, my voice frantic.

"Amelia took her?"

"I'd put Ava in her crib. Amelia showed up. She said she wanted us to leave with her. When I refused, she knocked me out."

I push past him, each second that passes feeling too long and dangerous. I rush to the front door, swing it open, expecting to see Amelia's car has disappeared. I stop in my tracks when I see it is still nudged between two others on the curb. She has not driven away, which means she must have gone somewhere on foot.

And she has taken Ava with her.

"I'm calling the police," Evan says, the phone already held up to his ear.

The rain is still pouring down in heavy bursts, the night dark except for the random streetlights and squares from bedroom windows.

"She must still be close," I say, turning my head from one way to the next. "I couldn't have been out for more than a few minutes."

Running back into the house, I find Amelia's keys on the floor.

"That must be why she didn't leave in the car," Evan says, then turns his attention back to the telephone. "Yes, I need to report a child abduction. The address is…"

I run to the patio overlooking the beach. The entire area is shrouded in darkness. A chair is flipped on its side. It could have been in reaction to the storm, or this might have been the route Amelia took to get out of the house unseen. I squint, trying to see into the distance, but all I see is blurry blackness.

The ocean and the rain create a cacophony of water around me, drowning out the sound of anything else. And then there's something. A noise. A cry. It's Ava, I know it.

"She has her on the beach," I shout to Evan, jumping over the back gate.

I don't have time to wait for him. I grab my phone, still in my pocket, and switch on the flashlight. Usually so bright it's blinding, now it only illuminates a few inches in front of me. I scan it across the ground, my feet sinking deeper into the wet sand with each step. The farther I get from the condo, the more alone I feel, not sure which direction to turn.

Then, another cry. It sounds closer, but the wind whooshing past my face can be misleading. I run in that direction. A few minutes later, I can hear Evan coming up behind me.

"Police are on their way," he says, using his own phone as a light. "Surely, she wouldn't take her out here in the middle of this."

"She has nowhere else to go," I say, stopping, trying to listen for more cries. The fear inside is overwhelming. I can't stand for Ava to be out here without me, and I don't trust Amelia's mental state.

Another whimper, closer this time.

"Amelia," I scream, my voice useless against the heavy winds. "Amelia, please. Don't take Ava. Don't hurt her."

My eyes begin to adjust to the darkness. Not far ahead of me, there's an outline of something on the empty beach. As I approach, I hear another cry. I hold my hand forward, shining the light. It's them. Amelia is huddled on the sand, holding Ava.

"Don't come any closer," she says.

It's amazing how quickly you'll obey when someone has your child. I freeze, holding my other hand back, instructing Evan to do the same.

"You don't want to hurt her," I say.

"Of course I don't. All I ever wanted to do is love her. Love you. I would have been a good mother. All I ever wanted was the chance. I finally had it, but he ruined it."

"Who did?"

"Bruce!" she screams, raising her face. "If he hadn't made so many mistakes, if he hadn't messed with those girls, Sarah would have left you with me."

"If Bruce was dangerous, she had every reason to take me with her."

She knows I'm right. Her silence confirms it. She wipes her nose with the back of her hand and clears her throat.

"She didn't kill him, you know." She rocks back and forth, holding Ava in her arms. "I did."

I fall to my knees in the sand, staring at the horrible sight of this confessed killer holding my child.

"Sarah gave him a good beating. I don't think he would have survived, especially with that wound on his head, but he was still alive when I came outside after I realized Caroline was gone," she continues. "He was on the pavement, asking for help. But how could I help him when he'd just cost me everything?"

The question is rhetorical, and I'm too full of fear and disbelief to answer her. I stay completely still, watching her every move. I'm stunned. This crime Mom has been running from her entire life wasn't entirely her fault. Amelia killed Bruce.

"I covered his mouth and nose with my hands," Amelia says. "He was already so weak. It didn't take much force. I didn't let go until I knew he was gone."

"You did that because you knew he was dangerous. You did the right thing, Amelia. You made sure he wouldn't hurt anyone else."

A burst of red and blue lights spreads across the beach. The police have arrived, although they are still in the condominium parking lot. Amelia sees them, holds Ava tighter. Evan rushes toward her, but I hold out my arm, signaling him to step back.

"You can still do the right thing," I say. "I know you don't want to hurt Ava."

"I didn't ask for any of this."

"And neither did we," I say, the wind blowing hair into my mouth, sticking to my wet cheeks. "Please, don't take my daughter from me."

Amelia scrunches her face, falling over on the sand. Ava rolls from her grasp. Without instruction, Evan leaps toward her. He swoops her up, running away from us. There are voices behind us.

I see the intermittent blasts of flashlights as officers run to meet us on the beach.

"I'll stay with you," I say to her.

Amelia remains in the fetal position, wailing. She has finally given up, released the last of the secrets she's been keeping all these years.

CHAPTER 50

Now

Marion

I'm sitting on the living room sofa with a blanket wrapped around my shoulders. The police have separated us so they can get our individual statements. They have taken Ava to an ambulance to check her vitals. Each second I'm away from her feels like a punishment. Even though I believe she's safe, this knot in my stomach won't untangle until I can feel her body against mine. I rock back and forth, the blanket doing little to warm my drenched clothes and hair.

"Let me in," I hear a voice at the front door.

There are two officers blocking the entrance to my living room. I don't have to see past them to know the husky voice yelling obscenities belongs to Des. They try to reason with her, an impossible feat.

"Let her in. Please," I tell one of the officers.

He steps to the side. Des lumbers into the room, her arms outstretched. She kneels on the floor in front of me.

Des' face is pale. She has always had a weak stomach, and last I looked, there was a nasty bump on the side of my head. "My goodness. Are you okay? You look like you've been in a car accident."

"It feels like I've been in one."

"Ava. Is she okay?"

Ava. I just want to hold her. My mind flashes back to the beach, the overwhelming terror I felt watching Amelia wrestle to keep Ava in her arms.

There's another disruption at the front door. The officer steps aside. Evan is standing there, holding Ava in his arms. I stand, charging toward them. I take her from him. Her face is perfect, undisturbed. She's safe. She's here. I smile through the tears, holding her close to me.

"Everything's okay now," I say.

Evan nods. There is nothing else to say, at least not in this minute. This minute is for appreciating Ava, giving thanks that she's back. I've never been so close to losing her, and my body will forever remember this feeling, ready to react again if forced.

Des pats Evan's back. She walks over to the sofa and takes a seat, relieved. I know she wants to love on Ava, and she'll get her chance, but she must be happy to know we're both out of harm's way.

I close my eyes, swaying Ava from side to side, whispering prayers.

When I open my eyes again, Evan is watching us, smiling. His presence tonight was crucial. He didn't come to my rescue, but he came to Ava's. If that's not enough to make me fall back in love with him, I'm not sure what is.

CHAPTER 51

Now

Marion

There's a certain type of electricity inside threatening to burst. And yet, I can't quite label it. Is it excitement? Dread? I suppose the combination of those two emotions would be anxiety. I don't want to set my hopes too high, knowing there's a strong likelihood they could all come crashing down.

It's Mom's day in court.

Carmen is negotiating a plea deal for the remaining charges against Mom. After Amelia confessed to Bruce's murder, the most serious charge was dropped. Carmen is hoping to prove that the other crimes Mom committed were done so under extreme duress.

Jamie ended up coming forward, sharing her account of what happened back at Phillips Academy all those years ago. She identified Bruce Parker as the teacher who attacked her, as the teacher who was rumored to have assaulted other students on the campus.

Except now it's not merely rumor. Once word got out that a deceased Phillips Academy teacher had committed assault, other former students came forward. Back then, they were young girls. Naïve. Ashamed. Afraid. Now, they are women, and at least three of them have agreed to open up about what happened to them, considering how much is at stake.

The press jumped all over it, of course, knowing that the slain father of Baby Caroline was accused of something so terrible.

The Baby Caroline saga has a new spotlight; it's hard to catch a morning news show that doesn't touch on it. I can't blame them, really. There are many new developments that have obliterated the narrative spun for the past thirty years.

There is also a storm of questions surrounding Amelia. After she was arrested on the beach, police and press began piecing together her true involvement with the crimes Mom had been accused of committing. Adoption documentation was never found because Amelia never submitted it. She had a legitimate birth certificate for Caroline Parker. When police tried to track down the doctor listed as delivering the baby, they learned he had died over ten years ago. As he was the Parker family's personal physician, there is no telling how forthcoming his testimony would have been. I'm sure there have been more than a few people paid off over the years. We'll probably never know the full story, but it feels like we have enough to understand who was really at fault for this tragedy, and it wasn't Mom.

We're hoping a judge will agree. Carmen's presenting her case today, hoping the court will accept her proposed plea deal. Although I'm the first to admit that Mom walking away without some form of punishment is unlikely.

I'm supposed to be at the courthouse within the hour. I arrive at Carmen's house and knock on the door. As expected, Michael answers. He's wearing a robe over a T-shirt and sweats.

"You should already be downtown. Carmen left over an hour ago." He sips the coffee in his hands. "How are you feeling?"

"Scared."

"It's almost over, okay? This is the homestretch."

"Unless the judge denies the deal."

"Don't think that way," he says. "Stay positive. I know nothing is going to make you feel better right now, but she's been rehearsing what she's going to say all week. I've never seen her more prepared."

"That's good to know," I say, looking across the street at my car, then back to him. "Hey, she told me you're about to launch your own real estate agency. How's it going?"

"I'm feeling surprisingly good about it. It'll take a little pressure off Carmen to have me working again."

"It doesn't feel like much time has passed since you left your old job. Now you're getting ready to start a new one. Lucky."

"Yeah. I guess it feels longer to me." He looks back at the open door. We can hear the children's voices from where we stand. "I should check on them. Good luck today."

He turns to go back inside, but I follow him. "You know, Carmen has been great about keeping me in the loop. She's shared almost every detail of the case. Everything she's uncovered about Mom's and Amelia's pasts. Carmen is thorough. Not much gets by her."

He turns to face me again. "That's the truth."

My hands in my pockets, I take another step forward.

"There is one thing she missed, though. It's small. Won't help or hurt Mom's outcome, really. But it's something I noticed."

"Oh yeah?"

"After Amelia was arrested at my house, the police did a complete search of her hotel room. They uncovered all the research she did over the years. All the information she'd tracked down after she finally figured out where Mom was hiding."

"You think she knew you were in North Bay this whole time?"

"Not this whole time. She said she found out where we were after Mom was arrested. Turns out, that wasn't true. She knew where we were first. She's the one who told the police. And it's because someone tipped her off."

"Wild."

He looks back at the open door. The children's voices have quieted. They've probably followed each other upstairs. I know he wants to check, but I've not finished with our conversation.

"She had all sorts of random stuff. More recently, she had the names of local journalists. Looks like she was the one leaking those stories about me and Ava to the press. She'd kept a careful record of all her contacts. When we were sorting through the evidence photos, I found this." I slide my hand out of my pocket, revealing a photo of Amelia's papers in the hotel room. "Why did Amelia Parker have one of your old business cards?"

Michael cocks his head to the side, a quick movement. He squints. "My business card?"

"Yeah. You did a lot of work in New Hutton before you left your job, right? Did the two of you ever cross paths?"

"I think I would remember her if I did." He wraps his palm around the back of his neck. "I mean, it's possible, but I don't think—"

"I could never figure out how she finally found us. She always offered a reward, but what were the chances of someone stumbling upon Mom after all these years? It would have to be someone who really knew her. Knew her well enough to think that she might be Sarah Paxton."

"Sure. I just—"

"And those articles. The one about how I became pregnant with Ava. There's no way Amelia could have had that information. Even if she hired someone to look into me, only the people in my life would have known some of those details."

Michael's expression freezes as he slowly exhales. "Marion, what are you saying?"

"It's convenient you have enough money to start a new business. I mean, you left your job, what, a month before Amelia showed up? What are the chances?"

He opens his mouth but freezes. He doesn't know what to say.

"I can't help wondering if you didn't run into Amelia at your old job. At least hear about her, know her story. Maybe you looked into it one day, when you were bored in your high-rise office, daydreaming about quitting and starting your own business. You might have noticed the large reward she was offering for any information."

Michael pinches the bridge of his nose, slides his fingers down to cover his mouth. "I thought it was a long shot. Online, I found a picture of this Sarah Paxton lady. I mean, Eileen looked a little like her, sure. But I had no way of really knowing. Carmen told me how complicated your past was. Eileen's past, really. I thought, maybe it might fit."

"So, you're the one who told Amelia about us?"

"I didn't know everything would play out like this. I thought I was being paranoid, really."

"But you still told her you believed Mom was Sarah Paxton."

"Trust me, if I knew everything that would happen, I never would have said anything. I was under the impression Eileen had committed an awful crime. I thought Amelia was suffering, still searching for answers."

"How fortunate that providing those answers gave you enough money to start your new business." I shake my head. "And what about everything else? The press leaks. Did you give her that information too?"

"She wanted to know more about you. I thought she was your biological mother. How was I supposed to know she was out to hurt you?"

"She kept paying you, didn't she?"

"Yes." His words are filled with shame. "Marion, I didn't know Amelia's motives in all this. If I did—"

"Does Carmen know?"

"No. Definitely not. She never would have allowed me to do it."

I believe him. As shocked as I was to find that card, to toy with the idea Michael might have turned Mom in, I could never think Carmen was involved. Especially after watching how hard she worked on Mom's case. She'll be even more devastated about Michael's involvement than I am.

"Carmen is my best friend," I say, my words filled with enough anger for the both of us. "I thought we were friends, too."

"We are!" he shouts, turning for another look at the door. "This whole thing just fell in my lap. It seemed like an easy way out at the time. You have to believe me. I'm sorry for all the pain it caused you and Eileen."

"I need Carmen's head in the right place. We're going to get through today, then I'm telling her."

"No, Marion. You can't." He's off the porch now, chasing me as I walk to my car.

"Goodbye, Michael."

After today, I know one thing for sure: no more secrets.

CHAPTER 52

Now

Amelia

The lock clanged against the bars when the officer left Amelia in her cell. She had been there for months, but it still hadn't sunk in that this was forever. That she would stay here, in this cold, hard place, accompanied only by her thoughts.

At least she had her memories, most of them grander than the average person would ever experience. She would close her eyes, could almost feel the desert heat on her face. Could almost hear waves crashing on the other side of the wall. She could almost feel Bruce's hand on her leg, back when they first started dating. They had been happier in those days, a far cry from where they ended up.

But it wasn't always the happy memories that Amelia would conjure. Sometimes the painful memories, the ones that brought her to this place, crept in. Like the spiders in the corners of her cell, she'd stomp them out, but they had a way of returning.

She hadn't meant to hit Cliff with her car. Not really. That certainly wasn't her intention when she spied on Sarah that day, as she had so many times before. It had become a weekend routine of sorts. Watching this pitiful girl made her feel better about her own life. She followed Sarah and Cliff to a nicer part of town, watched as they went inside the apartment complex.

For hours, Amelia stayed in her car, listening to music, waiting to see them again.

At long last, they appeared on the sidewalk. Despite their cheap clothes and blemished skin, they appeared happy. That was the first time Sarah looked like she was actually pregnant. Another passerby would no longer look at her and think it was just bloat. No, this girl was having a baby. That goofy boy at her side was having a baby. And Amelia, with her large car and expensive jewelry and custom clothes, had nothing.

Amelia pulled her car into the street so fast, she wasn't sure what she'd done. She was speeding, racing against her own thoughts, fighting to get away from her jealous desires. Her envy ceased when she heard the thud of Cliff's body hitting her car, followed by the squealing of tires, the screaming of civilians on the sidewalk.

She drove home in a panic, not sure what her next step would be. *There will be police and media*, she thought. Someone would come and arrest her.

No one ever did.

After a few days, the lack of interference confirmed what she always thought: certain people didn't matter. No one would ever take her from the luxury of her life to punish her for ruining the nothingness of someone else's.

She was free.

It was an odd moment to reminisce about now, detached from the world she had known. Separated from the people she once knew. Isolated from the many others who never knew the real Amelia Boone Parker.

She thinks back to the woman she used to be. The woman who spotted Sarah that day in the center. Their roles seemed so defined then. Which person was meant to be a mother, which one was meant to make a mess of her life. It seemed all Amelia had done since that day was take from those around her, mastermind ruin and corruption, even if it didn't feel that way at the time. To Amelia, her actions had felt right, justified.

How ironic that Sarah ended up besting her after all. More than that, she succeeded in being the mother Amelia herself never deserved to be.

EPILOGUE

Ava turns two years old today.

I spread a plastic tablecloth over the picnic table, watching as the wind lifts and furls it. I fasten down the corners with decorative weights and start unpacking two-liter bottles and plastic cups.

This year's party isn't as extravagant. We moved it outside, enjoying the warm weather on the beach underneath a community pavilion. I only invited those who play an important role in our lives, which I realize now is still a good amount of people. One by one, they arrive. First, Des, clutching two gift bags in one hand and balancing pizza boxes with the other.

"Let me help you," I say, taking the pizza.

"Beautiful day today," she says, standing with her shoulders back, taking a deep inhale of salty air.

"Cake, Mamma. Cake." Ava stands by me, tugging on my shirt.

"Just a minute, honey," I tell her, resting my hand on the top of her head.

It's amazing how much Ava has changed since last year. She no longer looks like a baby, although I guess in my mind she'll always be one. She's grown taller, her shoulders and hips filling out. She is turning into a child. My child. She's talking more and more, the two of us beginning to have brief conversations. Each milestone makes me more thankful for the time we have together.

Next, Carmen arrives, with Preston and Penny leading the way down the ramp. Each is holding their own gift-wrapped box, and Carmen has a designer purse hanging from the crook of her arm.

"Sorry we're late," she says, kissing my cheek.

"No worries. It's just us. We're still waiting on a few others to arrive."

"Evan says he's stuck in traffic, but he'll arrive before we start opening the presents."

When Evan first moved back to North Bay, his plan had been to start his own firm. After Carmen kicked Michael to the curb, she decided she needed a different type of partner: a business one. She invited Evan to join her practice; the two have been working together for the past six months.

Evan has been around a lot more lately. We haven't fully labeled what we are, but I believe the feelings we had for each other never went away. The way he and Ava look at each other, it's like love has always been there between them, too. I can finally admit I can't imagine a future without him.

The kids are already tearing into the pizza. Ava throws her crust on the sand. Minutes later, a bird flies by and swoops it up. The children giggle.

"Cake. Cake," she says again, looking down the ramp.

I turn, looking in the direction to which Ava is pointing. Mom is walking toward us, carrying a small white box.

"I told you it would be just a minute," I say.

Mom sits beside us, letting Ava crawl into her lap. She squeezes her between her arms, craning her neck to kiss her cheek. "Happy birthday, my precious girl," she whispers.

Carmen's plea deal worked. After uncovering the allegations against Bruce and the manipulation by Amelia, the most serious charges were dropped. Because of the cancer, Mom was granted a compassionate release for the remaining charges. As long as she meets the terms of her probation and stays out of trouble, which I don't foresee being a problem, she won't spend time in jail.

Amelia, on the other hand, will likely spend the rest of her life there. Assault. Home invasion. Witness tampering. Murder. Even though she is fighting every charge with a pricey lawyer at her side, she won't return to the real world. It seems fitting; she stole Mom's life, forced her to live her best years in hiding. In more ways than one, everything appears to be coming back around.

The boards on the pavilion creak as another person comes walking toward us. A woman. Mom and I both stand.

"Is that her?" I ask.

A smile spreads across Mom's face. "I think it is."

The woman has dyed red hair and is wearing a black crochet top. As she gets closer, she holds out her arms. Mom walks to her and the two women embrace.

Jamie's decision to come forward was crucial. Once she heard there was an update in the Baby Caroline case, she was conflicted about what to do. When the media began reporting Mom had been attacked, it was the push she needed to reach out to me. She'd been calling the hospital asking for me for days, too afraid to contact me another way; she wasn't sure what my reaction might be. She and Mom have been in touch in recent months, but this is the first time they have seen each other in over thirty years.

They walk closer.

"Jamie, I'd like you to meet my daughter. Marion," Mom says.

There are tears rolling down Jamie's cheeks as she smiles. "She's absolutely beautiful."

She pulls me in for a hug, smelling like expensive perfume and cigarettes.

"Thank you. Thank you for everything," I say.

It wasn't just how she helped in the aftermath of Mom's arrest, after all. She played a crucial role in helping Mom avoid detection all these years. She believed in her when many others would have chosen to look the other way.

"It was nothing," she says.

Jamie and Mom walk along the shore, catching up on a lifetime spent apart. Every so often, Mom will throw her head back and laugh. Jamie will lean over, slapping her leg. It feels good to see them happy.

As promised, Evan arrives just as we are preparing to open gifts. He stands behind me, his hand on my shoulder. After Ava opens the last one, he leans in to kiss my cheek.

"Great party, Mom," he whispers.

Carmen and Des help wrangle up the trash and consolidate the remaining food in Tupperware. Eventually, everyone scatters out across the sand, the children fruitlessly chasing birds and the adults having their own conversations. I watch the entire scene, feeling a warmth inside. Growing up, it never felt like I had a whole family. Someone was always missing, it seemed. Now I realize I have more support than most people, and I can share all that love with Ava.

Mom walks over, her arms crossed, and stands beside me.

"You know, it seems like I spent most of my life trying to avoid people," Mom says. "I went about it the wrong way."

"What do you mean?"

We don't bring up the case often, or even her past. But when we do have a conversation about it, there is no longer that barrier there. We talk about our lives openly and honestly.

"For so long, I believed people were out to hurt each other. And all that is true. That's why I made it my life's mission to protect you." She looks at Ava, then me. "But I forgot to appreciate the good in people. People like Jamie and Des. I never would have survived if it weren't for them. And I wouldn't be here today if Carmen hadn't fought for me. They show me a different side to people. A better side."

"You were lucky to have them," I say, squeezing her hand. "And we're lucky to have you."

I'm aware our time together is limited. All our time is limited, whether you lose your life in an instant, like my father, or slowly to a disease, like my mother. It is why we have to make the most of the moments we have.

"Cake," Ava says, stumbling toward us. She has been patient enough.

"I'll cut three slices," Mom says, holding her hand as we make our way back to the pavilion.

We sit and we eat. We enjoy the fantastic breeze and the beautiful view. We appreciate this moment together, which has always been, and will always be, enough.

A LETTER FROM MIRANDA

Dear Reader,

Thank you for taking the time to read *Not My Mother*. If you liked it and want information about upcoming releases, sign up with the following link. Your email address will never be shared and you can unsubscribe at any time.

www.bookouture.com/miranda-smith

What I love about the crime genre is the opportunity to take ordinary scenarios and explore them a step further, to a desperate and dangerous place. For this book, the scene of a woman being arrested at her granddaughter's birthday party stuck out to me, and the rest of the story developed from there.

I was fascinated by each character's determination to be a mother, whether it be Marion, a single mother by choice, or Amelia with her obsessive manipulation. I'd also like to mention that I'm a huge supporter of adoption, and I hope none of the themes in this fictional story suggest otherwise.

If you'd like to further discuss the novel, I'd love to connect! You can find me on Instagram, Facebook, Twitter or my website. If you enjoyed *Not My Mother*, I would be thrilled for you to leave a review on Amazon. It only takes a few minutes and does wonders in helping readers discover my books for the first time.

Thank you again for your support!

Sincerely,
Miranda Smith

           MirandaSmithAuthor

           @MSmithBooks

           @mirandasmithwriter

           mirandasmithwriter.com

ACKNOWLEDGEMENTS

Thank you to the Bookouture team for continuing to publish and market my books like no other, especially Jenny Geras, Kim Nash, Noelle Holten, Sarah Hardy, and Alex Holmes. Special thanks to Jane Eastgate and Liz Hurst for fine-tuning my manuscript and finding any mistakes I missed (of which there were several, I'm sure).

As always, thank you to my fabulous editor, Ruth Tross. Your attention to detail takes each story to the next level. Thank you for helping me work through the plot, even when I felt quite lost in it.

Huge thanks to the book promoters and reviewers who continue to praise each novel. I appreciate every tweet, comment, share and recommendation. To my readers who continue to follow me from book to book, thanks for joining me on this journey. I hope the ride isn't too bumpy.

Thank you to my very supportive family, both near and far. So much of this process consists of being locked away in my room alone. It's thrilling when we get to celebrate the finished product together. I'm hoping for many travels and gatherings in the near future!

Thank you to my parents for believing in me. Chris, thank you for helping me juggle the madness. You are the best hype man ever.

This story is about mothers and daughters, and for that reason, I've dedicated it to my daughter, Lucy. All my children are too young to read anything I write, but I continue to thank them in each book because they are a fundamental part of who I am and what I do, in all aspects.

Harrison, Lucy and Christopher: I hope one day—much like when Marion reads her mother's letters—you'll read my books and feel proud. If I can do this, you can do so, so much more.